WHERE IVY
DARES
TO GROW

WHERE IVY DARES TO GROW

MARIELLE THOMPSON

KENSINGTON
PUBLISHING CORP.

www.kensingtonbooks.com

KENSINGTON BOOKS are published by
Kensington Publishing Corp.
119 West 40th Street
New York, NY 10018

All Kensington titles, imprints, and distributed lines are available at special quantity discounts for bulk purchases for sales promotion, premiums,
fund-raising, educational, or institutional use.

This book is a work of fiction. Names, characters, businesses, organiza-
tions, places, events, and incidents either are the product of the author's
imagination or are used fictitiously. Any resemblance to actual persons,
living or dead, events, or locales is entirely coincidental.

To the extent that the image or images on the cover of this book depict
a person or persons, such person or persons are merely models, and are
not intended to portray any character or characters featured in the book.

Special book excerpts or customized printings can also be created to fit
specific needs. For details, write or phone the office of the Kensington
Sales Manager: Kensington Publishing Corp., 119 West 40th Street, New
York, NY 10018. Attn. Sales Department. Phone: 1-800-221-2647.

The K with book logo Reg US Pat. & TM Off.

ISBN: 978-1-4967-4263-6 (ebook)

ISBN: 978-1-4967-4262-9

First Kensington Trade Paperback Printing: July 2023

10 9 8 7 6 5 4 3 2 1

Printed in the United States of America

For Beau, in every timeline

The whole series of my life appeared to me as a dream; I sometimes doubted if indeed it were all true, for it never presented itself to my mind with the force of reality.

—Mary Shelley, *Frankenstein*

Contents Warning

This book contains instances of infidelity, vivid dissociative episodes and mental health struggles, gaslighting (particularly in regard to mental health), consensual sexual content, emotional manipulation, grief, terminal illnesses, and extensive discussions of off-page parental death and childhood neglect.

Chapter 1

I feel like I might disappear, and I almost wish that were the truth.

There is nothing but gray up here at the top of the world, bleeding the road and the sky into one. Damp grass expands on either side of us, a steady spread before the land drops off into the black pit of the ocean below, only air and the jagged rocks of the cliff between them.

The knuckles of Jack's left hand have blossomed white where they grip my thigh. I shift, my legs pressing farther into the sleek tan interior of the passenger side door and his hand falls away, mindlessly drifting back to mirror its partner's grip on the steering wheel. We cut through clouds of fog hovering just above the road as we speed through the fading afternoon light, our disjointed breathing and the thrum of the engine the only sounds. The car envelopes us in a warm bubble of protection from the raging of January beyond the glass and metal.

I reach across to run a hand through the light coif of Jack's hair, my knees still pressed away, my body facing the door, the window, beyond. There is no light to glint off of the diamond wrapped around my fourth finger, but it still draws my eye, catching my breath as it dances between the golden strands of hair. He doesn't lean into my touch, doesn't even seem to notice the spiritless play of my fingers across his scalp.

"It'll be all right," I say, and I wish I could mean it.

He says nothing because there are no words, not really, and I wonder if he even hears me, even knows I'm here. But then his eyes dart from the road, landing on my face for just a moment.

"Yeah. Thanks, love." His tone is flat, but it's enough. It's the best that could be expected of him, all things considered.

We'd known that his mother's health had been deteriorating for far too long. She'd been fighting her battle for years now. Even back when Jack and I were still building the foundations of our life together, she'd been on the cliff's edge of health. But now not even the best medicine that Britain had to offer was enough to pull Alice back. It had tipped us all over the edge with her.

So it was no surprise when, the night before last, Jack had come through the door of our flat, tie hanging askew, a heavy weight pulling down on his gaze. These days, it could have been anything, but I knew what it was immediately. I wasn't sure that he'd ask me to join him and his parents as they retreated to their family estate up north to hibernate together for his mother's final months, weeks, days.

But he had. I could've said no—I thought about it as I sat there on the stiff leather of our couch, in our flat whose rent I couldn't afford, our television that I had not really been watching droning listlessly behind his words. *Ours, ours, ours.*

But I had looked into Jack's eyes across the space that we shared, that we had built together, and I knew that saying no to this would be saying no to much more, and so the word could not make its way off my coward's tongue. I had nodded, said, "Of course." I had kept reciting my script the way I was meant to.

He hadn't hugged me, hadn't laid his head across my lap

and let me stroke my hands gently across his hair, his skin, his lips, like he did when our relationship was still in blossom. And I hadn't let my eyes attack every inch of his appearance, looking for a stray golden hair of the work colleague whose smile opened too wide for him, or a distant gaze that meant his mind was somewhere else, on someone else. I had stopped looking for a reason, stopped caring who had filled the ocean between us, afraid to find that it would be my own empty-eyed reflection staring back at me.

And Jack had simply nodded once, placing a numb kiss upon my forehead as he drifted past me, making his way into the bedroom. I hadn't followed him.

The door handle of the car's interior bites back at me as Jack guides the car to the right and for a moment I think he's leading us over the edge of the cliff at last. But then a line of sturdy-backed trees rises up through the fog, guiding us off the main road and onto a private drive.

The estate—Langdon Hall—has been the cornerstone of Jack's family for longer than my own family can even trace our lineage, the shining star of the Page family's extensive ownership. I wasn't surprised when he told me this is where they'd gather now, the house full of memories of summers spent in childhood along the rocky English coast, the scent of salt spray and money on the air. No map sat unfolded in the car with us—Jack knew the journey there as well as he knew himself.

In all our years together I had never been, the weekends away always coinciding with my own familial visits, dissertation defenses, bachelorette parties. Jack's mother could be powerful with a planner when she wanted to be. But I didn't have any of those things, those people, in my life anymore. I only had Jack. And so here I was.

The historian in me was always fascinated by Langdon, this piece of the past that the Pages owned. I had thought of the house often, guessed what of time's secrets it hid, what tales it could tell. But even in my most wild, vivid imaginings, I had never pictured the grandeur that rises up before us, the slate gray of the fog parting to reveal steepled stone in the distance, protected from the outside world by a looming, intricately woven iron gate that now stands to greet us. I almost expect a footman to be conjured from the mist to guide it open, to welcome the prince home. But it is 1994 and the mere press of Jack's fingertips across a digital pad out the window are enough for the gate to creak open with a slow ominousness that makes my palms itch, the last moment of escape sliding from my grasp.

The car presses through the gates and deeper into the swirl of fog across the base of the dusky building.

It is another world.

Age has collided with the brutal English weather to turn the stones deep brown, stacked atop one another like soldiers, a fortress of peaks and archways, made all the more dominant by the sudden disappearance of the land around it, the sole inhabitant on the threatening point of a cliff. Ivy creeps up and around the sharp edges of the home, softening them, like emeralds wrapped around the thin column of a neck. Narrow, rounded turrets reach up toward the thick wall of clouds above, tiny windows nestled beneath threatening iron peaks.

A hundred windows, nearly all darkened even in the slanted evening light, stare back at me as the car edges closer, falling beneath the great silhouette of Langdon. The glass eyes seem to gaze down at me, assessing, finding me wanting. The building is weathered and worn but still immaculate, wearing its history as proudly as the Pages do.

It is terrifyingly beautiful, this looming being of stone. I imagine that once it was simply beautiful, and I wish that I could have seen it in such a state. But instead I see it as the dark form that it stands as now, a building made of shadows knit together.

"You'll be good, right? You can manage?" Jack does not look at me, does not explain himself. He does not need to, we both know what he means. He did not used to ask these questions, though I can hardly remember those times anymore. *Even if I was not, it's too late to turn back now, isn't it?* "Of course. I've been doing well."

Like a child to a parent, I want Jack to affirm me, tell me he sees me trying, tell me that he's proud of me. That he's here.

He simply nods.

That's been the worst part of it all. Everyone stops believing you. So much so that maybe, eventually, you start thinking that you shouldn't believe yourself either.

I used to know Jack so well. Now he's grown distant, become a stranger. I do not know who I need to be to keep his love anymore. The pressure to find out is a ticking clock as loud as our silence.

The crunch of stone and gravel beneath rubber ceases as we pull to a stop behind the form of a black sports car, a favorite of Jack's dad, often left unused in the wake of Alice's grumbling. The car is a rare sighting when the Page matriarch is around, refusing to even step foot inside the vehicle. But perhaps when Edgar drives off the lot in it in a few weeks' time, he doesn't think he'll need to worry about coaxing Alice into the passenger seat to leave. Because that's why we're here, isn't it—because Alice will likely not be leaving Langdon at all.

The manor yawns as the wide wooden doors swing open, the dulled edges of a man barely visible through the dimness within. Jack hurriedly exits the car to greet his father, the slamming of the driver's side door rattling those of us discarded items that remain within. With the trepidation of a decision made that cannot be revoked, I unfold myself into the expansive driveway.

Nighttime has crawled in, the gray of afternoon slipping into the navy of evening. The emptiness of the ocean, of the cliffs beyond, of nothing but air, devour the estate, casting a darkened blanket across its face. I head steadily, unarmed, into the mouth of the beast.

Chapter 2

Jack has already disappeared into the bowels of the estate. There is only one man left lurking in the doorway, his back to me and the outside world as he watches his son scurry off with the privileged air of familiarity.

"Ah, Saoirse." My name pulls his voice down. Edgar turns to face me, an afterthought to the arrival of his golden boy. His flaxen hair is heavy with pinstripes of gray now, but his broad shoulders and reaching form still mirror that of his son, age not yet a weight on his back.

"We're glad you could take time off from school to come. I'm sure Jack'll really need the support about now." His tone is familiarly condescending, frosted by the sharp spears of the ice that live within him.

I try not to let him see me bristle at the cavalier, though expected, way in which he dismisses my PhD as mere school-work, as if it is simply a childlike commitment. The wound they've created there has long since scabbed over. I no longer hear the echoing chuckle of Edgar as he tells his mates that *"Saoirse studies old pieces of paper and whatnot,"* like the study of history no longer bears any consequence when it doesn't have the Page family seal.

The night I met Jack he'd had to lean close to my ear, his

breath hot and damp across my cheek as he told me over the crowded sounds of the pub that he "worked in finance, love, and family business." I remember being charmed by the low smoothness of his accent, so at odds with the sharp points of the American tongue that I'd left the week before. He was charming and confident in a way I never was, not even then. Immediately and instinctively, I wanted him and I wanted him to want me in a way no one had before, in a way that would last. I was swept up in him so easily, in the effortless way he floated through the world, the way I could stroll along in the path he set. The way his face lit up as he discussed a cricket match, the way I would happily sit beside him in a pub for hours while he smiled up at a game I did not understand. I wanted to be there so I could see him cheer, so I could be the person he grabbed to celebrate when his team scored. Jack drew the eyes of everyone in a room, that was just his way. But he had always been looking at me.

It was only once I knew him that I realized the family business was receiving a paycheck for wearing the Page name and nearly any old job title could be attached to it.

I should have known then.

There is no impressing these people. There is no job title I can hold that will ever be enough. Not even fiancée.

I should do better now.

But I do not.

There is no sense pushing against a brick wall and hoping it will sway. So I pretend I do not see it. And that is something the Pages themselves do so well.

"Of course," I reply to Edgar. I can hear that my voice is pinched, flat, lifeless, but I cannot remember the last time I was a woman who spoke in colors.

My future father-in-law leans toward me, his left arm and my right almost making one complete hug together, enough air between us to whistle as the stinging wind rolls through the still-open doorway.

As Edgar guides the heavy wood closed, the deep hum of finality echoes through the wide cavern of the entryway, like the top sliding over a tomb. The air stills, dark and potent. Stone floors, blanketed in modern crimson carpets to weaken the spread of chill from building to foot, are dulled by the grandeur of the staircase that expands before us, a velvet-covered marble walkway up into wealth. Light glints off the cream railing from the chandelier above us, its buzz a better conversationalist than Edgar or I could ever be for each other. The air smells deep and metallic, life long since rusted, buried beneath stone.

The rounded edges of the room are hidden from the light's reach, heavy doors once likely meant for the use of butlers and staff obscured. I would not be surprised to learn that the Pages could still count a few people in their employ. Perhaps those darkened alcove doors would have been more fitting for my entrance.

I pull my sweater tighter across my body as a bone-chilling draft sweeps across the room, a wind across the moor or a ghost through hallowed halls. But I am no Cathy, and I certainly have no Heathcliff awaiting me here.

I see Edgar's eyes catch on my hand for the briefest moment as I move, the sight of the Page family ancestral ring around my finger halting his thoughts with the same dark cloud that appeared when he'd first seen it there a year ago.

The Page family. I'm meant to be one of them by this time next winter. A little bit of me falling away with the passage of every month until that name locks into place next to my own.

"Come." Edgar turns his back on me as he begins his ascent up the gilded staircase, his shadow lengthening and coiling in his wake, a dark path of invitation to follow.

Slashes of light cut across the portraits guiding us up the stairs, highlighting the peaks and valleys of paint that form the faces of Pages long since passed. Edgar doesn't pause long enough to let me drink in the sights, to get caught in the rows of dark hair and hazel-eyed gazes looking down at me, empty stares protecting their home. Edgar raises a hand to a few of the portraits as we pass, saying something or other about their subjects, but the steely, painted eyes steal my attention. I feel those ghostly eyes on my back like a cold fingertip down my spine, the press of chilled lips on the nape of my neck.

The thick of the carpet swallows our footsteps as we make our way up to the second floor, stepping out into a large sitting room eclectically yet tastefully merging modern and dated furniture, signs of old wealth enduring. The faded colors of the menagerie are all offset by the prominent white gilding that joins wall to ceiling. A line of windows taller than I am allows the flat blue of the early night sky to become our guest as we stand already raised above the world after just one floor.

"Alice is taking her tea just through there." Edgar's eyes fall to a door of faded blue and gold in the near wall, eyes still glancing over his possessions rather than landing on me. "Jack's already visiting with her, I presume."

I'm not sure whether the information is meant to be an invitation to enter and pay my respects to the matron of the house, or a warning of where I am meant to steer clear of.

"Better to be seen than to be heard, sometimes, yeah?" Jack had said once to me, his hand on the small of my back and a smile lifting his face as he guided me through the doorway of his parent's expansive full-time home down in Surrey. I had thought he was joking then. I know better now.

"Harry will take your bag." Edgar makes the decision for me, though his face is still pinched tight in the middle, as if he is as displeased about the outcome as I am.

But there is no avoiding Alice forever. I am already a fish caught on the Page family hook.

A man in a crisp shirt and trousers appears from beyond the stairwell, coaxing my duffle bag from my grip before returning to the darkened hallway, possessions in tow. I am too aware of where my sweater frays at its hem, even as I tuck the fabric into my fist. I step forward, contemplating knocking on the door, but whether it be Alice, Jack, or both, I doubt there's a soul behind who cares whether I enter or not, so instead I simply push it open. I am shy, have been since I was a girl letting my brothers speak for me, but I cannot help but admonish myself for the way my hand trembles against the wood. More than nervous to speak but afraid to be seen, to be perceived by the people meant to know me, to be my family. I don't think I used to be like this, but that woman is so far gone now, so who is to say if I was ever more than a dim phantom. The hinges creak as the door tilts open, the sound both grating and haunting with the hesitant slowness of my movements.

Another sitting room, larger, filled with more staunchly upright chairs that look ready to collapse with age and a twin of the couch Jack had bought for our flat. A grand piano rests in the corner, ivories darkened with age, jagged and cracked like a mouth of rotted teeth.

Jack sits in a chair facing his mother, a teapot cooling on the small table between them that Jack leans over, their voices dulled over the angry howl of the sea and wind beyond the windows. Jack's back remains turned, the golden halo of his hair blurring into the matching, perfectly styled waves resting atop his mother's sharp features. Sharp features that look up now while still, somehow, looking down at me. The conversation dies as quickly as I enter, the silence of me filling their mouths.

"Hello, dear." Alice reaches her hand out to me in greeting and I cross the room to take it in my own. Her knuckles are hard knobs made prominent by illness. It feels like a trap, the term of endearment for once spoken with something like tenderness rather than bite. *Dear* is a title that should always be gentle, but it is often made sharp in Alice's mouth, endearment whittled down to pointed condescension.

Alice looks smaller now, bones visible through the thick of her crisp cardigan, shoulders sitting lower, but her chin is still lifted, as always. I know better than to think there could be any weakness in this woman.

I take a precarious seat in the chair beside her, instinctually running a hand across the back of Jack's scalp as I do, a meager offer of comfort in the face of his mother's withering. He looks at me at last, as though he's just remembered that I'm here. Edgar's gaze mirrors his son's, the father still lingering in the faded edges of the doorway. I hold all of their eyes. I pull the seams of my sweater down over my hands, the chill of this house inescapable. They have given me the stage. So I must act.

"How're you feeling?" It's a stupid question and I regret it immediately as Jack's eyes fall back down to the intricate weaves of the rug.

I wish, just once, I could pass their tests. I wish Jack still gave me the answers.

"Yes, fine, fine." Alice's voice is crisp. A shallow answer meant to keep me on the outside, and it does. "It's so nice that you could make it out. I figured you'd head back to Boston while Jack is busy. I know he's mentioned your family home being a bit too . . . petite to fit extra guests. Though it seems you don't see your family much, do you?" And there's the familiar swoosh of Alice's sword cutting the air between us.

I try not to let it gratify me, in a small, sick way, that she's faded since I last saw her nearly eight months ago. Then there was still enough of Alice Page for a true fight as we sat across from each other in a sun-speckled restaurant in Mayfair. My leg had rocked our table as I jostled it endlessly. I was uneased by the high prices on the menu before me, by all the unfamiliar faces of fellow eaters around me. It had been so long since I was surrounded by strangers that weren't in the mirror.

It was me who was faded then, a sepia woman not prepared for Alice's colorful attacks, her mentions of how lucky I was that I could simply take off from my PhD and its meager stipend for four months.

"How nice for you to have Jack to live off of, isn't it?"

"Is it really all that much work at the most of times—medieval studies, no?"

"Well, now, I've never known anyone who needed to take mental leave, dear."

"Stress worsens my . . . condition," I'd said, but my voice was too small for her to hear.

Jack had taken my hand in his beneath the table, a hidden gesture of unity, though his tongue had long since frozen in the emptiness of his mouth, his ears willfully unable to hear my unspoken screams.

The chair creaks precariously as I shift, the little bites of winter draft nipping at my skin as it sweeps in from the window behind me.

"Of course. There's nowhere else I'd rather be."

I wish my smile was larger, stronger, but my fingers twist and falter instead. Jack doesn't grab my hand. There isn't a reassuring squeeze anymore.

Alice's gaze sweeps over me and for a moment it is only the sea crashing on the cliffs that makes a sound. But then she sighs, and it is tight. Her eyes move from me, letting me know I am no longer of fascination or importance or even curiosity.

"I'm quite tired, I think I'll head off to rest." Alice slowly sways her way onto her feet, her white fingers threading into Jack's hair as she kisses his head in passing.

She and Edgar slowly make their way through the doorway and into the hall, and Jack and I are left with the ghosts of his family, this home, ourselves.

I don't feel like I'm alone.

I suppose I'm not—Jack is drifting across the room, flat-topped fingertips leading buttons back out of their holes. Our shirts and pants color the rigid backs of dated chairs that are dispersed around the bedroom as though our nighttime activities are expecting an audience. But it's no longer unexpected to feel alone in Jack's fluttering presence, two worlds bumping against each other.

It's more. It's as if there are eyes watching me from the dark swoop of fabric over the canopied bed, frenzied breaths drifting in from the peeling wardrobe whose door sits ajar. As though Alice's dark eyes have been sewn into the wallpaper, always assessing, always watching. I swipe a hand down my bare arm, but I cannot scrub away the goose bumps that rise there.

"Not exactly any old country house, eh?" I say lightly, desperate to put words out into the air before I choke on the quiet, before I start to hear the whispered tones of whoever's gaze makes me burrow lower beneath the heavy down duvet. "A place like this must have quite the history. Do you have any idea when it was built? It's sort of neoclassical, right, so I'd venture sometime after Elizabeth I. Renovated around then, at least."

The sound of my voice wakes Jack up as he tosses the last piece of his outfit onto the dark stack of its companions.

"Hmm?" He looks over his shoulder, eyes widening to find me in his bed. Our bed. The bed. "Ah, yeah, you'd have to ask Dad more about it. I mean . . . I told you it was quite large and old, didn't I? Very important to my family and whatnot."

"Sure, but most holiday homes don't look like the set of a BBC drama. Or have a butler and hundred-year-old furniture."

"Closer to two or three hundred years, really," he says mindlessly as he slides beneath the covers beside me, a chilled breath of air between our bodies.

"Oh, is that all?" I chuckle.

It falls flat between us. This is no longer the Jack who would've rolled his eyes at his own pretentiousness, who would've even acknowledged it as such. Maybe it's his mother's decay that's robbed him of that self-awareness, that lightness. Maybe it's my own withering that was the thief.

Now my jokes sound like weapons and I must scramble out from beneath them.

"How are you, baby? Really?"

"I'm fine, Saoirse. I expected this. This is what we're here for."

He won't say it out loud, won't vocalize it, won't put a name to the thing that eats at his family, but still I know that he means these words. I've watched him prepare and accept, make lines and rules out of things beyond his control in an attempt to bring them back within it.

But still, the air is heavy around us both with the sorrow-to-be.

I'm not sure it's his mother's death that we're grieving prematurely.

I let my gaze take in his hazy form in the darkened room, the last lamp extinguished. His light hair still gleams, as perfectly and meticulously placed as always. Dark brows pinch down to meet each other in concern, the strong swipe of his jawline in profile accentuated as his teeth grind together, his eyes still staring ahead, broad shoulders propped up against the intricately carved wooden bed frame behind us.

Nothing in me flutters.

I reach out to him and my hand pauses for a moment, trapped in the empty night. I almost expect my fingers to press into the cold skin of another between us, something ghostly, something more alive than us. But my hand passes through nothing but air before I stroke it down his shoulder.

I wish he would look at me.

I wish he would never look at me again.

I want to pull his head onto my chest, be his shoulder to cry on, be his comfort.

I don't.

Instead, my hand just rests on his arm, the vestige as unfamiliar to him as it feels to me. I squeeze timidly—or my hand does—and he leans over to press his lips gently against my own, his eyes closed before he can even take in the face of the woman who's to be his bride.

Until death do us part.

A wish and a curse.

I press up into his mouth before he can retreat. I use my lips, my tongue, to beg without words, to bring him alive.

Please, please.

Jack lets me guide him through the motions unseeing, lids still pulled down over his eyes. His hands are ice across my body, the chill from within and without meeting somewhere in my bones.

His face presses into the pillow beneath me, his motions steady, organized. Four hands meet the bedding, the sheet, the air, anything to avoid skin.

The fabric of the canopy sways, and I watch as the crimson red weaving spreads into the golden stitches around it. Waves of blood flowing above me. In and out, back and forth.

I let the tides of fabric pull me under until Jack's body disappears from atop me, the cold, dampened air my lover once more, running its breath and hands across me.

Jack turns onto his side, his back stretching out before me, and I roll to meet it with my own, two pairs of eyes peering out into the night rather than at each other. I look at the seats at the end of the bed and the eyes of the night are gone, no audience to our crumbling now.

Chapter 3

"Baby!" Jack's voice echoed down to me, twisting around the winding staircase. "You doing all right down there?"

The honking horns and screaming babies of London faded as I climbed my way up toward him, the two stacked cardboard boxes in my arms swaying precariously as I went. The staircase opened up into the narrow hall of the top floor, one perfect little blue front door propped open, Jack leaning against it, his hair like liquid gold as the morning sun backlit him.

"I'm doing all right down here."

He kissed my smile, taking the boxes from my arms to place them just beyond the doorframe.

"Welcome to our home, love." Jack stepped back, pulling me into the space with him by our joined hands, fingers interwoven with a thoughtless familiarity.

It wasn't much yet. Wide wooden floors buffed smooth, boxes and suitcases resting in corners, the sofa sitting crooked in the middle of what would be the sitting room.

It wasn't much, but it was more than anything I'd ever had before.

It wasn't much, but it was *ours*.

A space lit in stripes of hazy morning light streaming in

through the far windows, painting this place and us in gold, warming us all.

Back then it never felt like I had to try for Jack. Like just being *me* was enough, whoever that was. I don't remember her much anymore.

Jack pulled me against him in the middle of the room, situating us in a square of light, his hands resting on my waist, the steady thrum of his heartbeat in my ear as it pressed against his chest—my favorite sound.

But even now my heart could not slow to meet his, could not ignore the little thing that clawed up through me and made me call it anxiety.

"What's happening in that head of yours, huh?" Jack could always tell when I'd gone elsewhere, when the cavern of my mind started to look like all there was.

He ran a hand down my hair, guiding my chin up to look at him.

"It's just . . . this is your space, you know? And I have all this stuff, and I'm worried I'll get in your way, or what about my bad days and—"

"Sersh, this is *our home.* I don't care who signs the rent check. And wherever I am, there will always be space for you, you know that."

His thumb stroked across my cheek, his own face tilting down so he could look into my eyes, so I could follow the hazel back out into the world, our world, this little nook of comfort that we were creating.

"Thank you. I'm sorry."

"You never need to thank me and you never need to apologize." He lifted my left hand to press a kiss against my knuckle, just above where that diamond ring would eventually come to rest.

I didn't choose to believe him—I just already did. I let the gold of our home warm up the space inside me.

I looked around at the chaos of the room, seeing how the books could rest on the shelves, how the throws could be tossed across the cushion backs. Building this *us* in my mind.

"It might be an absolute mess in here at the moment, but I did make sure to leave the kettle nice and accessible." I stepped back, cracking open the box roughly labeled "kitchen" in my familiar, sprawling hand. "Shall we christen the space with a cup of Earl Grey?"

"Ah, I can't, love." Jack was stepping away, gathering his wallet and keys from where they had been strewn on the cluttered countertop. "I've got to meet my parents, remember? They've driven up to take me out to lunch."

"That's today? Are they going to come take a look at the flat later?"

"Nah, likely not."

"All right, I guess. Why'd that have to be today? It would've been nice if we could settle in together."

"I know, baby, I wish I could. But they insisted." He'd shrugged. *What can you do?* "Why don't you ring your mum? Tell her all about the new flat? Phone's already all set up." He gestured to the heavy white telephone wired up on the kitchen wall. All that would do was make a good day bad, but Jack could never quite understand the way the telephone line felt empty when I called my family. His was always so full.

"That'll just make me feel lonelier." I could hear how pinched my voice sounded just at the mention of my mother. I knew Jack could too as his face shuttered, just the slightest bit. I chided myself for breaking my own rule of even touching upon my mother's indifference, my own failing. Jack didn't need to see that. I vowed that I wouldn't let him, not when he and I were finally blooming, laying down our roots. I wouldn't tarnish us with my past.

"I can come along if you'd like? I haven't seen your parents in a while," I deflected. Jack's face smoothed.

"They said they had things to chat with me about. You know how they can be."

I didn't, not then. I know now.

"Tell your mom and dad I say hi, then."

"Will do. I'll be back before you know it, love." He kissed me, hand already outstretched to rest on the door handle. "And I'll miss you every moment I'm gone."

I rolled my eyes and laughed, the tightness in my stomach loosened. I still had Jack. His smiling face leaned forward to linger by mine until I pressed up onto my toes to join our mouths once more.

"I'll miss you too."

Jack stepped back into the doorframe, falling into the shadow of the hall, halfway between the soft light of our space and the world beyond.

"It'll be all good, love. There's nothing to worry about. Stop letting that mean brain of yours be mean."

The worry at the edge of my mind was still slowly bleeding in, but I smiled at him, at the affection in his eyes, at the way his body tilted toward me even as he was pulled to obligations elsewhere.

"What do we always say?"

"We'll figure it out together," I replied obediently.

"Exactly, we'll figure it out together. It'll all be all right."

I believed that then. I think Jack probably did too.

He pushed through the doorway at last, pulling the door slowly closed, his last words finding me through the shrinking gap.

"I love you!"

That day, in some swanky café downtown, Alice had told her son of her diagnosis at last, of the way that the ticking clock of her life now seemed to move a bit quicker than it had before. And when Jack had returned home that afternoon—

to our home—he seemed to bring the shadows in with him, with a little fleck of dark in his eyes that has not left since, that has grown and seeped out into us and between us and became us.

I love you too.

Chapter 4

The bed was empty by the time I woke, but I could still feel the ghost of heat radiating off the other side, could see the faint indent in the mattress that continued to bear the weight of a sleeping form. I used to always be the one to wake early, to brew the coffee that would stir Jack, guiding him into the living room for that quiet morning moment we would share before the split hecticness of our days. Now there are days I cannot bear to see the sun at all, days I cannot be brought from bed. Now I wake alone.

The heat of the bed is replaced by the same damp chill that runs throughout this house, the chill that guides me, searchingly, from the bedroom to the expansive dining room I now cautiously enter. The sound of my footsteps is thrown back at me as I make my way across the wooden floor. The sound does not draw the eye of the room's occupants.

The Pages are already seated around the long expanse of table in all their haughty glory, backs as straight as the wood between them. At home, Jack usually meets our dining room table with his left leg up, ankle kissing knee, or knee kissing chest. Here, both feet firmly ground him, his body a taut string.

Strains and remnants of toast, tea, and fruit dot the table, though all the plates before the occupants have long since been cleared. The family of three chatter quietly to one another, voices clear and dignified, but not ringing back from the high ceiling, too many years of practice speaking beneath gilded arches.

My chair complains loudly as I sit upon it. Alice's left eye pinches at the screech, but her gaze remains turned toward her husband at the table's head and her son, seated across from me. Still pretending as though he cannot see me, cannot hear me. As though I do not exist. Maybe I do not.

They do not want me here; I knew as much before I even crossed Langdon's threshold. But suddenly the days, weeks, until I cross it out into the world once more seem never ending, and guilt pinches me to think that I wish the time would pass quicker. They want me to disappear, are willing it so, and I do not know how I will survive my time here.

It is like I am not here at all. I might as well not be.

The window at my back casts dampened gray light across the table and me, muting it all.

"Good morning." I hate how loud my voice sounds in this space, as though I'm yelling over the soft tilts of the Pages, announcing that I do not belong here. "How did you all sleep?"

The purse of Alice's mouth, the same narrow lips that meet on Jack's face now, tells me I've asked the wrong question again. I am reminded of Jack hanging up the phone one morning, stress having slashed lines into his forehead, the tinny ring of Alice's voice telling him that she has lost another night to wakefulness, coughing up bits of herself.

I hate that I can never seem to ask the right questions, hate how it makes me hate myself. I hate how these people make me hate myself.

"Fine, thank you." With his curt dismissal Edgar lets my body slide from the sword of guilt in my belly. "The . . . nurse should arrive around midday, I'm told. Very highly recommended, Dr. Black has assured me." The patriarch's eye returns to his wife once more, Jack's own sweeping in its wake, and I have faded away once more. I almost wish I had screamed. To let them know—to let all of us know—that I am awake, I am here.

I feel that potent, deep ache in the pit of my stomach, that especially awful kind of loneliness that spreads out to your bones, that feeling of being alone in a room of people, that sense that you exist to no one but yourself.

That darkness inside me calls out. I do not answer. No, not anymore.

The toast is flavorless in my mouth as I chew, the crunch echoing back at me, even as I soften my bite, shrinking. Alice lets out a small huff and I swallow heavily, reaching instead for the bowl of fruit with an outstretched hand that doesn't really feel like mine. My arm brushes a mug, a too loud clatter, tea washing across the table.

"Oh, now, honestly." Alice, who can never let it rest, whose words are chafed with annoyance.

"Mum, it was just an accident," Jack says. For once, he says something, and the weight that lives on my chest eases its burden just a bit. "Saoirse didn't mean to—"

But then Alice's waifish frame is racked by coughs, chest jumping and trembling with the force. And just like that, I lose Jack, the olive branch snaps. He turns a heavy, disapproving gaze on me as I wipe up the mess with these hands, these hands that are someone else's. As though it is my incompetence, my carelessness, that ills Alice. As though harshness toward me is some sort of apology for ever daring to dispute his mother.

I never chose a war with Alice Page, would never ask Jack to choose between us, but it's clear he has. I can't even really fault him if his dying mother outranks his fiancée. There are two kinds of sickness, and Alice's trumps mine.

I am brought back to my body as a sheer wave of blue strokes the arm of my chair, the curtain dancing away from the movement of a figure behind it. A figure that cannot be there.

My eyes catch on the fabric, on the clear press of an outlined body against it, the line of an arm up into a shoulder, a man in passing hidden by the curtain. But then the fabric floats down, landing on nothing but air.

I'm almost driven to my feet, heart plummeting, but I freeze, hands still gripping the stiff wooden arms of the chair. The faces around me are not shocked, not terrified, but irritated. It is as though they did not see whatever it was that has made blue satin whisper against my arm, made my hands tremble. All they have seen is my response.

I want to speak, want to ask, but my tongue has disappeared before the stares of people waiting to see me slip.

With little more than a quirk of an eyebrow and a shake of his gray-topped head, Edgar makes his way around the table to help guide Alice's quaking form up from her chair, her eyes on me sharper than the protruding notches of her body.

"It's time for your mother's medicine," he says in passing as they make their way through the door.

My ability to clear them from a room, with no effort or desire on my end, has been a skill perfected for years now.

"What was that? They were busy sorting things out, Saoirse. You didn't need to try to, I don't know, get attention or something, acting all afraid," Jack sighs.

No, no, not you too.

I know what I saw. What I felt.

"It wasn't that, I—"

"I should probably get started on the things in the attic." Jack does not let me finish, mind made up. He pushes himself up to stand, his chair sighing in relief. "It's full of old shite, I guess. Dad wants me to sort out what to keep or donate up there since we likely won't be back for some time."

"I'll help." I go to stand, but Jack raises his hand and brow, stopping me in midmotion once more.

I want to help, I want to be with him, I do not want to be left alone here.

"No need, Saoirse. You haven't even finished your breakfast."

I tuck a piece of toast in my mouth, the bread as dry and stale as our words.

"I'm hardly hungry, baby. I'll eat as we go."

I can almost still feel the whisper of the blue fabric on my arm, but I ignore it because I can see in Jack's eyes that he wants me to and I want, so badly, to pass a test here.

"Besides, I'd love to see your family's artifacts. I'm sure there's plenty to learn from it." I smother the slight quake in my voice, but I am not sure Jack notices me enough to pick up on it anyway. I smother the pang in my chest that my fiancé did not think I would be curious, that he does not know or care of what may interest me. I smother the fear that is still clawing at my chest.

Jack doesn't concede and he doesn't say no, he simply makes his way to the door, shined black shoes carelessly indenting the thick carpet. His silence is a little lash of shame and I feel its sting, replacing the gentle touch upon my arm.

As we trudge our way up the grandiose stairs, peeks of darkened sitting rooms and heavy closed doors flashing by us, I cannot resist looking over my shoulder with nearly each step. I don't feel the weight of eyes on me, and for that I'm thankful, but I can't stop the quick, rapid breathing in my chest, expecting a phantom arm to snake itself across my shoulders at any moment. Jack does not notice, eyes not even trailing behind him to look at me, much less someone who may never have been there at all. But I cannot shake what I saw, the form of a man made from air and dust and the fear that has nibbled at me since we drove through Langdon's gates.

I wish I could remain quiet, but I cannot. The words will burn my tongue until I free them.

"At the table back there . . . did you see that?"

Jack doesn't pause, doesn't look back. He keeps climbing upward, away from me.

"Do you mean the curtains?"

"Yes!" *It was real, I am here still, it is okay, I am here. The darkness cannot reach me.* "I'm certain it looked like there was someone behind it but then—"

The sharp exhale of Jack's breath takes the power from my tongue. One breath and I am small, shrinking into the velvet beneath our feet, a child reprimanded so many times that they've learned the warning signs of the lecture before it begins.

"Come on, Saoirse, it's an old house. There are drafts." His voice is tight, but it lingers, sullying the air between us as he pauses. "Look, are you . . . feeling ill again? Is that what this is?"

The punch of his words hits me in the chest with all the impact he'd intended.

"No, Jack, it is not my depression nor anything else." I do not lower my voice, do not fade away, even as he winces at the sound of the word ringing through his hallowed halls.

His sigh now is all rounded edges, concession. He goes down one step, no longer a looming figure, takes my face in his hands, his grip pushing auburn strands into my vision. His hands are gentle on my cheeks and I almost believe that this is where he wants them to be, almost melt into him again.

Something stops me, as it always does now.

"Of course. You know I just worry about you, love." His lips are still tight with the words he does not say as he presses them to my forehead. "It's a large, old house. Sometimes these things happen. It's nothing."

He is the prince here, and his words make it so.

Jack dashes up the last few steps to meet the sloping wood of the house's final floor, leaving our conversation behind, resting it beside me on the staircase.

The small door tucked away up here screams in protest as Jack forces it open, the bronze skeleton key that lives in the lock a shaky duet. It would be enough to raise the hairs on my arm, to put me off this place if I was not already. We duck beneath the flaking doorframe, the shadows of the forgotten Page family legacy standing like an army to greet us from within.

"So what're we meant to clear out exactly?" I wish that my voice, too quiet, too patient, didn't make it so obvious that I want to smother the ripples left behind, ghosts of the waves that have just raged between us, weaker now that we've lost the anger, the desire, the love, to even truly fight.

I wish I didn't feel like it was my job to steady our ship, but I am too afraid to not try and see that Jack would not either.

Jack's nimble fingers pull the cord of a light toward him to no avail. We stand unspeaking, my back pressed to the peeling yellow wallpaper, as though I am a fixture of the house, choking on dust and history. Then Jack fumbles his way to a little stained-glass lamp and the room is thrown into a golden glow and I come alive again.

The attic, with its tented roof and porthole window showing the raging waves beneath us, does not feel like the air is made to feed the ghosts of this home. It is quiet, it is empty, it is only us, Jack and me, that make dread scratch its ever-sharper claws along the base of my belly. We are what haunts this room.

"Any and everything. There's just too much stuff in here, loads of it—likely junk too." Jack's voice is empty, words spoken to the floor as he leans over to peer into an open chest in the center of the room. "Dad wants me to sort it out a bit, see what we can bin and what's Page important."

Page important, a favorite phrase of theirs, an adjective that carries the highest worth, the steepest rank. *Page important*, like Edgar with his rich family legacy; like Alice, who wove her own thread of pure lion's blood and sterling into the Page family tapestry; like Jack, who could do no wrong, who has whittled himself down from the charming, carefree, loving boy I met on a sticky floor in Hackney to the perfect image of his parent's deepest longings—the only blemish on his life the girl who wears his family ring on her shaking hand.

Page important.

Two years ago I would have gotten lost up here for hours, hands not able to grab objects quick enough to satiate my curiosity, fingers scribbling notes and questions to take to the library. I would have wanted to learn every secret this "old junk" could tell, find out what it said about the house, about the Pages, about Jack, every corner of him a place I wanted to explore. Now I sort through things as mindlessly as he does.

It is nearly nightfall by the time we have separated the room into three piles; the shining gems of worth on the right— jewelry that still catches the fading light through the window even after years of neglect, vintage gowns with the high waists of the Regency era and the shortened, beaded, hems of the jazz age. To the right, hidden from the light, sits the items ready for discard, portraits of Pages not worthy of the stair- well and its golden frames, hastily stacked atop one another, their faces obscured and buried, like their names.

And in the middle, before where Jack is crouched on the floor, the last few remnants left to sort of the task that is surely Edgar's idea of distracting his son from his mother's breathing decay.

I reach out beyond Jack's shoulder, my hand no longer shaking, the sense of emptiness in this room almost bliss now from the suffocating feeling of *presence* in the floors beneath us. My fingers brush against the hem of Jack's body and I nearly apologize and I almost wish that I did not have the de- sire to retract a touch from the man who is meant to be mine.

I claim a book of deep brown leather, its only mark a stamped Tree of Life across its face, the spine splintered with signs of use and the pages yellowing and curled with age.

The book opens for me reluctantly, showing faded swirls of black ink that I can tell were made long ago, written by quill. The once-bright glow from the lamp has dulled its usefulness as the sky outside turns onyx, throwing shadows across the page that hide the words within them.

"What've you got there?" Jack leans across me, a gap of intention between our bodies, as he tosses a rolled map to the right.

"A journal it looks like. Not sure whose, though." No name mars the pages, but the steady press of the hand remains the same across each of the opening sheets, the latter ones left empty.

Jack's eyes glance off of it in a way that is so familiarly distant that it makes a fist squeeze within my chest.

"We've got most of the records from my important ancestors. You can toss it in the to-bin pile." He has already dismissed us, the journal and me, placing the final item to be determined—a jewelry box—beneath the dance of starlight, worth affirmed.

As I feel the thin, aged paper on my fingers there is that rush I had forgotten, that has been lost with all the other parts of me, that feeling that told me I was a historian. I miss that, the way a book, an artifact, a letter could give you the glimpse that let you fall back into the past. That made the past come to life.

I glance back down at the journal, letters too quickly scrawled to make out with just a look. But I see the word "alone" and I cannot relegate the journal to be forgotten just yet.

"Do you mind if I hold on to it for a bit?"

Jack's sigh is a string taut with tension and I feel my breathing shallow in response.

"If you'd like." He shrugs to tell me that he cannot understand me, but he has not understood me long before we set foot in this attic. I swear, in the haze of my memory, that he used to. "We should get down for dinner. Harry'll clear out what's left."

Jack walks through the doorway and back into the brightness of the stairwell, where the gloom hides eyes, gazes that I already feel before I follow Jack out into the light.

Chapter 5

Jack is gone again. We have been here only three days and yet he has made a routine in Langdon that does not include me.

But I can't find it in me to worry as I make my way around the twirling stone staircase on the estate's western wing, the leather journal I unearthed yesterday icing within the chill of my grasp. Jack had mentioned, as he buttoned up his shirt this morning, eyes on the window and with his back to me, that the library sat at the head of the estate's farthest left turret. It was a suggestion meant to distract, to occupy my day where he would not have to see me, would not have to worry. To tuck me away in earnest, the way his parents already had, regardless of my presence in a room.

The promise of a library is all the more appealing for its location in the farthest corner of the house. I am all too happy to be far from the voices of the Page family in the sitting room where I'd first seen them, my absence so unnoticed that my presence could never be necessary. Never be desired. Perhaps the stories of this place will hold answers, will tell me who died here and who lives here, and why this place seems so much fuller than the four of us that move within it like mice in a maze.

So I welcome the cool stillness of the air as I climb, the way that the buzzing lights turn the stairwell into a golden tunnel, stretching upward forever. The ache in my joints has begun, with each step carrying me above the world. But the little bursts of pain are me, are mine. They keep me here, within my body.

The path reminds me of the swirling, narrow steps of Notre Dame that Jack and I had climbed on our holiday years ago. He had held my hand loosely in his, smiles tossed casually over his shoulder, raising my heartbeat more than the endless steps, journeying upward together until the heaven of the Parisian skyline unfolded just for us. Now my hand holds nothing but the journal and I do not know where Jack is, not really, and I do not mind. I am solitary in the stillness of my steps upon stone.

The cold burns into my skin, but I'm thankful for it. I hold my shoes loosely in my hand, having discarded them the moment I was free from the watching gazes of the house's occupants. There is a chill on the thin skin of my soles, but it is worth it to be rid of the pressure of thick seams and suffocating fabric. They would be keeping me from touching, from being grounded into the here.

I twist the bend, but the upward climb does not cease, leading to a heavy red curtain lain across a sliver of window at the top of the curve, blocking out the afternoon gray from the stairwell. I continue toward it, pace steady, grounded. *I am here.*

But then the thick red fabric sways, lifts above the steps, long before I can reach it and be the catalyst for the curtain's movement. A ringing sound echoes down to me, the hardened sole of a shoe glancing off of a step as someone climbs, the footsteps of the ghost of this place. It is as though the house itself has come alive, is breathing, is holding me within its sharp-toothed jaw.

There must be someone else here, someone real, though invisible to my eye. Is it real or is it merely the house? Is there a difference?

Goose bumps rise along my arms in waves, the chilled draft of the stone steps, stone walls, stone heart, no longer innocent. I want to close my eyes, to take a deep breath, remember that I am not trapped, I am free, *I am free*, this stairwell, this house, is not a tomb. Months of my heart screaming out to not be alone and now I fear—now I know—that I am not. And it is sickening.

I am afraid to look behind me. Afraid to continue upward, to see what awaits me around the bend of the winding stairs.

The curtains hang lifeless now, but I cannot trust it. I can nearly see those red arms waiting to reach out to me, to wrap me up in them. The journal is trembling in my grasp.

I rush up the stairs in a burst, my bare feet slipping across the pale ridges of the steps. My body absorbs the cold from below in my frenzy, the hem of my dress slashing against my ankles. I pass the curtains and they do not reach out to trap me, do not even move at all. I am the only thing alive here now.

Nothing awaits me around the corner but a massive dark wooden door, worn metal hinges blessedly still as it sits ajar, a peek of bookshelves beyond calling to me, telling me my journey of terror is, for now, complete.

I stand before the door for a moment, breath held, ears sharpened for any shoe soles meeting stone. My eyes rove over the steps, awaiting a phantom to emerge or a finger to glide across my skin. But nothing comes. Perhaps nothing ever came at all.

I am alone again, and I always was. Maybe I'm just a silly girl. Maybe Jack is right, maybe my illness has reared its head once more—not just the depression but the darker bit—come back to pull me under for good, to take the final, fatal blow against me.

I hate that my first thought is that it may bring Jack joy to be free of me at last. His beautiful bride, too fucked in the head. He could cut the ties and no one would blame him. And I would not really be there to blame him either, would I?

"Saoirse, here, but not here at all. That's what we worry about," the doctor had said. "That's what we want to avoid, you understand?"

Jack's hand on my leg but his eyes distant as the doctor spoke, the hazel of them clouded over with the thoughts written across his face: What have I gotten into? *His eyes, cutting to the ring already on my finger.* What have I done? *he did not need to ask.*

"I can fix it, don't worry, it's nothing to worry about. I'll rest and I'll be fine. I'll fix it, I'll fix it."

Then he'd started to slip away. Or maybe the ocean that would be between us was already a pond by then, we just had to drift a bit more. And we had. I have learned that sometimes love has conditions.

Jacks wants the woman he met, the woman he fell in love with. I do not know her anymore.

The cold air of the stairwell pulls forth the water from my eyes, moisture gathered and quivering, ready to spill. I push my way into the library and press the door closed behind me, a barrier between me and the spirit of the house, the empty twists and my own mind.

My hand presses into the wood before my face, my chest heaving, and the fear that has dissipated with distance rises once more as I am face-to-face with that ring, that string of diamonds. It is my branding, the price of my cowardice.

They say that brides will never forget the moment of their proposal and it's true. I will never be able to hide that memory away.

I loved Jack.

I love Jack.

But sometimes you can't see the truth until the man you love is on his knees before you.

The yes came forth anyway because I knew he expected it, everyone expected it. Even I expected it. Even Edgar and Alice, with their sneers and their snobbery, had assumed that I would say yes, though surely they had hoped that I would not.

Because saying no was impossible, inconceivable. Who would deny a Page of anything, especially when agreement came with a diamond and the comfortable assurance of money and a golden weight upon your tongue to keep you silent?

So I had said yes. I had ignored the little part of my brain that was screaming because by then I was already suspecting I could not trust my own mind. Jack, my first and only love, was now to be my last. It didn't feel right, felt too snug at the collar, but I ignored it all because I could not believe that anyone—much less someone like Jack Page, from a family of money and genuine love—could choose me. There is no saying no to that. There should be no reason to.

I had waited my whole life to be chosen, held my breath waiting for it. I couldn't let it pass me by. I knew I might not get another chance. This was the first chance I'd had, to love and be loved in return.

I wasn't loved as I was—as I am—perhaps, but it had been so long since I'd known who I was, since I was anything more than nightshade blooming, made to cope. I had a blank pallet of self, so I swore I would do my best to become whoever I needed to be to keep Jack's love. My childhood had showed me enough to realize that, whoever I was before I was lost to the eclipse of my mind was not someone worthy of love and attention.

My family had taught me in their quiet, violent ways that love came with conditions. So I would meet Jack's. That's all there was to it. I would say yes and I would try to be better.

If Jack is the first to love me, there is nothing to say he won't also be the last. His desire, his love, could be a mere fluke. I could not say no.

I had not said the truth and instead it had choked me. The weight of words unsaid had seeped out of me and created the ocean of oil between us, a gulf that we are both too afraid to acknowledge, that will consume us. It had not felt right, even then I had known, through the haze of light that was our love, that saying yes planted a heavy stone in the pit of my belly. But I also knew that it shouldn't be there, that I didn't want it to be there, that I loved Jack.

Or maybe I had meant it then. Maybe my memory just paints ash across hues of pinks and purples so that the scene will match everything else I see. A world in shades of gray for a colorless woman.

Some days—the bad days—the only thing about myself I'm certain of is Jack. Even when I am hardly Saoirse, I am still *Jack's fiancée.* This relationship, this dying thing . . . I know it is not the best part of me. But when it is the only part, well, I can't just let that go.

And what is Jack's excuse? I see the way he looks at me now and the way he does not. Jack is just playing the hero. He's long served better as his mother's white knight than mine.

What did it mean to simply not be in love anymore? No good person would feel this way.

But I suppose I am not a good person.

The shame bubbles to the surface and it makes the darkness start bleeding in through the corner of my vision, and I fear that it will wash me away.

No, no. Please *no. Not again.* I cannot, will not, bear the shadowy depths of my mind, jammed with aching, suffering thoughts. Or worse, the hollowness, the times when I feel like I have no mind, no body, no emotions of my own, a robot, a shell, merely an idea. *Not again.*

I am not crazy. It is these people, these words unsaid that I cannot breathe around, the glares, the expectations, the cliff that they lead me toward.

I am not crazy. It is this damned house.

Breathe in for four, breathe out for six, slow your heart, Saoirse.

Do not look at the darkness and it cannot get me.

Breathe in, breathe out.

A crack sounds behind me, the walls full of books absorbing the echo, but the noise still pulls me from falling down inside. I spin to see the rounded curves of the walls, bookshelves reaching up to the ceiling along every surface, leather faces welcoming me. The crackling emanates from a fireplace on the far bend, licks of orange and yellow bringing it to life, ready for me.

It should not be lit in this empty room. I know it should not. But I do not feel the fear here. The stillness in this small place is not the quiet before the storm, it is the world muffled in snowfall—delicate and safe.

I stare into the flames until my vision blurs to nothingness, a steady fuzz, and my heart rate slows to match. Whatever awaits me in this house—and something does await me—it does not feel insidious here, now, in this tower.

The names I've heard so many times on Edgar's mouth jump out at me from the shelves, men whose titles sit on paper spines and whose bodies occupy seats at the Pages' table. But tucked among them are rows of aged brown and green and tan, the words of decades, of centuries, nestled together. There is an original Dickens stuffed in beside the words of some man who has nothing to say for four hundred pages, the former priceless, but not even a gleaming jewel among the riches of this family.

An old rotary phone sits on the hulking desk in the corner, a thin layer of dust settled across it, dulling its sheen. When I see it, the first, stupid, thought in my mind is, *I want to talk to my mother. I do not want to be on my own with whatever else is in this place.* I could call her, I know distantly. Maybe she'd even answer, with only the slightest pinch in her voice as she heard it was me. Maybe she'd be annoyed or distracted by my presence, like she was when I was a child, too loud and needy in the heavy quiet of our house. The child who had the green eyes, the small smile, and the red hair of her recently dead husband. The child who was too hard to look at, so my mother did not look at me at all, and silently taught my brothers to do the same. Even after her grief had settled like dust, I had learned to be quiet and passive and peaceful to be loved. But I think it was already too late for her.

Maybe I learned how to be from watching my mother. She spent my life half-awake, glazed eyes never quite landing on her daughter no matter how much I cried or preened or people-pleased. She just kept watching the distance, as though my father would walk through the door, alive and well. She seems to be better now, close to my brothers, who have stayed behind. But I'm gone, far from home, and her newfound attention has never fallen on me.

But maybe if I called my mother now, she would tell me about her friends and her day trips with my nieces, would treat me like little more than a sounding board, would forget to even ask how I was. That was how it tended to go—quiet, cooperative Saoirse, an afterthought to her life, even when I was a child she saw every day. A child who needed her but had no choice but to boil down to nothing.

Pushing thoughts of my mother from my mind, I settle into a fabric-backed wooden chair that sits waiting for me beneath the narrow stretch of window, the rotary phone to my back. The chair's clawed feet are well sunken into the swirls of navy on the carpet, its place here unchanged and earned. A thread of ivy snakes beneath the shuttered window, weaving along the frame and onto the wall, like an intruder sneaking in through the cracks. It is a little piece of reckless beauty, a living thing daring to grow in this decaying place. I wait for something to bang against the door, the fists of a Page, living or ghost, but no one comes for me. The thud in my heart lessens, the walls seem to take a deep breath themselves, expanding outward, air refilling the room and my lungs.

So I open the journal in my lap, the worn yellowing pages like a lover's body as they glide beneath my fingertips, gentle, adoring. Dates jump out at me from the very first page, numbers further back than I could have imagined—a relic that belongs in a velvet box more than it does tossed about in an attic.

August 15, 1817
My dear Nell is out in society at last, stationed in the quarters of our aunt in London. It is for the best. Iris is now well married, and Nell is a young lady, eager to see the world, to make her own place in it beyond the walls of Langdon. Beyond the reach of her eldest brother.

But I will miss her dearly. Home feels less so without the sounds of her laughter echoing against the stone, without her spirit coloring the roses in the garden.

But there is much to be done to keep the estate in order, work aplenty to keep a bachelor busy. I am to journey to Bath in a fortnight, and the Lawrences shall visit in two days' time, Albert with his new bride.

Nell will do well to be beyond the reach of the estate. Its hold on her is nearly as strong as it is upon me. I hope she will find the life and love that she seeks.

The words are brief, the passages narrow, but they say so much to ears like mine, ready to listen. I know little of the nineteenth century, my years of study poring over centuries long before, but still I am pulled in by the voice of a past tucked away.

September 21, 1817
I am to leave for London tomorrow. Aunt Mildred tells me that Nell has met a man and been courted. It is to me to facilitate the affair, of course, to deem him worthy of my youngest and dearest sister. I knew that she would be the belle of the Season—she is a charming young woman with the Page name to give her rank. Perhaps too much rank, unreachable by many men.

But I had not anticipated a courtship with such speed. One must only hope that it is a man worthy of her.

The girls have been doing their best to lure me to Town all Season, Nell telling me of the beauty of the girls that fill the ballrooms and Iris reminding me that I shan't die an old bachelor, Langdon's hallowed halls left to her and Charles.

I make jest, for who shall care for the dog in my absence, who will keep the home? But, in earnest, the eligible misses of the Season shall never lure me to Town.

I have been lucky to have shared affection with many women, to not have a string of bastards in my wake. But I seek no bride. Iris may give the Page name to her babes, may have the estate when I have passed.

Whatever it is that binds me to Langdon, that awaits me here, here I shall be to meet it.

The ink runs across the pages in splashes, the hand calm and crisp on one page and dotted with pools of black on the next. I can imagine the hand that held the quill, smooth with the ease of aristocratic wealth, the feather hovering, ink dripping to collect in the valleys of paper as he pauses, waits, as the words come to him.

There is no name to distinguish the penman, but a man he must be. A man who seems to feel the breathing presence of this estate on his cheek, just as I feel it breathing down my neck.

I am not crazy. Whatever is here, whatever makes this place alive, I am not the only one who knows it. Or rather, the only one to whom it makes itself known.

October 17, 1817
James, a familiar face of my boyish days down at Eton, has called upon the estate to rest and visit but for a few days. He has brought his bride, the girl barely out of leading strings but a charm nevertheless.

James is still adrift in his rakish ways, his eyes and hands drifting to the girls in my employ, even to his bride's own sister, a child of insolence and avoidance, in my esteem. If the whispers of the staff are to be believed, his bride is with child.

A brilliant mind, a talent with a quill, a quick tongue—as James can well boast—does not make a good man.

It is these marriages, the ones of love in its all-consuming newness, that bring the ruin of both hearts. It is unions like this that forced my hand in rejecting the courtship of my sister. I must hope that dearest Nell will find forgiveness in her heart, that the clouds of youth will drift and she will see that my decisions are not made to hurt her.

The world is not easy for women, this I know. I dare hope that one day she will be glad that she need not pass through it unaided before she reaches the arms of a worthy husband. So many women must contend with lonesomeness that leads them astray, toward men racked with foolishness and cruelty. I shall not allow the same for my sister.

Our sister has found companionship and joy with a man of honor, worth much more than foolish new love, and someday Nell shall too, such is a union that will receive my blessing.

Intimacy and history splashes across these pages, written by the hand of a Page deemed unworthy of remembering. If this is what the Pages I know are willing to forget, to push aside, who am I to think I have worth here?

The light streaming across the page grays as clouds shift beyond the window. I stand, the carpet stiff and aged beneath my toes, and place the journal on the small table beside my seat. I leave the stamped tree side facing up to the point of the ceiling, so its leaves may grow.

The dark gray of this place has broken, the sky an icy slate as snow falls down, flakes kissing the frozen hedges, stacking atop one another in fresh layers of winter. The greens and browns of the garden expand far behind the house, a wrought iron fence keeping us all from seeping down into the waves over the cliff's edge, raging as the snow gets swept away with each beat of water on the shore. The window fogs over quickly, snow clinging to the glass and spreading it opaque, desperate to find a place within this estate where it can't be forgotten.

The fire that bores its slashes of color behind me no longer feels inviting but a heat trapping me here, burning me up. The world beyond calls to me. I want the ice outside to be inside, I no longer want to be burning, burning, burning.

I turn to snatch the journal, to begin my descent, but my hand finds nothing but air. I press my palm into the dark wood of the table, as though the journal has faded into its face but will make itself known to me by a touch. It does not rise, of course. It is not on the table, not waiting for me in my seat. It is simply gone.

I whip around, the faces of hundreds of books mocking me, having taken the journal hostage, making a joke of me. Rows and rows of leather that have stolen it, swallowed it whole. The thud of my heart begins aflutter, cheeks flushing, as though I can hear the manor leering at me, watching my confusion and fear. What an easy toy I must make for whatever it is that lives in these walls.

But then there it is. The brown leather of the journal sitting patiently, waiting for me, placed almost carelessly across the front of a shelf by the door, far beyond my reach. I did not put it there, I would have remembered. I am not crazy, I did not do this, something is here, something is mocking me.

As I look toward it, a dark figure appears in the doorway just beyond, looming beneath the arch. It is there for only a moment as my head turns, and as I look again the body is gone, the room noiseless, only my ragged breaths echoing back at me.

I will not snap, I will not spiral, I will not let this place break me.

Stay in the light, Saoirse.

But the hairs along my arms refuse to stand down as I make my way across the carpet, the creak of each step stealing my breath, awaiting the violence of Langdon, whose reach has grown long. Whose dastardly, ghostly arms have strengthened.

I am a smart woman. A modern woman. But I was weaned on the stories of ghouls and fetches, and they are stories I shall not soon forget. I do not need to have seen to believe, but I have seen nevertheless.

I snatch the journal from the shelf and make my way out the door, praying that the spirits will not follow me down, will release me from their grip before I am lost.

I am not alone, but oh, how I wish I were.

I fear what this house has in store for me.

Chapter 6

The velvet carpet hugging the stairs slips beneath my feet as I frantically make my way down the largest stairwell, down into the heart of the home. If Jack and his parents are anywhere to be found, the walls have smothered their voices. The only sounds are my muffled footsteps and harried breathing. And for once, I wish that they were here.

I cannot be alone with this house. I cannot. For I fear that it will never let me be alone, and that is the problem. I want to feel the hand of the man I love, not the icy fingers of a phantom.

I want to throw the journal from me, to scatter the pages, to let the draft that haunts this house carry them over the cliffs and out to sea. I want to keep the journal pressed to my chest, call it not a villain but a bystander, another victim of Langdon Hall.

A shadow in the corner of the staircase, sewn into the darkened wall, peels itself toward me, stepping into the light and into life.

No, no, no.

My hand skitters across the smooth gold of the banister, desperate to hold on, to stay on my feet that are flying beneath me, for I must get away before it consumes . . .

"Saoirse, what's wrong?" Jack steps forward.

The sight of him freezes me, and I do not know if it's in relief or fear. My body ceases its escape and we are still.

We look at each other for a long moment, hazel pressing into green across the expanse of carpet and stone between us.

"There's someone upstairs." My voice is breathy, my throat raw with fear and exertion.

"What do you—?"

"Some*thing*."

The worry on Jack's face falls off of him like a coat, his head ceasing its search for another figure in the splashes of artificial light. He slowly turns back to me. I know to expect the exasperation etched into his features before I even see it.

"Maybe having some time to yourself this morning wasn't the best idea after all."

I know I could push back. I could insist that what I experienced was real, that I'm not crazy, I'm not crazy, I'm not crazy.

But the disappointment in his tone, the way that worry has pulled his skin into little hills on his forehead—not worry *for* me, but *about* me. It steals the words from my lips.

There is nothing wrong with me. I know that what happened was real. But Jack will not believe it. I know that too.

"Nothing, never mind." I do not believe my voice, but Jack will because he wants to. "I think I fell asleep and had an odd dream or something. It's all fine."

My breathing still comes in rapid puffs and it fills the air for a moment as Jack waits, deciding if he will choose to believe this lie. I almost wish he would reach out and hold my face in his hands, running the smooth side of his thumbs across my cheekbones. Look me in the eye, truly for once, and actually see me. But I fear that his touch would suffocate me in the pity, the concern, the unspoken wishes that he could be free of me and all my endless problems.

I do want to get better. I'll fix it. I will again become

*someone worth Jack's love, not his unease, or his pity. I'll
fix this.*

"Okay," he breathes. He does not ask if I am sure that's all
it was, if I am okay. He does not want the answers, he wants
words that he can swallow down easily.

My hands are still shaking, the journal quivering in my
grip. Jack's eyes catch upon it.

"Are you reading that thing? Is it frightening? Maybe it's
best not to read much now, while you're still . . . delicate. You
know how easily your mind can get away from you. Maybe
do some journaling of your own instead, yeah?" He plucks
the journal from my grip and I know that he does not mean to
be cruel, but how can he not see the way that his words are
like a palm across my cheek leaving a stinging redness in its
wake?

Jack tosses the journal onto an awaiting table through
the doorway of the sitting room and I almost laugh that he
thinks it will remain there, that whatever haunts this house
will not move it and hide it just as they already have. But I
make a note to remember where it is, to come back for it, to
discover the tender words of a Page who knew that this house
had a heartbeat and a will.

How can Jack not feel the house breathing, sense that we
have been devoured by a living thing and are now stewing in
the acid of its ill intent?

"I was just heading off to make some tea for Mum and
myself. Would you like to join?"

Perhaps this is Jack's way of reaching out, not far enough,
or perhaps it is a mere nicety, him reading his lines as well. I
do not know anymore. I cannot be alone, but having Jack by
my side will not solve that ailment, so I will at least be outside
of this stone casket.

"No, I think I'll go for a walk." I try to make my voice
sound steady and I hate that I do. Why do I feel like I need to
convince him? Like I need Jack's permission to be free?

"It's freezing out, Saoirse," he says to the window, speckled with flecks of white.

"I could use the fresh air. I thought I'd check out the garden a bit."

We are months past when he would begrudgingly ask if I wanted him to join me, years past when he would offer with joy. So he does not ask and I do not offer.

I begin down the final bit of stairs, the sight of the large wooden door, my warden, nearly within reach.

"Don't forget shoes, Saoirse," Jack calls to the child that I am not. "And don't take the main door, it's loud and it bothers Mum. There's a small door beneath the stairs and the tunnel will lead you straight out into the garden."

I nod and he dismisses me, back turning as he disappears into the depths of Langdon.

The thick leather of my boots melds to my feet with ease, as though all of me is eager to be out of here, to feel my lungs chill with January's bite. My jacket is nowhere to be found, but I'm unwilling to search for it. I fear the house has hidden it, another means to keep me trapped inside itself.

So I wrap Jack's heavy wool scarf across my shoulders, welcoming the chafe against my arms that tells me I am in this body, I am awake, I am alive.

I stalk across the chilled stones of the ground floor, beneath the grand staircase, and hide away behind a wooden door that is silent as I pull it open. It closes behind me of its own will and I am in a darkened corridor. I wait for a reddened gaze, invisible to my eye or not, to emerge as I make my way quickly toward the opposing door at the far end. My footsteps clattering across stones echo as I move, the sound in pace with my heartbeat. I worry the darkness will never end, but then I am pushing open the door and stepping out into the bright white of winter.

A forgotten garden has been painted in ivory. The maze of high hedges is wearing a hat of snow that matches the ground that laces between them, pure, untouched. There are no foot-prints in the freshly fallen snow and I am alone, but in the best way. I press deeper into the cold embrace of the hedges, hoping that they will hide me from the house's prying eyes, from its ever-looming presence.

It is the house, that is all. It is not me. I'm not getting bad again.

Jack loves this house, wants me to love it too. He wants me to become someone worthy of this place, a person it could love back. *I am trying.*

I carry on my steps, for the garden is as free as I can be, as far as the leash of my life extends. The icy air stings my lungs as I walk, but the sensation is real and I am thankful for it. I enjoy the way that my fingers quickly redden and stiffen as the wind makes its way from the sea below and up onto the cliffside. Soon I am adrift from the sea, the estate, the world, as I get lost in the twists of the garden, the hedges reaching high up above me, hiding me away. But this time I am hidden because I have chosen to be.

I pass fountains, the stone figures blued with disuse, trapped goddesses without water to flow across their mouths, their hands, their breasts. Flowerbeds sit empty amidst the deep frost of winter. I can still feel the house behind me, tick-ling my hair as its stones surely swell and fall with each of its breaths. But it feels safer out here, amidst the monster's feet rather than trapped within its jaws.

I come to a fork in the path, both sides bright and spotless with snow, but from the left-hand path peeks a glimmer of red, the petal of a rose somehow still blooming within the ice of a hedge. I feel drawn to its beauty, turning the corner and choosing my own path.

I immediately wish I had not.

For around the bend, pressed into the once-spotless snow, are the deep imprints of footsteps. The manor and its phan-toms have found me once more.

I turn back, desperate not to meet whatever fate this house has in store for me, but the footsteps line that path as well, larger ones that cross atop my own.

So I push forward, hands trembling within the folds of the scarf, and in my fear I hardly notice that as the footprints fade away, so does the snow. Rich green grass takes its place along the path. The cold gray of the January sky no longer washes this place of color, but instead the gold of a sunny afternoon splashes across the hedges, bringing forth the vibrancy of the flowers that now sprout from its branches.

And around the corner is the broad form of a man. The sun catches the strands of gold within his dark hair and the fine threads along his spotless white collar. His crisp lapel ruffles in the mild wind that twists its way between the greenery to dance on our skin.

This is it, the step off the deep end, falling from the cliff within my own mind, lost at last. Jack was right.

But then the man turns to look at me. And he is real.

Chapter 7

"Excuse me?"

The words should be mine, but they are not. It is the man who questions me, his voice deep and smooth with an aristocratic English accent.

"The estate is not welcoming visitors at this moment, miss. How did you find your way onto the grounds?"

I should speak, I know I should. But I cannot move past how sweat has begun to prickle around my neck beneath the scarf, how there is suddenly no snow or gray skies to be found anywhere. No matter where I cast my gaze, I land upon a lush, green garden in spring, sitting happily beneath blue skies. My mind cannot move past the man, tall and dark and odd, so odd, standing before me. He is like no man I have seen before. He trades jeans for white cloth trousers that bubble at his hips and sit beneath a buttoned jacket of the darkest green and a wide, frilling white collar. A relic of another time stepped right through the past and come to life.

Nineteenth century, probably. Pre-Victorian, a voice in my head supplies as though by instinct, while the rest of me remains stunned into silence.

I know, immediately, that this man should not be here. Or

perhaps it's me who has gone somewhere I should not have. Whether within my mind or without, I am not yet sure.

My panic, my fear, has subsided to make room for confusion, an unerring instinct to understand.

"Miss." His voice has grown softer, a touch of concern now replacing shock as he takes a tentative step toward me across undamaged, green grass. "Are you all right?"

Probably not, almost certainly not, because this man seems real to me. His dark brows pulling down together above hazel eyes and high cheekbones seem real. The light wind that strokes its fingers through the hair that brushes his shoulder seems real.

The way that he is looking at me seems real.

I have not lost my mind, nor gotten lost *in* my mind. This man is really here.

"Who are you?" I'm surprised to hear my own voice interrupt the peaceful afternoon stillness.

The man pauses for a beat, as if considering whether it is safe to speak to the nonsensical woman I must appear to be.

Nonsensical, crazy, crazy. The words—accusations—that haunt me as much as anything else within this house.

The sun glints off a round of purple petals reaching up toward the sky, casting a colorful hue across the man's hands, hanging clutched before his stomach.

"My name is Theodore Page." He bows forward slightly at the waist, the gesture unnervingly formal. But everything about the man is a relic of another time, from his clothes to his manner of speech. "Miss, are you sure you're not unwell?"

Page. It takes me a moment to process his words. His name.

The Page family, much to Edgar's dismay, has grown smaller with each passing generation, and those Pages who remain are boastful enough for their roster of names to be burned into my mind. And there is no Theodore among them. Certainly not one who appears to be only a few years older than Jack. Memories of his woeful stories of a youth of familial solitude swirl through my mind.

I have met all of the Pages and this man has never been among them. His face is not one I could easily forget.

"I'm fine, thanks. How did you get here?" My eyes cut to the looming facade of the estate behind me, its many windows now dark, soulless eyes unwilling to see me, to come to my aid. For all of my wishes to be free of the house, to be away from the Pages and their judgment, I wish the door would spit out someone to come to my side. But looking at it now, I know I can trust nothing and no one who comes from that house. It is a trickster beast that has twisted itself into something new before my eyes.

All dustings of snow atop the bricks of the house have disappeared, the stones are cleaner, fresher, beyond the way that the sun glints off of them happily. The ivy that twists between the windows and up to the turrets is plentiful and thriving, somehow more alive and doubled since I first and last saw the estate's exterior days ago.

The home has freed me to the outdoors, to a new time. It has freed whatever it is that is happening now. But I fear that it has not released me from the same place. Could this be some other Langdon, some shadow of the Langdon from which I came? But if one is the shadow of another, it seems it is the estate I know that is the embodied darkness. Everything is wrong here, but a beautiful, gentle, glowing wrong. The sky is blue and the flowers are rich in color, and the pit of fear that has come to live in my belly since I set foot in this place is gone.

As the heat grows across my skin, I unweave the scarf from my shoulders, sure to keep my eyes on the man, lest he try to rush me or escape, though there is little escape from this cliffside except into the depths of the ocean. I see the man's gaze sweep over my body, his eyes catching on the peak of my boots, on the swaying of my patterned dress in the sea-salted current. I cannot help but blush. A crinkle forms between his brows as he takes me in. His mouth matches as it falls into a frown.

"I do not mean to scare you—" He takes a step toward me and he's wrong. I am not scared. I do not want to be scared. I can choose not to be. Whatever is happening here, I will not let this house strike fear into me any longer.

"I'm not afraid of you."

His frown cracks, a small smile spilling out to take its place. It is not sharp but soft and genuine, his tone no longer that of someone trying to calm a cornered animal.

"No, it doesn't appear you are. Are you of the Page family, miss?" And now it makes sense why his gaze ponders my face, takes in my hair as the wind lifts it up around me. Alice may have added a golden hue to the Page lineage, but there is certainly no hint of my auburn locks there.

But I'm nearly a Page, or will be, aren't I?

"No, I'm . . . a friend of the family." The words choose me. "How exactly do you know the Pages?"

"As I said, Miss . . . ?"

I think of the moment Jack had informed me that I would wear the Page name, the pursed lips of Alice, the downcast eyes of Edgar, as they'd both agreed. I had no words, no say.

"Read." I wish my mouth would not open so readily for him, beyond my control. But my own name comes forth.

"As I said, Miss Read, I am of the Page family. This is my home."

"Jack didn't tell me that any more guests were expected." Jack hadn't told me anything in so long, though. And who would bother to share information with Saoirse, who can barely hold her head?

"I am no guest. I own the estate. I am in residence here. And I do not know the Jack of whom you speak."

"Nobody lives here."

"Strong an argument as that may be, Miss Read, I do, in fact. Now, from where did you come? How did you find yourself in my garden?"

I point back toward the door through which I'd exited, nearly invisible behind the hedges.

"I came from inside the house." I want to find my footing, want to keep the upper hand. One of us is not meant to be here. I have not left that home in days, I know that. So it cannot be me, can it?

I think of the strong iron gates that wrap around Langdon, protecting it even further from the outside world. They are the final barrier, as if the cliffs and recklessly rounding roads, the emptiness of the world up here above the ocean, were not enough to deter.

"I am fairly confident you are not among my staff, nor do you appear to be a tradesperson." His eyes move across me again and he shakes his head, a twirling, dark lock falling down across his forehead. His eyes grow in size as he looks at me, chest suddenly rising in quickened, shallow breaths. "It couldn't be . . ." His voice is pinched. "Miss Read, what is the year?"

Doom slithers back into my vision, memories of that same question replacing kisses on Jack's lips, the horrified, disgusted look on his face as he watched his love sob and slip and he used his words to cut deep, to show how little he thinks I hold on to reality.

I knew then and I know now. I know.

Pain or something like it must splash across my face, as Theodore's shoulders fall, face smoothed out into sympathy.

I wish everyone would stop looking at me with sympathy or with pity or with judgment. I wish someone would just look at me. As I am.

"I do not mean to disturb you. I am merely trying to solve our predicament and I fear I may have my suspicions as to what is occurring at present. The year, Miss Read?"

"1994."

Theodore takes a step back, surprise finally, properly, crossing his face. It is as though I have wounded him without even knowing that I held a blade in my hand. Perhaps I am a Page after all.

But then I see something like resolution break through his features, a small smile, a hard, affirmed set to his jaw.

"The folly of youth," he scoffs to himself. And then, as though remembering I am here, there, wherever we are, he looks back up to me.

"Are you certain?" he asks.

"Of course I am. Why, what year do you think it is?"

"It is the year 1818."

So perhaps it is not a question of where we are, but when.

Chapter 8

Theodore is so certain, words so steady, gaze resting assuredly upon mine.

Perhaps it is not just this house that is playing tricks on me.

"I'm sure you're confused, Miss Read. I will do my best to explain."

"That's not possible. Is this some sort of a joke?" Everything about the man himself may seem dated—far past dated, in fact—but that is not possible. Being in another time, another century, it can't be true.

"If you keep studying all those old artifacts, you're going to become one one day," Jack laughed, placing a kiss on my head as I'd hunched over my desk, dated books strewn before me, gripped by an academic fervor that has long since faded with the rest of me.

"Am I?" I'd asked idly.

"Absolutely," he'd said, fingers finding my shoulders and working out the knots that collected there, *"or fall right through time yourself."*

"Well, that would certainly help me with my PhD, so I'll take it."

"I assure you, I am in earnest. Please, let us sit and I will explain to the best of my, admittedly limited, ability." Theodore's face is stoic, with no sign of mockery or tricks.

I say nothing. The constant screaming, the looping, the fear in my brain has faded, and I find that I have no words. Theodore steps forward and lays a gentle hand on my elbow. The press of his fingers into my arm is so solid, so real, that I cannot deny that it must be. He guides me around a bend in the maze before depositing me onto a stone bench that I am sure was not there before. The hardness presses into my bones, but the physicality does not wake me from whatever this dream is, it does not throw down a rope to save me from the dark depths of my mind that I must have fallen into. Theodore settles down on the opposite end of the bench, so that he may flick his eyes worriedly to the estate that looms somewhere behind me.

I want to say that it is impossible, that he is lying, he *must* be lying. But the estate is visible now and the years of weather and neglect have suddenly fallen off of its face, a face that no longer breathes maliciously down my neck. The world around me has suddenly slid from the stark gray of January to the comfortable sweater of spring as the sun beats down upon us, and I fear that it may be true. It is that or I am finally gone.

No, no. I fixed it.

So this all, impossibly, is real.

I cross my legs at the knee, a worthless attempt to quell the shivering that runs throughout my body. The hem of my dress falls as I do, the breeze blessedly dancing along the pale skin now exposed between knee and boot. Theodore loudly clears his throat and I look over to see the man reluctantly but dutifully pulling his eyes from the hint of skin to squint at the clear green roils of the cliffs beyond.

"Are you all right, Miss Read?" His gaze returns to me and his hazel eyes are just like Jack's. Startlingly so, I realize now, with the strands of gold that seep out from the pupil and illuminate the world. But this man's eyes ring a deeper true green around the edges that opposes Jack's rich, warm brown.

"Sorry?" It has been so long since someone, especially a Page, has asked me that question in earnest that it hardly breaks through the mist of confusion in my brain.

"I know you must be feeling rather baffled and quite over-whelmed, I would venture. But are you all right? I believe I know the truth of our situation, but I do not wish to expose you to more if you are not prepared."

I don't speak for a beat, tongue lost among the green in the hedges, the clifftops, and his eyes. The color, with its enveloping presence, slowly pulls me into this moment. This moment that may truly be real. Real in that this man is no joke or conjuration, real in that the heat spreading across my shoulders means that this sudden change in weather is not the result of my finally expired mind. Real in that I am here, in Langdon, but somehow it is not the same Langdon that swallowed me into the pit of its belly days ago.

"I'm confused, but I'm all right, yeah." My eyes keep cutting to the house behind my shoulder, noticing how the ivy across its stones has suddenly been revitalized. It's thriving in abundance. Even the sitting room window lacks the harsh yellow cast of electric lights. The house looks as though it shook off its old skin, like the shedding of a snake, and now wears a face that is more pristine and renewed.

"Though everything in your countenance and appearance seems to tell me it is true, I must ask once more, Miss Read. What year did you come from?"

"I came . . ." *I did not come from anywhere, I've always been here, haven't I? How long have I been in that house? Days, days of only those walls. I came from here.* "It's 1994."

Theodore nods, face somber.

"Ah, but I fear it is not." His deep voice is smooth, meant to calm, and it does. "Some places are more than just places.

They're . . . beings. Langdon is one such place. This house is quite magnificent, and it has been known to play with time within itself. I believe that may be the fate that has befallen you today."

I tug at the high neckline of my dress, the fabric suddenly suffocating me as his words shock me fully back into my body. I am all too aware of the way that the dress touches me, of the sweat that pools beneath it, in the hollow of my clavicle, beneath my arms.

"Playing with time? What the hell does that mean?" The kaleidoscope of Theodore's eyes widens, the sun splashing them in gold.

"Take deep breaths, Miss Read." I had not realized the audible staccato my breath had become. "I do apologize for overwhelming you, but I believe it to be the truth. This may be your first time experiencing Langdon's oddities, but it is not mine."

I do my best to fill my chest, but the air that slips between my lips is shaky.

"I have lived at Langdon for a long time. I was born here. I know this house well and it knows me well in turn. It's . . . when I was a boy it was difficult to live in Langdon, isolated as it is, with only my sisters for company. Then one day a boy about my age appeared in the hall quite suddenly, his speech and manner of dress as unfamiliar as yours. He was of another time, but the house brought him to mine, almost every day for an entire summer. In his own time, he was as lonely as I was, but Langdon made it so we had one another.

"When my parents passed years ago, I retreated to Langdon once more. One day there was a young woman in my kitchen, a woman from a century before my own, my own ancestor living in the manor, having just lost her sister to illness. Langdon saw our shared grief and brought us to one another. I don't . . . I cannot understand how the house does it, what magic must live in the roots of this place. But however it is done, it is as though the house sees when people are fated to meet one another in a way not even time can deter." Theodore looks away from me to the sea, taking a steadying breath, and I instinctively mirror him. For a brief moment, there is only the waves slapping against the jagged rocks beneath us, a sea bird calling in delight as it swoops far overhead. The rampant, rambling tumbles of my mind spin, unable to find purchase on if this could be the truth, so the thoughts find handholds in nothing at all.

"I know I sound mad, but I swear this is the truth as I know it." His voice is genuine, his gaze piercing, and I find that maybe it is not so difficult to believe the words that he says. "Within Langdon's walls, somehow, time ripples, all of its lives are lived at once and it may decide to thin the veil between them. I should have realized. For days I have seen shadows come to life, have found my belongings scattered from where I have laid them. I thought the house was merely playing another of its tricks. It appears it has done much more than trickery."

His eyes sweep over me, as if I am the wonder, but I can only imagine what I look like now in my frenzied state. My chest nearly hurts with the quick pattering of my heart. Not because I do not believe him but because I know that this could be true because it is exactly what has been happening to me. The footsteps, the figures, the phantom arm beneath the ripple of a curtain. These instances weren't ghosts or my illness, but spirits of another time, sparking my fear only for being peculiar to me, to my time. Here one moment and sometime else another.

"That shouldn't be possible," I breathe.

"No," Theodore says simply, "it should not." And he offers no further explanation, but nevertheless I'm drawn to believe him. These words are what my brain wishes to cling to, what settles my swirling mind. What tells me that I have not fallen into myself, have not gone mad.

"I am sorry if you have found yourself here when you do not wish to be. But there must be a reason you are here, now. You came to the estate willingly, yes?"

Yes and no both seem like the correct answer, yet I find that neither one would sit quite true for me.

"In a sense."

"Good, yes."

There are questions that I want to ask, but there are too many of them. My brain is alight, a blazing switchboard. I feel alive for the first time in too long. I have forgotten how words can sit on my lips eager to be in the air, how my tongue can be light and not weighed down by shame.

"Are these time warps common? Have others in your family experienced this?"

"No, never." Theodore runs a hand through his hair, dark curls standing charmingly upright in the wake of his fingers. "When I told them as a boy, I am certain my parents thought me mad. And my elder sister too. But I am not. I am certain of what I have seen." His words come forth as though he's uttered them many times, not only to convince others but himself. It is like hearing my own thoughts, my rambling reassurances, spoken.

Something dark passes behind his eyes and I recognize that fleeting memory, others' words of confusion and mistrust masked as scorn. I hear them every day from Jack. For a moment my hand twitches toward Theodore. I tuck it beneath my leg. I do not say, *I understand, I know what it is to be told the reality you see is not. To be called crazy.* But I do understand. Too well.

"Nevertheless I have always known that the estate is more than a house. When I inherited it, I knew that I must remain here. Must be its caretaker, in more ways than most bachelors of means."

His accent has grown familiar now, the dated lilts of his voice engrossing. It is an accent that mirrors the Pages I know—this man's *descendants*—but raised with a formality and distinction that Alice and Edgar would long to achieve.

"Langdon is alive, in a sense. It must be cared for. Tended to like a child. But it is a fickle and mysterious creature."

I was right, this house, it breathes. I feel as though I'm tottering on the cliff's edge, nearly believing his words to be true, almost wishing that I could fall over into the richness of the world he teases.

But I do not let myself go beyond, not yet. Not until I see more, not until the change is so clear, so stark, so undeniable before my eyes that I have no choice but to take it as truth.

"Mr. Page, um, could we maybe go inside the house?"

"Have you caught a chill?"

"No! It's just . . ." A shrug. Tongue twisted. Asking for what I want is odd yet familiar, long untasted.

He hears me anyway.

"Ah, of course. Why should you merely take my word as truth?" Theodore lets out a brief, bitter chuckle.

He knows what it is to not be believed.

And yet he told his truth to me as though it was the only one. Unbelievable or not, I cannot find it in me to be another stone-faced unbeliever.

"It isn't that. It is just . . ." I falter.

He does not know that there has already been more than his word, that I have already seen the world tilt from winter to spring in a moment. That it is myself, my own eyes, my own mind, that I cannot trust so easily.

"Yes, I imagine you will find the interior of Langdon quite different from the time whence you came. Progress is a quick fox."

He stands, offering his hand to me once more. Pushing through the grip of awkward hesitation dancing in my stomach, I place my fingers in his. Theodore's grip is strong and warm as I allow him to guide me to my shaking feet. Our hands drop and we each, instinctually, take a step away from the other, still finding it difficult to acknowledge, truly, that the world could be much more fantastical than I imagine either of us has ever dared to dream.

He turns his face back out toward the sea. "Blackjack!"

Before the word has fully left his lips, I hear heavy, pattering footsteps rushing toward us, and my body tenses until I see the form of a large black dog barreling our way, bursting through the path of the hedges, pink snout first.

"I do hope you're not fearful of dogs. Blackjack here is my constant companion." A smile splits Theodore's serious face as he looks down at the dog who smiles right back, tongue lolling from his mouth with joy.

The animal's dark, burly frame is so similar to the dog I had growing up that I am immediately endeared to the scruffy fur and oversize paws. Blackjack noses over toward me, sniffing his way up the leather of my boots, his nose dampening the skin of my ankle as my hem dances around me. I lean forward slightly, the dog large enough to meet me without much reaching, the tufts of his fur between my fingers coarse and thick.

I look up at Theodore whose his smile has grown, his eyes taking in the two of us; Blackjack's face lifted toward the sun happily as I tickle beneath his chin. And somehow I feel calm, almost too calm.

"Not everything is too good to be true, Saoirse," Jack had said. *"Don't sabotage everything in that head of yours. That's part of the problem."*

"He's not precisely the friendly sort, but the old boy seems to have taken a liking to you." Theodore's tone is no longer the too soft of delicate footsteps across eggshells or the pointed corners of suspicion. We have landed somewhere among genuineness. "Come, Miss Read, let us enter Langdon."

And I am surprised to find that I no longer see a guillotine before me as our feet guide us toward the house.

Chapter 9

Immediately, I am forced to accept that this is a different place. Or maybe even as Theodore said, the same place in a different time.

For he is now leading me through the tunnel that runs beneath the house, connecting garden to foyer, and it is not the darkened and dampened space of abandonment that I had rushed through earlier. The underground hall is splashed in light. The golden fixtures attached to the walls sport lit candles that throw waves of yellow across the dim stone walls. I can see what is before me as we pass through, and what I see is Theodore, his wide shoulders strong and his step confident as he guides me into the house.

"I apologize for the path we've taken." He gestures to the stone walls around us, though he cannot know that the space is so much more comforting than it was before. Or maybe, if he is correct, than it will be. "There are, of course, the grand stairs into the estate, but the doors are quite difficult for the staff to tend, so I prefer to leave them closed unless I am expecting guests." He throws a smile over his shoulder, a tilted smirk more playful than I have seen from him before. "You, of course, Miss Read, are quite unexpected."

The door opens for him easily and Blackjack bounds past

me, paws beating into the stones of the entryway. The stones are a lighter ivory than they were just moments before, when I was here, fleeing from the arms of this house. Arms that don't seem to be choking me anymore as I walk through the doorway, held open by Theodore, his back straight.

A woman in an old-fashioned black dress steps forward, hands lifted eagerly to help, unblinking as the dark form of Blackjack races past her and up the stairs. Her eyes snag on me for a moment, pale eyebrows raising as she takes me in. Her eyes roam over the dress that I dug out of a discount bin and the red hair that falls down past my shoulders, presumably far too loose for the time, sitting in stark contrast with her own tight bun.

"Some tea for you and your guest, Mr. Page?"

"Please." He hands her his jacket, exposing the loose-fitted white top that is now the only thing between his skin and the humid air.

The woman looks to me, but I have nothing but the wool of Jack's scarf. I keep it draped over my arm, pulled close to my body as though she'll decide to snatch this piece of cloth that feels like the only thing grounding me to the Langdon I know. Not that that is a connection I particularly cherish. The woman disappears up the stairs with a curt nod.

The stairs are nearly nothing like what I saw in Langdon before. There are no light bulbs casting their neon glow across the room in a short reach. Instead, a large chandelier hangs from the high ceiling, dozens of lit candles illuminating the dark wave of Theodore's hair and banishing the shadows that existed here in my time. Instead of darkened, empty stone walls staring back at me, landscapes painted in rich greens and blues and purples are mounted, swathed in gilded frames.

Velvet still hugs the path up the steps, but it is fresh, lifted, unburdened by the deep imprints and grooves of centuries of feet. The faces that line the stairs here are few, only four eyes gazing at me—Page hazel, all the same. The two portraits are nestled among more painted scenes of swelling oceans and stretching meadows.

"My mother and father," Theodore supplies, following my gaze to the dark-haired subjects. "Do their portraits still sit in your time?"

In my mind, I conjure the paintings of the Pages from my time and they blend, nothing but hundreds of judging, cold hazel eyes.

"I'm not sure. Sorry."

He nods brusquely and I do not ask about the wound that sits beneath the movements.

"Come, Miss Read. The house has not brought you here just to admire my art, I am sure."

He leads me up the stairs, the sound of our steps absorbed into the velvet lining. My eyes get lost between the steady bob of his shoulders and the wide-open lands paused within paint.

How can the world have shifted so suddenly and resolutely? How can this be real?

No darkened sitting room meets us at the top. Instead, the room is brightly lit by the glow of candles resting in sconces upon the wall, the windows and curtains thrown open to welcome the spring afternoon.

I find that air fills my lung easily, freely. I do not hold my breath in wait of phantom eyes upon my back, a ghost of a touch upon my arm. There is no presence here, no shades seeping out from the corners, down the walls. Langdon is now a place of light.

I recognize some of the chairs, pieces of wood suddenly stripped of their splinters and stains, brought back to life in a mere moment. Leather-bound books adorn nearly every surface, words tucked away everywhere until they are a foundation of the house. There was only silence in the Langdon I knew.

Footsteps ring out all around the home, characters dressed in quiet Regency garb moving in and out of frame in practiced motions, the heart that keeps the home alive. Most exchange small smiles and nods with Theodore as they pass, and he greets them in turn, a few curious gazes catching on the out-of-place woman beside him.

Things are different but in smaller, quieter ways. It doesn't feel as though I've stepped back in time two centuries, but more so like I'm merely living another day that had occurred and was occurring and would forever be occurring within the grounds of Langdon. In a sense, it is as though Langdon is the world.

"Is it diff—" Theodore begins.

"I believe you." To pull such a fit of trickery would be impossible, a prank of too great a feat, a humor Jack would never have or desire.

Theodore turns to me, green eyes earnest and voice to match. His quick nod is to assure and comfort us both. If this is all real, and I am not mad, then neither is he.

"I am not sure why the estate brought you here, Miss Read. But it has, for reasons mysterious to us. I suspect we will find out why it is you and I were meant to meet. But until then, you must know that you are most welcome here."

Our eyes hold for a long moment and I am not sure why his voice is so gentle, why it drifts across my skin, across my mind.

I think of Jack and I do not know why.

"Would you care for some tea?" Theodore's eyes cut to the door of blue and gold that Alice once lurked behind, its colors now rich, Theodore's large hand gesturing out toward it.

I nod, my footsteps following in his path as we move.

Light streams out from the doorway, the far window sitting open, the blue sky shining beyond it.

"Are you a visitor of the Page family then, Miss Read? In your time, of course."

I do not know what the right words are, am not even sure of the truth.

"Um, yeah, I—"

I step beneath the doorway and the gloom floods in, the chill returns deep within my bones, plunged from the sun back into icy waters. The room goes gray and the only sound is the howling cry of the wind.

"Saoirse?" The man turns to look at me from his rest in a dilapidated wooden chair, hazel eyes darkened by confusion and annoyance, their tenderness long since strained out.

I am once more met with the cold gazes of three Pages and the heavy stillness of loneliness, firmly back within my own time. The hope and the light slip through my fingers like water, my mind returned to the gray.

Chapter 10

I feel like I'm being hidden away here.

When I had stepped, dazed, into the gray little room where the Pages of the twentieth century were sitting in hushed chatter, I had hardly gotten a word out before Jack had whisked me out into the now-darkened hall, arm like a vise around my shoulders. Something like shock had come over me, his words passing through my skull like ghosts, the phantoms of *"What's happened to you? Are you feeling ill, is that it? Come, Saoirse, Mum is having a rough day, she doesn't need the excitement,"* standing out in sparks of red.

I had heard *"Jack, please, listen to me"* fall from my lips to be ignored, my words trapped in the ether to wither away.

I was simply shepherded up the stairs to the bedroom, where they could hide me away, an unwanted spectacle, as always. I do not think more than a word left my lips in the face of Alice and Edgar—no screams, no tears. Yet even my silence was too much for them. I was still lingering in surprise, still too numb to even try to be who they—who Jack—wanted me to be.

If only they had known what I've just gone through. They would be horrified that all I had met them with was silence.

Did they know what I'd gone through? Have any of them ever been the victims—or maybe the chosen?—of this house and its apparent wrinkle in time?

They may be Pages, but something told me they would not have welcomed their beloved estate making a mockery of reality.

The bedroom door creaks open as Jack pushes his way back in, a plate of food held in his long fingers. He does not speak as he comes toward me, his eyes skeptical, worried, as he paces toward the wild animal that they've made me.

"I feel fine, Jack." I am as surprised as he is to hear the defiance in my voice, to hear my head breaking above water. "I was just walking around in the garden for a while, I didn't mean to surprise you all when I came in."

The lie comes easily and I do not regret it. But it is a single stone in the tower that is the truth, surely.

"In just your dress, Saoirse?" He does not believe me, he never does, and neither of us knows what words he wants to hear anymore. "You strolled into the room like you'd seen a ghost."

I almost laugh. We can no longer reach each other. We are so far from each other that he doesn't even realize how close he's glided to the truth.

"I honestly don't know what has been happening with you lately. I don't know how to help you anymore." The soft edges of Jack's concern are sharpened by the exasperation beneath them.

There are roils of waves within me—how could there not be—but I hate to think that there are waves that we must battle between us. Waves that are my fault, a roughness on the ocean born from my mind and the struggles it brings us both. *I need to get better. I thought I was.*

"I'm just having an off day, I guess." It's a phrase we'd heard from my mouth a thousand times before the dam broke. But then an off day had become a brain and body that felt like it belonged to a stranger, bringing tears and quiet and grief for nothing. But I have tried so hard. It is no longer our norm, my norm, and I do not want to bring us back there.

I have gotten better, I am getting better. But it feels as though Jack can never quite forget the aches of my past. I hate that we both remember me as a woman who needed to be cared for, another stressor upon his life. I hate that we are both unsure if I am still that woman.

"I'll just rest up." I do not say that I am afraid to leave the sanctity of the bed that he deposited me into, afraid that every doorway will leave me spinning through time.

Afraid that it won't.

"I think that's for the best." Jack leans to set the dish on the table on the far side of the bed, and both of our eyes catch on what already occupies the space.

Among the clutter of a mug, pens, my discarded glasses, rests something else. The journal sits innocently, the elaborate Celtic Tree of Life pointing up to the ceiling. I feel the invisible arm of Langdon run a finger down my cheek, murmuring its ghostly words just for me.

"Did you bring that up?" My voice is a whisper, the question sitting between us for a beat.

"No." Jack casually tosses the journal onto the bed toward me, where it bounces for a moment before it settles within the pillows.

This house has not yet freed me from its arms, it would seem.

I do not know the truth of what has happened to me or what I have seen. But I choose to believe it, for I cannot believe that the arms of this house can only reach out to pinch and bind and trap. I want to trust Theodore. I cannot be another nonbeliever who makes him question his reality, not after what the house has shown me with my own eyes. So perhaps he is right, maybe the house seeks to guide. Toward what, I'm unsure.

"You'll eat, yeah?" Jack looks at me for a long moment until I unfold from the covers, the cold immediately biting at my ankles as I grab the plate and the journal, making my way toward a chair in front of the fireplace Jack has lit for me. He places his hand on my shoulder, the weight heavy, as he gazes into my eyes and I do not know what he's looking for, but I hope that he finds it, or that he does not. I do not have the rulebook; I no longer know what game we are playing here.

"You're freezing." His fingers rub across my skin quickly, almost harshly, but the touch sparks little warmth, even as the air from the fire soaks through my skin. "Just rest, yeah? Please."

"Yeah, I will." A nod.

For a moment I think that he will lean down and press his lips to my forehead, his heat becoming a part of me once more. But his hand only lingers against my neck before making its exit and then so does he, closing the door with a clash of finality behind him.

The fork is cold on my fingertips, the food tasteless in my mouth and after a few empty bites of mash, I find myself setting aside the dishes and hauling the journal into my lap instead. I expect it to feel different now that it has been in the grasp of phantom hands, moved across several floors of the house. A much greater feat than the jump across the library just this morning. But the thought of the movement does not quicken my heart with fear this time.

It is merely the shallow breaths and itching mind of intrigue. This house has shown me how controlling, how intentional, its movements are. If it brought me this journal, many times over, it is choosing to do so.

I carefully flip past the pages already familiar to me, the yellowing paper worn smooth beneath my touch.

November 8, 1817
Langdon has been abustle of late. Many new faces passing beneath its stone archways, faces familiar and welcome and those decidedly less. I cannot deny that I have been feeling weak, losing a day to bedrest. The physician has come to see to me, but his news holds nothing of weight. For I am on my feet once more, the worst long since passed.

Iris has come to visit once more, with the exciting news that she is with child. A new heir to the Page name is to come. It is a heartbreak that neither Mother nor Father has survived to see it, but I do hope that the children will come to know Langdon, perhaps even that Iris and Charles will make a home of the estate.

For every soul who has lived in Langdon always shall, and our beloved parents will be able to watch the babes grow through the eyes of the manor.

Nell still resides in London and has refused response to any of my correspondence. Though both Aunt Mildred and Iris assure me that my youngest sister is well and is making herself an honorable place in the society of Town. I do hope that she sees the truth of my actions or at most if she cannot, that she will not bar Langdon from her heart.

The wind screams in anguish and I lift my head to see that the brightness of snow has once more retreated to a dark slate of rain beating down upon the window against the blackness of the night sky. The lamp on the mantel highlights the descent of one heavy drop, slowly slithering down the window before it disappears into the depths beneath. My eyes and my mind begin to comfortably blur as I watch its movement.

Then the stillness of the air is split by a sharp creak and I turn my head quick enough to catch the door of the wardrobe, flaked with age, carefully creeping open. The draft of the room hangs low, swirling about the ankles, but the door is opened with the precise force of a hand invisible to my eye. It hangs open for a moment before slowly, deliberately once more falling closed.

I can almost feel the ripple of time around me, the way that the house thins the lines of possibility, the way it scratches at my brain to make sense of it. But even knowing what the home can do, that it can bring me to beautiful places, I cannot stop the way that the small, pale hairs on my arm rise.

Is it Theodore's hand that opens the wardrobe, preparing for sleep or for a morning within Langdon's walls? Or is it Jack's great-grandfather decades ago or some future Page, centuries from being born?

I watch for a long moment, the room pregnant with a silence that is anything but quiet, though the space and all it contains remains steady. I turn back to the journal, the presence of the wardrobe behind my back still loud, the tickle on my neck more familiar now, no longer an intruding omen of fear. It is almost like something of a friend.

December 13, 1817
Autumn has bled into winter, the chill of the season making itself especially known out upon the cliffs. Much to all of our chagrin, we find ourselves much more bound within the fickle walls of Langdon, forced to make do with our own company.

Thankfully, the estate never remains silent for long. Iris and Charles both have returned for the season, Iris already the matron of the home, the very image of Mother herself. I cannot help but recall my own boyhood, Mother's laughter ringing through the halls as she strung holly across the banisters, waking up to see Langdon awash in green and red.

My eyes flicker to the top of the pages, finding swirling numbered dates that I had somehow drifted past before, a time period far beyond my own niche studies. It is not just any journal, not just any life, that the house has put into my palms.

It is Theodore's. Of course.

It may not be quiet today, but the sounds are not the same as I once knew. The silence will be all the more once Iris has returned to Town. I long to follow, I do, but Langdon cannot remain empty. I am bound to it, for someone must be, and that shall be I. It is for the best interest of all.

Nell says that she will not be returning for the season, spending the winter instead in London.

The words are filled with a deep familial love, but the undercurrent of loneliness, of longing, is strong. It is a sense that I know well, a feeling that has been compounded and illuminated within the walls of Langdon as I know it. This place is making our paths cross twice over, weaving our strings together, and I wonder if it sees that same dark thread within us both. That same pitch of solitary song, making a duet of us.

I jump in my seat as Jack's voice rings out over the sound of the bedroom door swinging open, both accompanied by the howling outside. His brows pinch together as he takes me in, hunched over the journal, hands twisted together, food chilled and forgotten.

"I'm not sure what's happening with you, Sersh, but you should really be in bed. I can tell your sleep has been restless lately." Jack moves on from me, shrugging into the thick knit of a sweater that was draped across the back of my chair, careful not to touch me as he extracts it.

He does not guide me to the bed with his hands but instead with tiny admonishments. I am drifting back beneath the covers, the journal on my bedside table once more. I have become the phantom of Langdon in the time that we know, the voiceless form of a wife, the ghost that haunts these halls.

If the look on Jack's face—the confusion, the distance, the frustration at my very existence—is to be believed, I am the thing to be feared here.

Chapter 11

My desire is nonexistent, my appetite gone. I'm almost thankful as there are few things that make me shrink more than sharing a meal across the table from Alice, her sharp eyes stabbing a million little holes in me with every bite I take.

This morning neither of us eats and I feel the tension in the room at her absent hunger, the way that Edgar's eyes cut to the untouched bread upon her plate, Jack pushing jam, tea, anything toward his mother's shaking hands. More of her fades every day and she does not have the energy to replenish herself.

We are more alike than Alice realizes. I feel the guilt as I think it, but I know I am where she is, the illness within instead of without.

No, not anymore. I've fixed it, I'm fixing it.

Allow yourself to get better, Saoirse. Be proud of how you've gotten better.

This is not all you are.

It's easy enough to tell myself that. Harder to make others believe it.

Like Alice, who still finds the strength to rake her eyes across my skin, burning in her wake.

I wonder if they always sit unspeaking, or if it is merely for my benefit, a punishment for being present.

You invited me here, don't you remember?

Why don't you want me?

Jack does not look at me, but I see my face caught in the reflection of his periphery, hear the screams of his unspoken fears that his future bride will act up, speak up, flare up. Jack used to tell me that he loved every part of me, every day. I know Jack resents and fears what my mind has become in equal measure, resents me just the same for I cannot stop it, much as I wish I could be better for him. But I also know Jack loves the safety of the blanket that drapes over my mind sometimes, too often, the weight trapping me still, making me silent and cooperative at the best of times. Better to have a bride on the days her mind makes her silent than on the days it makes her sob with hollowness.

"I walked through the garden yesterday. It was lovely." I revel, just a little, in the way that my voice echoes across the expanse of the dining room and in the swivel of three pairs of eyes toward me. Lines of hazel darkened with annoyance, but I would have weathered these looks even if I had not spoken.

"Why exactly? Was it not frozen over in the snow?" Edgar questions at the same time as Alice's verbal weapons lash. "It's January, anything to see out there is long dead."

I am amazed to find that their swords do not meet my flesh today. I am in on a joke, a little joy, between me and the house they all love so much. I think of the sun glinting gold on Theodore's dark hair, the bright strike of blue flowers against green hedges, the contrast of Blackjack's pink nose sniffing along the grass as the air carries the scent of roses in early bloom.

"I guess I found something to appreciate." My shrug is the only jest I allow, suppressing my private smile.

They all look at me as though I'm crazy. Perhaps I am.

"Well, you always were an eccentric, dear." Alice dismisses

me, plunging the room back into the silence of finality, but I do not mind.

I resist the urge to push my fork through the food that grows cold on my plate, my fingers lacing and unlacing with themselves instead. They itch for the feel of the journal and I wish that I had brought it down with me, so I could steal away with it somewhere. But it was gone from the bedside when I awoke. I had almost expected it to be anyway.

I trust the house to bring it back to me if it is meant for me. My lips tug up as I think of the way that the fear I had of this place and its hold on me has so quickly grown into private joy, mutual understanding, even if the house never sweeps me deep into its embrace again. What was terrifying and new now feels familiarly thrilling when I can see that the Page's beloved estate has given me something it would never give them.

I can tell where I am not wanted and, for once, I untether from the impossible, unspoken rules that the Pages have set before me. I will hide away under the wallpaper if it is what they want, bide my days until Jack leads me back out the gates. Solitude is preferable to crowded silence.

I hear the sound of footsteps ringing out in the hall, heavy shoes across the wood, though the four lives that are within Langdon, now, all sit in this room.

Perhaps solitude is not my only choice.

My eyes catch on the door and the mystery of what could be beyond, but the rest of the Pages' gazes remain unwaveringly on one another. They are either too engrossed in the conversation they are having with just their eyes, or their ears are unattuned to these sounds, the noises for my notice only.

"Do you need help with anything today, Jack?" I almost wish that he would say yes, that he would ask me to spend the day in his company, but I know he will not. He does not. So I push away from the table, tell them I am off to explore the house, but to let me know if there is anything I can do for them today. We all know my absence is the best tonic I can provide for Alice, and neither of Jack's parents, nor the man himself, offer any words as I walk out the doorway.

My path is aimless, or rather, nonexistent. But I welcome the way that I can breathe freely out here in the darkened hall, the tightness in my chest slowly unraveling as I move beyond the gazes of Alice and Edgar. I pause at the junction of the stairwell, choosing between a dark descent or a dusky ascent.

I veer to the left, bare feet slipping across the velvet carpet as I climb the stairs, leading to an unknown destination. The draft carries the whispers of many voices whose bodies cannot possibly be found here, now. The words are unintelligible, muffled nothings, equal parts the whimsy of the house and the rickety foundations of my mind. The flash of a golden chandelier is the only beacon in a dark room, peeking out from a cracked doorway off the stairs, and I find my curiosity leading me toward it on an unbreakable leash.

In the moments between my lashes brushing my cheek and lifting again the light has shifted to a hazy gold and my legs are suddenly accosted by a black ball of fur barreling toward me.

"Blackjack!" The laugh is pushed out of me in a shock. I cannot deny that I am joyful that the house has once more taken me into its fantastical confidences, continued my secret within the holy Page space.

The carved white door, its color suddenly so much purer than it was a moment ago, pushes open before my hand can reach it and I am face-to-face with the green eyes, the waves of dark hair, and the billowing, pressed shirt that make up Theodore Page.

"Miss Read!" The shock on his face quickly gives way to a small smile. "You've returned."

"I guess I have." I cannot help the smile that splits my face in return.

"Were you able to . . . erm, travel intentionally?" His eyes cut to a darkly dressed woman who passes by behind me, arms laden with a tray of dishes. She pays us no mind.

"No. No, I was just walking around the house and then . . . here I am." *Here I am meant to be, it seems.* I shrug and our eyes catch in the same pool of confusion.

"Well, a welcome surprise on Langdon's behalf then." He nods, body bending forward, something like a small bow, and when he leans back up there is a little smirk on my face.

I feel my cheeks rise to pink; the air here is so much balmier than it was moments ago in my own time. I am once again thankful for the stock of dresses I've packed to lounge about the estate in. Even if their light, swishing hems stand out in contrast to the garb of the passing staff, I cannot deny that they allow a bit more breathability and blending than most modern wear.

Passing eyes glance off of me instead of catching, and for once I am, within these halls, glad to not stand out as something of note.

"And such a quick return as well." Theodore gestures toward me.

"Oh? Was I here just yesterday for you too then?"

"Indeed." He nods and our conversation lulls, both wondering at how the ticking of the clock aligns in our separate worlds, our separate lives, within these shared walls. Wondering answers to questions that I suspect Langdon will never give us.

"I was just about to have tea. Would you care to join me?"

"Oh, um, sure." A sharp pang of guilt creeps in at the thought that my sudden presence has now infiltrated upon Theodore's day not once but twice. But then I remember the words strewn across his journal, a journal that he does not know I have, filled with days of silence and solitary pursuits.

He steps away for a moment to talk quietly to a passing man, fitted in the dark dress I've quickly come to associate with the staff here. It is a color scheme of employment that rings true even in the time I've just left, visions of Harry and his crisp black shirts cropping up in my mind. A color that allows them to blend into the house itself, to be seen only when they should be.

A standard in this time even if it does make my stomach pinch with discomfort, but entirely unnerving to witness still in my own. But it is no surprise from the Pages. Those beneath them should not be seen, and that is most of us.

"It appears to be a lovely afternoon. I thought perhaps we'd relish the rarity of the English sun and take tea out in the garden?" Theodore reappears before me, and I'm almost afraid to let him out of my sight again, for perhaps he is the thing that tethers me to this time, the thing the house brings me here to find. I'm not sure I'm ready to leave it behind yet.

I see the clouds drifting sleepily across a bluebell sky in the window beyond, imagining the mild air that I swear I can already feel across my skin.

"That sounds wonderful." Theodore's smile mirrors my own—or perhaps it is my mouth that rises in response to his.

He offers me his arm and I have to hold down the laugh, almost manic, that bubbles up as I put my own through, my forearm coming to rest in the crook of his elbow. A gesture so distinctly historical, so articulately Regency, that if I had any mind to deny that this is the truth, I could deny it no longer. Maybe I should switch paths after all, become a Romanticist, suddenly more qualified than any of the other PhD contenders.

We begin our descent down the grandeur of the stairwell, Langdon alight and glowing, in its spotless prime—the happiest form I have seen it yet.

Chapter 12

"Are you not curious about why the house keeps bringing me back here?" I ask, as we step out of the stone tunnel and into the sunlight of the garden.

Theodore holds the door open so that I can stroll through and Blackjack can make his bounding sprint into the masking green twists of hedges.

"Of course," he says at last, eyes cutting to me. We follow the dog at a measured pace, the bobbing forms of estate staff already visible in glimpses between flowers and stalks of green. I'm sure my presence here is already odd enough, so I do my best to resist the urge to offer to help them, to take some of the dishes and blankets they carry into my own arms. I know as much is likely not the role of a guest of the Pages in this time. "I do not pretend to understand the workings of Langdon, but I trust that the home had a reason that our paths were fated to cross, even if it remains a mystery to us."

Fated.

I contemplate telling him of the journal, *his* journal, that sits on my bedside table, but the words wither away like the flowers of my own January. It feels too intimate to admit that I've been gifted his words that were never meant for eyes beyond his own. But is that not the way of history, private words read, analyzed, and studied as markers of their time? But to Theodore, he is not yet a piece of history. He is himself. To him, this is now, this is what is present and real. "Perhaps the estate thought you could use a friend. Or rather maybe it is I who is in need of a lunch partner." He laughs, but I cannot deny the familiar image his words conjure, the steady penmanship stamped from the page into my brain, the strand of loneliness that I suspect runs within us both.

"Maybe a bit of both."

Theodore leads us into the hedges, the air taking on a crisp bite as we move toward the edge of the cliff, out to sea, the sun's light struggling to permeate through the high walls of greenery surrounding us. My arm still rests in his and I cannot deny the itch of unease, of something that is almost, but not quite, guilt. It grates at the side of my mind. My arm intertwined with one man—innocent as it may be in my time much less the one I am in now—while the ring of another sits on my opposite hand.

I instead choose to let my mind fixate on the press of grass beneath my bare feet, the faintest moisture of morning dew that has clung on into the afternoon, chilling me from the soles up. It is the same freshness, the same grounding that highlighted my childhood. I remember early mornings in the backyard in Boston, my brothers playing catch while I trailed behind them, the pink skin of my feet slipping across the damp grass as I scurried in their wake. The sound of the ocean lapping against the shore crashes beneath us now. It is the violent counterpart to the faint sound of the tide rolling in from my childhood memories. I used to sit on the back porch alone and listen to it, the steady flow easing my mind as it had begun to coil around itself in my teenage years.

These things that had grounded and freed me were mirrored here, now, in this place that, in my own time, had made such a mockery of my comfort. This Langdon is painted not in gray and beige and navy, but in the same rich tones of my youth.

As if he can read my mind, Theodore's eyes drift from the sea to the grass beneath us.

"Oh!" he exclaims, voice laden with concern. "My apologies, Miss Read, I have dragged you from the house without being sure that you're properly attired. Of course, I cannot apologize enough, I can—"

I laugh and I am saddened to realize that I had forgotten how those yellow and orange hues sounded coming from my mouth.

"It's fine, really. I actually quite like the feeling of the ground beneath my feet."

"Are you certain?" He is hesitant, brows rising, the green of his eyes overpowering the brown as they widen.

Jack had worn the same look once, as we had strolled through Regent's Park last year as spring was melting into summer and I had shed my sandals to feel the press of the fresh summer grass upon the most vulnerable part of my body. His eyes had cut to those around us, tones of concern on his face. I was stabbed by the sharp point of embarrassment as he'd pushed my shoes back into my hands, "C'mon Saoirse, we're not alone, be appropriate, yeah?" My body had blushed with shame, the heat so different from that of our first summer, when Jack had laughed with joy at the sight of my bare feet in the grass.

The memories flood back to me now as I gaze up at Theodore's face, so like his descendants' that will come to look at me one day. I feel the bright colors seep out of me, settling back into the grayness that has come to be my home.

"Sorry, I just, uh, I enjoy it, but I can go inside or—"

Theodore's laugh stops me. A laugh of endearment, of wonder, all smoothed edges and crinkles around his eyes.

"Is this normal of women in your time?" He smiles at me,

continues walking, and maybe I absorb the sunset hue of a passing tulip into my skin.

"I don't think it's *abnormal*, per say." I shrug.

"You are a very interesting woman, Miss Read. For any time."

I feel my cheeks pinken again, though the heat has grown no stronger. I keep my eyes on the flowers around me and not on the smiling man who moves at the edge of my vision or the little dark spot of something like guilt that nibbles at the pit of my stomach with stronger teeth now.

"You can call me Saoirse. Instead of Miss Read, I mean."

Theodore clears his throat, the graveled sound a rough contrast to the calls of birds circling beyond the grounds of the estate.

"In this time that is . . . far too intimate. Miss Read would suit me best, if you do not mind."

The shame comes back hot and quick and I wish that I was not so easily swayed to embarrassment, not so easily sliced with the sword of reprimand, even when it is not meant to be so.

"But . . . if that is more standard in your time . . ." he begins again, words coming forth slowly through the trickle of hesitation. "You may call me Theo."

We look at each other for a moment, perhaps both seeing the first threads of friendship that we have begun to weave between us with colorful hues, linking us beyond the dark wire of our shared loneliness. He squints against the sun at my back, but still the light brings out the spots of gold and green against the brown of his eyes.

"Theo, then."

"Miss Read." He nods back, the same small smirk raising on his face, eyes on me, *seeing* me. I am all too aware of where my forearm touches his, my arm still resting in his own, though we no longer stroll the gardens.

The posture links us in a casual closeness that has become

so unfamiliar to me, hidden away in the flat or Langdon or my mind, that it feels anything but casual.

"It's all prepared, sir." I almost jump, both of us turning to see the squat form of an older woman, adorned in the simple garb that matches the younger blond woman at her side, who smiles at us before scuttling back into the hedges in pursuit of the house.

Her task appears to have been completed, and what a task it was. A large blue blanket sits atop the grass, covered in a luxurious spread of meats and cheeses, small dishes of bright strawberries, and a gold wine that sparkles in the sunlight.

"Oh God," spills out of Theo's mouth on instinct as he takes in the sight. "Yes, thank you, Martha."

"Of course, sir." She returns his smile, hers much less forced than the one that has overtaken his face.

"How is your son? Is he no longer taken ill?" Theo's voice stops the woman as she turns back toward the house, his tight smile melting into the pinched brows of genuine concern.

"Ah, yes, he's much better now. It seems the cough is passing." The woman's accent is thicker than his own, heavy with her Yorkshire roots that surround the estate. "I cannot thank you enough for sending the doctor for him, sir. You needn't've."

"Don't be silly. You are family, Martha, and thereby so is Alexander. I'm glad to hear the boy is well."

The woman's cheeks turn red before she moves back toward the house in a brisk shuffle, leaving us with little more than a curt nod.

"I . . . cannot apologize enough, Miss Read," Theodore says, eyes taking in the picnic spread before us, and I'm surprised to find that his own cheeks have been painted pink.

"For what? This looks amazing."

"Yes. But, well, I fear that my staff has become rather excited at the sight of a woman on the grounds and they seem to have gotten the wrong idea about why it is you find yourself in my company today."

"Ah." And there we stand in the sunlight, both of us with matching blushes like a couple of schoolchildren. I pinch my fingers together, a fidget I cannot seem to break, and as the ring on my left hand presses into my skin, the dread in my stomach strengthens its bite.

There is no need. I have done nothing wrong, of course. Others misunderstanding is simply that.

"Don't worry about it." My voice is too heavy with the casualty that I try to inflict, but Theo either does not notice or he is kind enough to pretend not to. "No sense wasting a great lunch just because people might be a little chatty, right?"

"Of course." Theo holds his hand out to guide me down to sit upon the blanket, but I let my eyes rest on the sea beyond, as though I do not notice. I do not take his outstretched offering and in my periphery I see his hand falter for only a moment as he holds air before he joins me across the blanket.

The air between us suddenly feels a bit heavier, as though it carries more than the wind lifted off the sea. I find no words to remedy it, my movements as stiff as my tongue as I reach for a strawberry. Its dotted red skin is as fluorescently bright as everything else in the garden, as though the world I had seen before had never, truly, been in color. It has a taste to match, freshness and summer sparking across my tongue, melting to the touch.

"These are delicious, wow." I catch the barest moment of Theo's eyes on my lips before they return to my eyes as I speak, the pink across his cheeks not yet faded.

He clears his throat, focused on his task of pouring suncolored wine into the small crystal glasses that await us. They seem far too formal to be used upon the grass.

"Thank you, they were grown in the greenhouse." He tilts

his chin to gesture beyond my shoulder and there, just at the cliff's edge, is a magnificent structure of glass. The sun glints off of it, making the darkened vines of plants beneath it glow like green-gold veins.

"It's beautiful," I breathe.

"I am pleased you think so, Miss Read. It's my refuge, I must admit."

"Oh! You grow this all yourself?"

"I do, indeed. It's perhaps an unusual pastime for the lord of an estate, but I cannot deny the peace I find among the roots. Does it still stand in your time?"

Langdon in my own time already feels like my past, the edges blurred like old photographs, the way that memories so often are.

"I'm not sure. Truth be told, I've never wandered farther into the grounds than where I met you just yesterday."

"Ah, well, you must then. There is much beauty to find within Langdon's wrought iron. At least in this time, my time, I can say for certain."

There's an itch there between us, words he holds down beneath the surface, waiting for me to scratch it first.

"I'm sure you want to know what my time is like," I try.

Theo chuckles lightly.

"I see my curiosity is transparent. But, no, I will resist bombarding you with questions of your own era. I am a man who knows his place. I have no real desire to know of things that I shall never see. The things I do see, here, now, are aplenty for my taste. And if you are any indication of the future of Langdon, Miss Read, then I trust that it is a pleasant future indeed."

I feel my cheeks flame and I am grateful for the breeze that lifts up to bite at my skin—nature giving me a mask. I tell my heart not to quicken its pace, and it nearly listens to me. My tongue tangles around a response, but whatever I lack in social niceties, Theo sports in abundance. Likely a necessity of his time and position, but one that I am grateful for.

"I am certain you must wish to see more of this time"— Theo gestures to the sea—"than just the estate. Than just me." It feels like this is a challenge, an evaluation, a touch pressed tentatively onto the smooth top of a frozen lake, testing the waters and seeing how much weight it is willing to hold.

Where are my limits?

Why are you here, Saoirse?

"No, I don't want to see anything else." The words come forth quickly, against my will, but I do not question it or bury it into the rich grass beneath us. "I mean, I don't know if I could. Leave Langdon. I'm not sure that whatever keeps me here, now, would work outside of the estate. The power is in the house, after all, isn't it?"

If I wished to see some flash of disappointment cross Theo's face—and I don't, of course not—there is none to be found. He contemplates instead. The pink of Theo's lower lip falls victim to the mindless nibble of his teeth as he is silent for a moment, both of us wandering separately into the planes of thought surrounding this place, of what it is capable of and how. Of why—of all the people who have entered Langdon in all its lives—it has brought the two of us together.

"Yes, that could very well be the case. I suppose it's not something you would want to risk trying."

"No, it could be dangerous. Who knows? Besides, I don't mind it here." These are words that I never thought I would say or mean, but as I say them, I find that they are true. The Langdon of here and now is a place worthy of the awe and love that Jack and his parents somehow find for it in my own time, worthy of the devotion that spills out from the pages of Theo's journal.

Theo passes me a glass of pink glinting wine, and I do not

know why I make so sure that my fingers do not brush his, that they do not slot into place between his own long digits as the glass sits between us for a breath. But I cannot keep my eyes from watching the exchange, from noting the way that the pale of my hand contrasts and complements the slight tan of his own, as though he has lived beneath a sun I have not seen in too long.

"Oh." The word falls from his mouth and drops heavily between us, and for a moment I cannot identify the shift in his eyes, the sudden frown on his lips. There is a change in the air between us as surprise and tension radiate from him. "Where did you get that?"

Theo's eyes now sit on my left hand, on the large diamond that catches the light of the sun. It is a beacon between us, embodying the things I am ashamed to admit I had pushed from my mind, for just a moment.

"Oh, um," I falter, and I do not know why there is a barrier, why my mind contemplates what it is that I should say. There is only one thing to say and it is the truth and I do not know why I am afraid to bring it forth. Afraid to make my real life, my future, Jack, real in this place where it all feels anything but. I do not want to tie the weight of my reality to the place where I feel something that resembles freedom.

I hate that I do not feel free with Jack, with his ring on my finger, and I hate that I have known the truth of that for many months and have buried it for just as long.

The guilt that pricks from within my chest now feels more deserved. I do not question why it is there—no woman should want to hide the name of the man who put a ring on her finger, not from herself or from others.

"Miss Read. The ring?" Theo prompts when I do not respond, lost in the depths of my guilt and past and mind. "Did you find it in the house? I am not accusing you of theft, it is merely that that is—"

"A beloved heirloom of the Page family passed down for the men to give to their brides. Yes, I know."

The words are out, sitting between us. Theo tilts his head, like a confused puppy, sifting through my words, perhaps trying to find what I do not say. I see the moment that he finds it, face tightening before it bleeds away into neutrality, so quickly that I have to question if the flash of disappointment was real or if the house is merely playing tricks on me again.

"You're the bride of a Page man, then?"

"No, not yet."

The weight that has lived for months on my chest like my own personal demon returns. It is somehow heavier now that I have dared to forget its presence, dared to live without it for a moment.

"Ah, but you are betrothed. That is lovely." But his hazel eyes say that it is anything but as they tip down to the ground, his black lashes all that is visible to me. "Congratulations, Miss Read."

Congratulations to the happy couple! Our friends, Jack's friends in earnest, with smiles on their faces but eyes shifting to one another, smirks beneath the upturned lips. But still— congratulations!

I fucking hate that phrase and I fucking hate hearing it from Theo, hate that I have been reminded of this thing that I wanted to forget, hate that I even wanted to forget it. I practically wished Jack into my life. I'm lucky he stands by my side as my mind swallows me, swallows our life—even if his heart and mind have gone far from me. I should want to get him back, not to forget him.

"Thank you." And as those words leave my mouth so does the color that has begun to bloom, the wine turned to ash in my mouth. I am closer to the woman I have been for months, the woman who belongs and blends with the angry gray of my own Langdon, and I was a fool to think that I could be anything but.

I expect Theo to tell me what an honor it is to be made a Page, to feel the icy sting of Page pride, all the more potent as one who lives within the history that Edgar and Jack so often boast of.

"To know true love makes one very lucky indeed. You seem a lovely woman, Miss Read, you certainly deserve such joy."

His words sound genuine, and they hurt because they do. But he does not know the truth of how I struggle and how I make Jack struggle in turn as my mind shifts and warps. I am not so certain I deserve joy or that there is room for luck in my life anymore. But as our eyes lock on each other, the picnic between us is forgotten, replaced by the buffet of the life that I will have. The green of Theo's eyes seeps into me, and I let that little vine wind itself through me, the first hint of color restored as I look at him.

"Have you . . . are you? I mean—" I stammer, with none of the ease that a taken woman should have in the face of another man, conversation stripped of potential and what-ifs by the marker wrapped around her left finger.

Theo laughs lightly, brushing a dark curl from his face, but the breeze quickly brings it back to rest atop his brow.

"No, I have never wed." A cloud passes across his face for a quick moment and the sky above follows suit, as though this place is him, as though it follows his heart and mind. "I do not believe I ever will."

I am reminded of the distance, the loneliness, and the longing found on the pages of his journal, words written just months before where we must be now in the spring of 1818. I remember how I felt a connection to those words, to what they did not need to say, though our lives could not be more different.

"It is quite the honor of a man of means, to be the eternal bachelor." His chuckle does not reach his eyes, does not fill the little dark blot of hollowness that I see within him. But I rise to retain the humor, to lift spirits that have darkened between us.

Jack is not even present and yet he has brought the clouds. "Some would say it's the same even in my time." We share an empty laugh and I find my eyes catching on his hand, wanting to hold his fingers, to squeeze them, passing some light to him that I do not even have. I keep my hands to myself.

I think his face darkens further, but no, it is merely the clouds above us stitching themselves together tightly to cast sideways shade upon us, the air becoming thick with the promise of rain yet to come.

Theo's chin tips upward, the sharp edge of his jaw accentuated even in the gray light.

"I think perhaps it is best we go inside. The weather seems to have turned against us."

He pushes himself to his feet, his hand once more reaching out toward me in guidance. This time I set my fingers upon his, letting him guide me to my feet. I do my best to ignore the way that the heat of his touch flushes up to my neck. Once I am firmly on my feet I pull my hand back, burrowing it in my pocket until I can no longer feel the echo of his gentle grip. I catch Theo briefly run his thumb across the ghost of feeling on his fingers, before his hand too disappears into the pocket of his trousers.

It is nothing, turn away, Saoirse.

We abandon the picnic and the words we had there to the whims of the English weather, to be washed away and forgotten. We weave between the maze of hedges once more and Theo does not offer me his arm, and I do not admit that I am disappointed. Instead, he trails behind me, as though in being the last one to enter the home he can protect me from the onslaught of weather.

I round a bend and suddenly the rain crashes down.

I turn with a laugh already on my lips to tell Theo that it looks as though we hadn't been quick enough, but there is nothing but shadow and rain behind me. Even as I spin, eyes searching, I know that I will not find him.

I am here with only the darkened eyes of the Langdon I know, its crumbling facade once more looking like it is moments away from falling, from shedding its stone tears.

My feet slide across the grass as I run toward the building, though I wish that it was not this Langdon, not these Pages, not this life, that I am running toward.

Chapter 13

It is as though the switch of the world has been flicked off. The lights have been turned down and everything is plunged into night once more. I am numb from the cold battering of the rain, which is no longer the chilly drizzle of spring but instead the icy rivulets of winter, soaking into my body. I am numb from the cold, from the sudden plunge back into the icy waters that are my life.

That time in the past, with Theo, was only ever a moment of respite, to forget, a moment of air, stolen from a break in the freeze. But I have slipped back under, as I was always meant to.

I lose feeling in my toes and in the soles of my feet as I pad across the stones of the foyer, soaking up the draft that lives within the floors of this Langdon that even the velvet draped across the stairs cannot undo. There are no more whisperings of the staff, no sounds of feet or paws across the floors. It is all silence here.

So I do not expect Jack and Edgar to be waiting at the top of the steps upon the first landing, blond head bowed toward gray as the two share terse words, too quiet to be understood by the ghost that I am, haunting these halls.

"Jesus Christ." Jack rushes toward me and at first I think

I must look different, that I must be wearing the mark of some deceit that I have not committed. But it is my frozen form, dripping onto their beloved aged carpet, that unhinges Edgar's jaw, that lifts Jack's hands up between us, as though he wants to reach out to either fix or hide things but does not even know where to begin. "What were you doing, Saoirse?"

Edgar huffs, looking at Jack with eyebrows raised, the words that they have never said aloud sitting between them, *This is the woman you've chosen? This is certainly not Page behavior. What is wrong with her, Jack? Do you have no respect for this family, bringing her here?*

I shrink beneath those words unsaid, beneath the meaning of the hard glint in his father's eyes.

"Can I not leave you for even a few hours, honestly? Mum is really not feeling well. I can't be worried about both of you." Jack's annoyance is loud and sharp and I know that I have done nothing to deserve his ire, not truly, yet I always find it pointed at me. It is not my fault, I begin to remember that, even though the accusation that it is hides beneath every word he says.

Why did you bring me here, Jack?

Why have we not set each other free?

But what if we did? Where would I float without Jack to hold me to reality? I cannot let go.

"I just went for a walk; I didn't expect it to rain."

My words are not defiant, but there is the faintest edge to them, no longer whispered and cowering, and I see in Jack's eyes that he hears it too, that he sees me waking up, asleep for so long that both of us have forgotten that that is not merely my state of being. I am as surprised as Jack seems to be that I do not cower and morph into his image of cooperation.

Edgar still stands over Jack's shoulder, a witness to the tension that has long grown between us, so long hidden, so often unacknowledged, now beginning to peek forth, and I do not know why it has chosen now.

He places a steadying hand on his son's shoulder, bending forth to say something in Jack's ear before pulling back, a reminder that there are words that I am not yet privy to, that I may never earn a place to hear.

"Jack will go visit with his mother. Alice's hospice carer has just left and she's quite worn down, but I'm sure she would welcome some quiet company." His eyes cut to me, a gaze full of swords, sweeping down to my feet, where wet shreds of grass cling to my toes, soiling the floor beneath me. "Saoirse, why don't you go change into something dry and perhaps have a bath. Then we can meet in the foyer downstairs in an hour or so. I'd like to chat with you a bit. I think it'd be nice for you to learn about the history of Langdon, of why we treasure the estate so much. Certainly that would be of interest to you."

There is no question or invitation to Edgar's words, merely instruction, laden with disapproval and weariness.

Every word is a pinprick, creating holes meant to fill with shame. They have treated me like a small child since my first slip downward into my mind.

"With a careful eye I'm sure you can guide her back on track," the psychiatrist had said to Jack.

When did we stop trusting me to care for myself? When did I start to believe they were right?

I am dismissed now, the two Page men turning their backs to me, disappeared into the house's doorways.

I do not care that my skin is ablaze. I am thankful for the burn that seeps deep into me, offsetting the chill that this house puts in my bones. I am thankful for the sharp bite of the water against my frozen skin as I slip down into the bathtub, a stinging reminder that I am alive.

The bathroom that branches off of the bedroom Jack and I share is a relic of grandeur, with its ivy green tiles filled with the hair-thin cracks of age and the heavy clawed feet of the copper tub turning red with rust. It is a place that could be beautiful but instead has been forgotten, and I cannot miss the perfect irony of it all as I sit within the basin.

I sink beneath the surface and fall deep into the tub, the red of my locks floating out like a bloodstain across the water's surface. The yellow light of the bathroom is warped and distant through the wall of auburn. I do not close my eyes, instead welcoming the burn against my irises, the pressure that builds within my ears and inside my lungs. For a moment the world is silent beneath the water, and I wish that it could bestow the same calm to my mind.

I emerge from the water with a gasp, my chest tight. I know what Jack would say if he was here to witness me, the concern that would pinch his eyebrows as he began his questions of, *Do you want to hurt yourself or something, Saoirse? Why must you always push things to their breaking point?*

I do not push because I wish to fall deeper into the seclusion of my mind but because I want to crawl my way out, to remember that I am alive, that I have the power to find the handholds and climb to freedom.

I do, don't I?

Do you, Saoirse? Do you believe yourself?

Yes, yes, I do, I must. I will.

Their words are not your truth.

I waft the water toward me within the cup of my hands, watch as the heat blooms red across my neck and breasts, but the waves do nothing to bring my numb skin to life.

There is no creaking of doors, no padding of phantom footprints. The house is silent and I hate it for that. For leaving me alone. For making the only sounds the ones I make, the slap of water against copper, its ringing echo bouncing back at me.

You made yourself my friend, you living being of stone and glass and frost, and now you turn your back on me?

I do not know why the quiet that has become the norm of

my life feels heavier now. Nothing has changed, I am still me, Jack is still Jack, and the darkness is still my truth.

But I had forgotten what the balm of spring felt like and I resent that I have been reminded, unsure if it is better to live in ignorance, to forget that there is anything but the numbness of the cold.

But it is nothing, merely the darkness of winter without. There are still warmer months within me, between Jack and me, there is warmth coming, *there is, there is.*

There must be. For how else will I survive?

Chapter 14

An hour submerged in heat has done nothing to soothe me.

The chill of this house has already settled back into my bones, burrowing the cold deep beneath my skin as I stand in the foyer, damp hair twisted atop my head in a mass of burgundy. I am awaiting my reluctant tour guide, or, rather, my babysitter. Edgar tasked himself to look after me for the evening, as though I cannot be left to my own devices long enough to give Jack a moment's peace, as though I am not a grown woman, capable of being by myself, of *being* myself.

How would any of us know what I am capable of, when I instead have become what they see me as, what they treat me as?

Two days ago, I would have been eager at the chance to learn of the house's history, even from Edgar. But now I know the house is more than an artifact. It is a living being who has made me a part of its history, planted me time and again into the seeds of the past.

I hear footsteps on the stairs and for a moment my heart comes alive again, a bird fluttering against the cage of my bones. I wonder if the house has already sent me back and if it will be Theo, or Martha, or Blackjack that comes around the bend of marble.

But it is merely Edgar, along with the coldness of the air. The howling wind outside has not diluted, but has rather increased, as though the patriarch's presence strengthens the winter of this house.

"Hello. Are you feeling better?" His voice is tired, clipped, the way it has always been with me, long before his wife was truly ill, long before they deemed me to be just as sick in a different, quieter, shameful sense.

"I am, thanks."

Hollow, hollow lies.

Edgar comes to a stop on the last step of the staircase, resting a head above me, his gaze pointed down the slope of his nose and lifted chin. I had expected that maybe Jack would make an appearance for my Langdon Hall history lesson—my reprimand—but he remains hidden from me within the bowels of the house.

"I thought perhaps I could tell you a bit about Langdon since you have the pleasure of visiting." I do not roll my eyes or huff out my breath. "I'm sure Jack has told you a bit about why the house is so important to us?"

"Uh, yeah. He said it's been in your family for centuries." That much I know firsthand to be true, Theo's voice flashing in my mind. "That it holds a great deal of Page family legacy."

"That it does." Edgar nods slightly, a teacher almost mulled by a student's correct answer.

Look at how quickly Saoirse can learn to be a good girl.

"Come."

He begins his ascent up the steps, and I follow in his footsteps without even making the conscious decision to move, so well done is my conditioning by the Page family. I follow where I am led. Edgar stops at the first small landing, both of us stepping back to look up at the wall colored by the many Page family portraits, harsh eyes marking the space.

"These are, of course, some of the many Pages that have

inhabited Langdon. As a boy I was taught the story of every one of these figures, as was Jack. It is essential that the history of the Pages be remembered and preserved. That this knowledge is passed down by those that appreciate and celebrate it."

Is that the only history that matters? The one with your last name upon it?

"Of course," I reply, voice stale.

Edgar's eyes cut to me from the corner, sharp, but he does not find the rebellion of sarcasm in my face even if it has trickled into my voice.

"This is Barnaby Page, my grandfather." He gestures to the picture at our eye level, a blond-haired man with deep wrinkles by his mouth from decades of frowning, his glare already boring into mine, as disapproving of me as his grandson. "He was born in 1875 and served his country faithfully in the First World War."

Edgar gestures to the portrait beside it, the faces nearly identical, both hardened with displeasure, their features mirrored, despite the decades of age between them.

"That is my father, Harold Page. He was born in the winter of 1901, and married my mother, Regina—this is her here—in 1927." A cold-faced, sharp-featured woman glares down from within a gilded gold frame. "My mother was, of course, from quite an important lineage herself, much like Alice. Both women are from their own great English dynasties."

I hear the words he's weaponized, the women born to wealth themselves, weaned on his beloved English soil—two things I have never been and, perhaps worse, have never had the desire to be.

My eyes move away from Regina's glare, drifting across a dozen other equally dissatisfied hazel hues, most under carefully coiffed dark hair. I am drawn in by a somber family of

five, immortalized forever within a silver frame. Their clothing dates them back centuries before Barnaby, thick ruffles
binding vein-strained necks and the cuffs of wrists that rest
stoically on one another's shoulders.

Edgar sees my gaze, all too ready to educate, to inform, to
shame.

"Montgomery Page, born 1711, with his wife, Katrina,
their eldest son, Montgomery the second, born 1732. And
Elizabeth, born in '35, and Lewis in '37." The smallest son
stares back at me, a small smile tugging up at his lips in a way
that is immediately reminiscent of Theo, his mouth holding a
joke that is meant for no ears but his own. "Montgomery the
second passed on the battlefield and Elizabeth in childbirth
in 1754. Lewis, however, married one Jane Page and the two
had six children."

It's interesting, the way the Pages demean and infantilize
my studies, but here Edgar is, something of a historian himself. *But on the things that matter.* Though I have a feeling I
could memorize every Page on the wall, pore over their stories and immortalize them, and yet it would not be enough.
Edgar continues to speak, spouting off names and dates that
I will never care to remember, his voice falling to the back-
ground, a mere hum in my mind as my eyes sweep over the
wall, unashamedly catching the painted eyes of all the Pages.

If I can look at them without letting my gaze fall to the
floor, without shrinking in their stern presence, perhaps I can
one day do the same for the Pages here, in the flesh, made
of blood and bone. The ones who are more than mere paint
strokes.

But then there is one portrait, one Page, who catches and
holds me.

"Saoirse, are you listening?"

"Of course." My eyes do not look away from Theo's. They
cannot look away.

He looks different, younger maybe, eyes less green and skin more sallow, dotted with small differences to the man in the flesh. But I know, nevertheless, that it must be him. For there he is, the man I know, or am coming to know, ennobled in paint and canvas there on the wall. A space he has long occupied, looking down at the happenings of Langdon, at the movements of Edgar and Alice and Jack and me for days, an unspeaking, watchful gaze. Even when I thought I was alone, there he was.

"Ah, yes." Edgar follows my eyes. "As I said before, that's Theodore Page. An interesting ancestor, certainly. Born in 1788 right here in Langdon, as we all are. He never married or sired children, however, but the Page name was radically carried on by the three children of his eldest sister, Iris."

My mind is already worn so thin, from slipping between time and beneath hot water, that Edgar's words quickly fade into the distance once more as I look into Theo's eyes. Many of the frames house portraits of families of Pages together, husbands and wives, fathers and sons. But there Theo sits, no wife or children by his side, a mere "interesting ancestor," a small touchstone in the story of an ancestry that he did not— has not—forged himself.

Edgar's voice drones on, full of words like little daggers meant to poke at me with their sharp, hidden reminders that there is a rich history here that I am not a part of, that perhaps I do not deserve to be a part of. And yet, here I am, in some small, minuscule way, already connected to this family twice over, to the members that breathe and the one who hangs on the wall, and it was the house itself that made me so.

Edgar's hand falls to my shoulder, heavy, and I am pulled back to the present, woken back up to the dreary gray here beyond the strokes of Theo's eyes.

"Many of the women on this wall were not born Pages." Edgar's grip tightens and so does the hold of his eyes on mine, already saying the words that I knew he would lobby between us. "But they understood the importance and beauty of the Page name. I would hope that, as someone with such an interest in the past, you would too. They made sure that they could live up to such a title. Could make themselves worthy of it."

The words are dated, a relic of another time—another mind-set—and they should be shocking, but Edgar and Alice have been silently screaming their disapproval of me for years, and I know that no memorization of faces or names or years will ever remedy that, will ever redeem me in their eyes. The very place and family and history of me, or my lack of it, are at fault. There is no redemption that could remedy that. For them, I could never apologize enough for who I am.

But this house does not show a legacy, not really—it is the tombstone of a dying one. They want to blame me for this slow death, for a disease, a rot, that began in the Page name long before I came to it, a legacy that cannot survive the changing of times and cultures.

But that will not stop them from doing so.

"Do you understand what I'm saying, Saoirse?"

"Yes, I completely understand."

And unfortunately, I do.

Chapter 15

Has the house now judged me by Edgar's standards and suddenly found me as wanting as its inhabitants always have? For here I am, waking to the slant of gray light that could indicate morning, afternoon, or evening here, with Jack's back to me, and a whole two days spent very much so, very stubbornly, in the here and now of Langdon.

My thoughts must be loud enough to wake Jack, the pale expanse of his back stretching as he rolls to me, occupying the patch of mattress between us that sits cold and empty throughout the night.

"How'd you sleep, love?" The endearment slips forth, Jack not yet having woken up to the world, to us.

"Good, yeah." The lie comes forth on its own, my words so naturally now acting as an outstretched hand to keep him at a distance.

Jack's eyes drift across the bit of my skin exposed over the duvet's hem, the rise and swell of pale pink. He reaches toward me, tentatively, and when I do not say no in words or action, he rolls himself on top of me, propped on elbows to avoid any unneeded press of skin on skin.

"Should we . . . ?" His voice is quiet, a whisper, and he does not register the dispassion in my nod that matches the way that he too is merely going through the actions that we believe we should. Jack's touch on my skin used to feel like pure excitement, used to make my body curl in tingles that made me chase each touch for another. Now my body is hardly my own and Jack is hardly mine either.

His hand drifts down between my legs and the touch elicits nothing from me, an expanse of numbness making it so that I do not know or care where his fingers stroke and press. It's not entirely his fault—I've drifted from my body, from here, the past few days. Not far enough for respite, though.

The red and gold of the canopy dips low, falling into the shadow the morning non-light has cast upon us. And then there is absence, followed by the familiar pinch and slide, an entry into a body that feels too far, too unknown to be mine. He leans up as he moves inside me, but neither of us reach for the other, neither seek skin beneath our hands or across our chests.

The canopy sways from Jack's movements and the current created in the endless air between our two bodies, so devoted to distance. I watch the colors flow and bleed together above us, and for the first time in a long time I wonder if there is more. I remember a time when there was, when the press of Jack's skin against mine, inside me, would still never be close enough. Now we are merely actors walking through the markings of a show that the curtain has long since closed on.

My eyes move across the room behind Jack's body, but he does not notice, eyes closed, seeing something beyond me as well, I am sure. There are no clouds to move or part above us, just a wall of gray in the sky beyond the window. Gray across this room with its empty chairs and its bed that sits vacant, even when it is not.

But then, there it is, and I know that it was not there a moment before. The journal rests on my bedside table, innocent, far from the sitting room, where it had last been placed days ago.

Here it is now, the house reaching a hand out toward me—seeing my loneliness, even now when my body could not be more joined. Here is Theo reaching a hand out toward me, through this thing that we share, even if he does not know Langdon has brought his journal, his thoughts and feelings, into my grasp. Without thinking, I lift my hand to reach toward it, to feel the smooth brown leather beneath my fingertips, and the motion rockets me back into my body, and I remember that I am alive.

Eyes pressed closed now, I lift my hips, pressing Jack deeper into me, and the enthusiasm, the very presence of a reaction, startles him into sputtering thrusts for a moment. Then he returns, hips steady, a forceful press against my own, and I feel where he fills me, where the bones of his hips press into my thighs, where eyelashes tickle my cheekbones, where the journal rests beneath my flattened palm, so alive it's like it radiates the heat that should be between Jack and me.

My breath hitches, the flush from the book, from its words that I can see beneath my closed lids, spreading across my body, down to where my legs open. It's like the very touch is enough for those words to infect me like a drug, and I cannot stop the image of the man from whose hand they stream. One man presses his body into me, but it is another who is already inside me, in my mind, who sits smirking behind my lids. I arch my back as Theo's face comes into clarity in my mind's eye and I am unable to stop the breathy gasp that slips out from between my lips and I cannot believe that I am almost alive again. But then Jack shutters and sighs, and slides out from me, landing on the mattress with a thump.

The tunnel of air has returned between us, the draft of our relationship, and it wipes away the image that my mind has conjured against my will. The journal is like fire upon my hand, fingers and skin and conscience scorched. The guilt sets in quickly, an immediate stone in my stomach, but I will not acknowledge its source, will not look upon the deception that my mind and I have just committed. If I do not look, then I cannot see.

But the shame does nothing to extinguish my desire, still lingering and pulsing beneath the surface.

Jack's breath is shallow and quick, but I hold my own, ears strained for the sound of footsteps, of phantom bodies settling into chairs, something to tell me that the world is not just now, not just me and my fiancé and the ocean we are barely buoyed upon. But I am met with nothing but a dull ache of longing for someone I barely know.

The man I do know, or did once, is already lifting himself out of bed, trousers zipped and shirt buttoned, body quickly hidden from me as if there is still anything left unknown between us. Unacknowledged, yes, but unknown, no.

"Mum's hospice nurse should be pulling in any minute." Jack moves toward the door, eyes never glancing toward me. "You can handle yourself today, yeah?"

I can handle myself every day, you have simply forgotten that I am a person, that I am alive. You only see me as the being—the lack of—that you want me to be. That you made me be.

My thoughts surprise me because they are hot and alive, but mostly because they are true. It is the weight of my mind that strains Jack and me, but I am the only one trying anymore. And maybe I should not be.

But Jack does not wait for me to answer before the bedroom door is closing behind him, the moisture of his skin still clinging to my thighs.

Left in the room, I grab the journal without hesitation, pages soft between my fingers as I eagerly find my way back to Theo's words.

I could not have stopped even if I wanted to and I find that I do not.

January 11, 1818
A new year welcomed into Langdon Hall, and silence has
returned to the estate, Iris having returned to London once
more. She tells me that the ton already whispers of me, hopes
for my appearance this Season. But they will all be sadly mis-
taken if they expect such from me, no matter how often my
sister reminds me of the beauty of the many eligible women
in Town. My reasons for resisting remain my own, so I am
due to hear the incessant words of my eldest sister, likely
until the end of my days.

If there was a time for me to take residence for a Season
in Town, to seek a bride, that day has long passed. The quiet
of Langdon does often seem to mock me, the stillness of my
bedchamber at night. But it would simply be unfair, be fool-
ish, for me to seek a bride now. And what woman of Town
would wish to live in the isolation and distance of Langdon,
wealthy and esteemed as its halls may be? No, it is simply
not possible, no matter if I wish it were.

There are words that are not said upon the page, gaps that
remain between the ink, and I am suddenly longing to be
before Theo now, to ask him what it is that he harbors, what
is burrowed inside him that keeps him from reaching toward
the love he seeks. What irony it would be, the woman engaged, in a relationship where the love has long since lost its
color, asking another why he does not seek the same fate. The
companionship he so desires—the one he does not let himself
have—has been brought to him by his estate, in the form
of a woman whose mind is nothing but gloom and whose
thoughts are traitors.

March 8, 1818
I am still well. My spirits even remain high after a trip past
the border to Scotland with George and many of the mates

from our boyhood. Weeks at his estate, whiskey and hunting and the fresh winter air that is not weighed down with whipping wind as it is here at Langdon. Tiring, yes, but exhilarating nevertheless. Likely just as good for my lungs as the fresh sea air of home hopefully shall be. I have even received a letter from Nell. No words of apology or forgiveness, but the silence between us remains no more and for that I am grateful, though I do not know if she ever intends to return to Langdon, intends—

Footsteps from the other side of the door ring out, and my eyes freeze upon the page. The heavy footsteps of a man, steps that are not the familiar press of Jack's feet. It could be Edgar, I know this, but I cannot help the swelling rise of hope that comes forth in my chest. I throw the duvet back hastily, my naked form moving quickly across the room, not caring about—hardly even feeling—the way that the draft bites at my flesh, licks at my feet from the stone beneath them. I am a madwoman as I whip a dress from the discarded back of a chair, hastily pulling it onto my body as I strive to reach the doorway before the hole through time is gone.

I pull the door open and could almost weep to see candles lit in sconces upon the wall, to turn back to the bedroom and see life restored to the vintage furniture, the room suddenly in color rather than the sepia hues of my own time.

I pad down the hallway, already in pursuit. If Theo is around the bend, I cannot lose him, cannot remain without him in this time long enough that Langdon brings me back to my own. I do not know what it is that brings me here, much less why it holds me in this time, but I am lighter here, I am present in the past. And the only denominator I can find in my mind is the dark-haired man.

It is for that reason only that I seek him out.

It is, it is.

But instead I turn the corner and meet Martha, the woman's arms filled with a teetering, tall stack of folded bedding that is nearly startled from her grasp as she sees me.

"Miss Read! Oh, you gave me such a fright!" Then she seems to find herself, her eyes dipping low to the ground for a moment in greeting. "My apologies, miss, I had not realized you were to visit today."

"Oh, no, no, I'm sorry, Martha. It was, uh, a bit of a surprise visit. I'm not even sure Theo is expecting me."

Her eyes widen and it is a beat before I realize the intimacy I have shown in his name—nothing in my own time, but everything in hers, and I can already see the tongues that I have set wagging.

"Well, I'm sure Mr. Page will be very pleased to see you." The smile on her face says what her mouth cannot. "He's up in his study, if you would like to go to him?"

"His study?"

"Yes, miss. Up at the top of the left-most tower. I could escort you if you'd like?"

The room in the turret, the swaying of the curtain, the footsteps that rang without a foot in sight, the movement of the journal. Of course it was a place Theo could often be found, a place where the house has thinned the veil of time.

"No, no, that's all right. I can find my way."

I set off down the hall, wading through pools of golden candlelight that cast down from the walls, and there is a lightness in my step that I will not seek explanations for, but that has become unknown to me for far too long. I welcome it back with a heavy conscience that I willfully ignore.

Chapter 16

The twisting stone steps make my breath shallow as I climb, exertion and residual fear the cause in equal measures. But if there is a phantom to walk these steps, it is me, displaced from another time, dropped here by the wide-reaching arm of the house. Langdon still feels alive in this time, as though the wall closes and expands with its own breaths. But, if anything at all, it is a comforting, melodic rhythm. Reminding me I am not alone, that it has brought me here as I wished, that Langdon is more friend than foe.

And now it is not a mystery or a crisis of the heart that awaits me at the staircase's end, but Theo. Something, someone, that makes the climb slightly less fear inducing, even if he still causes a little hitch in my breath for reasons I cannot understand.

I pass the red curtain without incident, only my own fleeting form causing a flutter. My bare feet make no sound against the stone. I come face-to-face with the closed wooden door and as I lift my hand to knock, the diamond ring is once again in my eyeline. The reaction in my body visceral.

I choke down the panic and knock.

"Hmm? Yes?" Theo's voice is muffled by wood and stone, but it is clear that his attention has been pulled from elsewhere.

I contemplate turning away, leaving him to his privacy. I do not acknowledge that the thought could stem from the flutter in my stomach and the fear that that causes. But the choice is taken from me as the door swings open from the other side and then there is Theo, his face blank in surprise for a moment before the sun breaks through the clouds and his mouth lifts into a smile.

I feel my cheeks burn, the memory of his face in my mind this morning still fresh and burning.

"Miss Read! The house, it seems, is set on putting us in each other's company. I must thank it for that."

The journal, the regular journeys through time—Langdon links us in more ways than he knows. Maybe we both really do need a companion here. And even more, maybe we just need someone to believe us, someone who understands that the world is not always as simple as it seems.

"Mr. Page." I return the smile before I can even consciously choose to, but I would have anyway. I could not have helped it, I imagine.

Theo chuckles, the sound gentle and familiar. The kindness he radiates greets me as though I am an old friend, as though all are welcome in Langdon's rooms. As though there is nothing and no one he would rather see.

"I thought we had agreed upon Theo?"

"Well, maybe I felt like I should get into character a bit. Now that it seems like the house will be bringing me back to the nineteenth century regularly."

His smile softens, and it no longer feels like it's for everyone, but only for me.

"So it does. Kind of the house, truly. But I assure you this is no play, Miss Read. It is very real. So no character is necessary, you are more than welcome to simply be yourself here at Langdon."

The words are surely nothing to him, shallow pleasantries, but they spring a bit of moisture to my eyes that I do not expect, that I blink away before they fall or make themselves known.

Theo pointedly looks away, craning back toward the office barely visible behind him.

"Do you care to come in?"

"Oh, you sounded busy, I wouldn't want to interrupt."

Where else would I go? Why else am I here?

Why am I here?

"It is no bother, I was merely reading. And I assure you, Miss Read, there is no way I would rather spend my morning than visiting with a friend."

A friend, of course, is that not what we are?

What else would we be?

What else could we be?

Theo steps back, arm opening to welcome me in in a sweep of staunchly pressed white fabric. The full of his form is on display as I pass and the shock, the thrill of his attire—a confirmation that this is all real—returns in full force. What have I done that this house has deemed me worthy of flowing through a ripple in time, of spending my days drifting through the past with one of Jack's ancestors?

Jack.

He still does not know where I spend my days, tucked away into the walls and shadows of Langdon, and he does not ask. Perhaps it is simpler for him to be acquiesced that I am beyond the eye of him and his mother, and he wonders no further. Maybe it is good for me to have something that is my own, not a secret but something like it. Something that is mine, that reminds me that I am still me.

Of all the parts of Langdon I have seen here, the office-library is the most similar to how it still stands in modern day. Curved walls are adorned with shelves and shelves of books, and the wide windows show the expanse of the garden beyond. The high point of the ceiling is above us, and the thick carpet is beneath. Fire still crackles through the quiet of the room, splashes of orange and red dancing across the space, revealing the reality of the phantom flame I saw in my own era—wrinkles in time before Langdon ever opened the curtain enough for me to slip through. Even then, we were woven together in some way, the solidities of Theo's movements translating into the ghosts of my own, a language between us that the house struggled to translate.

Even much of the furniture is the same, newer here rather than made shabby with age, the chair and side table in which I first read Theo's journal still sitting patiently. But now they rest beside a large desk, the dark top strewn with papers written in the same hand as that I have come to be so familiar with, to be comforted and enthralled by.

Theo swings the door back toward its frame, leaving it ever so slightly adrift.

"Propriety in my time, Miss Read," he says as he sees my eyes fall to the gap in the doorframe that leaves us connected to the rest of the world. Not that I would ever wish for it to be otherwise. "You are betrothed after all."

It feels like a challenge, like a smirk, but it is only in my imagination, I am sure.

"Yes, I am." I am betrothed and lucky to be. And *happy* to be. I know most brides-to-be do not need the reminder of that the way I do.

But still, Theo's reminder feels a bit sharp, for reasons I do not quite know, and do not care to explore further, afraid to see what lies beneath the sensitivity.

How very typical of me, afraid to go into myself, afraid of the truth I'll see there. But it is no longer a deep, dark, devouring mind that I am afraid I'll see, but rather a spark of light in the darkness that certainly should not be there.

"After all, I'm sure Martha will be up with tea at any moment so she can set the tongues of the staff in motion," Theo laughs, as though he can see the way I've begun to slip into my mind and has thrown me a hand of laughter to help pull me out.

"Well, we wouldn't want to rob her of the chance to do that, would we?"

My gaze falls back to the desktop and there, at the center, I realize, is the very same brown journal, its spine cracked, a half-written page open to the sky and a quill sitting in a pot of ink beside it. Following my eye, Theo steps forward to close the notebook.

"The ink might smear if you keep treating it like that," I tease, but I cannot deny the flurry that his haste has started in my mind. What sits on those pages that Theo does not want me to see? Will the house favor me once more, putting those very pages before me in my own time, the security of two hundred years between us to keep Theo from obstructing my sight?

"I am certain it will be fine. Nothing of worth in there regardless." His words are tense, unnatural, hiding.

And I can easily identify the guilt that bites me this time, the truth of the journal—of what I know of him—as I face Theo. But how could I tell him now, when the very content of those pages has become so sacred, when the words he writes could become destroyed or altered or, worse yet, censored with the knowledge of my readership?

But I do not feel good as I prompt him toward the answers that I seek.

I walk to the window. My stride and my face do not feel casual, but I hope that is how I come across. Rain falls gently upon the garden, but the clouds are not the impenetrable wall that they are in my own winter.

"It's January in my time. Snow and hail and the lot every day. It's miserable. But it looks so lovely out there now."

"Lovely? I'm not sure most would call an English spring such, but I'm sure the year appreciates your compliments,

Miss Read." His voice has returned to its teasing tone as he comes to stand on the other side of the window, a chaste gap of air between us. But it feels hot and alive, opposing the draft that is the constant barrier between Jack and me.

"So it's spring?"

Tell me, Theo, tell me where in your pages I must go to live your life as you do, for your words and my mind to run parallel.

"Indeed. The fourth of April."

There it is, in my grasp, the pages of the journal I will seek out.

The fourth of April.

"Oh, hmm. I wonder why the house has brought me back to this month. Why not last January? Why not the next?" I say, to cover the truth of my curiosity.

Theo is silent for long enough that I return my gaze to him, and the tightness of his face is there for only a moment before he returns a shallow smile to it.

"Who could guess the whims of Langdon? I am certain greater men than I have tried and failed."

I smile in agreement, but that look on his face that lasted just a brief moment, that gaze that teetered between sadness and fear, is not yet wiped from my mind.

"So, what were you reading?" I nod to the book that rests on the windowsill, a thick slip of paper sticking out to mark the page.

"*Romeo and Juliet.*" Theo blushes and the pink brings his face to life, catching and setting the green in his eyes aflame. "An old favorite of my sisters. And I must admit I often fall victim to nostalgia."

As do I, so much so that I think memories are all that fills me anymore. A historian made of nothing but the past.

"Oh, you have sisters?" The words come on their own, a conversation built upon deceit. There is already so much I know of Theo's life that he has not yet told me, my eyes scavenging through the words of his heart in secret.

I wish I did not want to pry, but I have to see if he will tell me himself, if Theo will bring me into his confidence in person, the same way he unknowingly has upon the page. I don't want to be alone in the draw I feel toward the journal, perhaps even toward him. I want to hear that he is drawn just the same, pulled along in the tide that the house has set for us.

"Two, yes."

I think my brothers would like him, I realize. Too rich, too British, yes, in the way they joke about Jack being. That same aristocratic, assured *something* that made me chase Jack and his attention in a way my brothers had never felt compelled to do. They had been put off by it instead. But Theo wears his wealth, his title, without the tightness Jack does. Even if the world has questioned Theo, he has never questioned himself. There is an ease to Theo that is familiar, that same simple sort of peace that I always envied my brothers for. An ease that says that one has always known love and is softer for it, even if that love has been lost. Not the way Jack takes his parents' love, their lives, for granted. Not the way I have never known a parent's love, not truly, not as my brothers did, for flaws that must live in me, much as I try to scrub them away.

Theo lifts the book gently, handing it to me with care.

The green fabric of the cover is simplistic, the threads along the edge lightly frayed from many reads in the hands of many Pages.

"Both younger than I. My eldest sister, Iris, is in fact with child. The babe is expected in a matter of mere weeks. I am glad that I'll be here to see it."

"Will she raise the child at Langdon then?"

"Ah, no, likely not. She and her husband live in Town. As does my youngest sister, Eleanor."

I can hear the tenderness of the wound there in his voice

as he speaks of Nell, even if I did not already know the truth of it.

"She's actually due to visit Langdon very soon."

"Nell is?" I cannot help the surprise in my voice, knowing well the strain that has existed between the siblings for many months.

"Yes, I received her letter indicating as much just yesterday, though it was dated much earlier."

"That's awesome, you must be so excited."

"Awesome?" The word is clunky on his tongue and I cannot help the laugh that it brings forth in me.

"Wonderful," I supply.

"Yes, wonderful, indeed. *Awesome*. I await it eagerly. I believe you two would get along quite well, as a matter of fact."

"Well, then I'd love to meet her one day."

"I would love that as well." The tenderness has returned to his voice, to his face, and I hate the affection that it elicits in me as well.

"You said your sisters live in Town?" I move away from the delicate intimacy of his words clumsily.

"In London, yes."

"Oh, right. I actually live in London."

"Do you? I am not much in favor of it, though I imagine it is quite different in your day." Theo pulls the white collar of his shirt away from his neck as the heat of the fire drifts across his back, and my eyes catch on the column of skin that is exposed for just a moment before that smooth, hidden part of himself is once more tucked out of sight. "I gather that you are not originally from that area?"

"What gave me away?" I laugh, placing an extra lean into the smoothed edges of my American accent, a flutter in my stomach as I earn a smile in response. "I'm from Boston."

"An interesting place, Boston, I have heard. Does your family still reside there?"

"They do, yeah. My mom and my brothers." I am silent for

a moment, contemplating, but something in his eyes brings the words forth. "I don't see them much these days. We've drifted apart in the past few years since I've moved overseas to study and whatnot."

Since I gave my hand to a man who did not even try to get to know my roots, much less love them, since I sunk into him and then into myself. Since I got lost in my mind and the isolation there because I knew my family would not try to find me anyway.

"It is always so difficult. To accept the distance that grows between youth and adulthood."

"It is, isn't it?"

"Were you close with them when you were young? Your brothers?" Theo asks.

"They're both quite a few years older than me, so we were never too close. Not that we would have been anyway. It's just . . . they and my mom, they all have each other. They don't need me." I try to laugh, but I see the way my words fall between us, too flat, too heavy. I am not unfamiliar with the sad look in people's eyes when they switch from seeing me as a normal woman to someone even her own family cannot be bothered with. The pity, the searching for my flaws, the line drawn in the sand between me and normal.

I wish Theo would not look at me like that. I never should have spoken.

The air of the room has shifted toward heaviness, a blanket of chilled nostalgia sitting across us both.

But Theo is not looking at me with pity or horror, as though my words have not exposed my flaws. Though Theo speaks of his sisters with such devotion, I have seen the ache for lost closeness in his journal. I have read how he speaks of his youngest sister, how he burns for her returned affection, for the gap between them to shrink, just as I have in my mind for as long as I can remember.

Perhaps he would understand even this. But I am not brave

enough to say the word aloud, to risk seeing his expression close to me. It must be written upon my face, for Theo is graceful enough to change the subject.

"Come, Miss Read." Theo glides us past the blue, pulling me out of my twisting thoughts before I can fall too deep once more, a talent he seems to have perfected already. "Let me give you a tour of the books we have here."

"I would love that."

Theo steps toward the closest bookshelf and I follow suit. He tells me of titles long held in the family, and then of ones from popular writers of his own time, but I hear none of it, my entire world shrunken down to the spot where his fingertips lightly kiss the spines as he speaks, his hands strong and long and so gentle in their caresses.

Why is such a subtle, simple movement catching me so?

There is nothing to it. Maybe I am overtired, mentally working through a fog, prone to distraction.

But the way I cannot seem to look away from the finite movements of his gestures makes me uneasy.

We pass along the arc of the room, Theo's voice as steady as his steps, me trailing behind like his obedient, engrossed shadow. I step back, letting the air between us grow and cool and hoping that I can do the same.

Some of the spines before us identify themselves as hallmarks of the time; an Austen, so new the ink is practically still hot, a copy of *Waverley* purchased during a trip up to Scotland. So many of these classics of fiction are merely contemporaries to him. And still, there are so many amazing words yet to be shared with the world that he will get to see for the first time. He has no knowledge of Bertha in Rochester's attic or the fate of Ebenezer Scrooge. The words before us highlight the worlds between us and it is a distance that fascinates me, excites me, intoxicates me.

"This is a rather new title." He steps closer to the shelf,

placing his finger along a crisp spine. "The story is simply magnificent. I do hope that it is still discussed in your time."

I step closer to the shelf to peer over his shoulder and take in the title of *Frankenstein* stamped upon its spine. It is only when I release a small breath of surprise and see the way that it makes the fine hairs that rest on Theo's neck sway, that I realize how close I've leaned toward him.

There is no air left between us, with my chest pressing to his shoulder, and there is nothing between my skin and him but the thin, nearly translucent fabric of my dress thrown on in haste. Theo draws in a sharp breath and I know that he is also all too aware of the lack of distance between us. We are closer than we have ever been. Closer than we should be.

Works of literature, words as a whole, have slipped from my mind entirely. There is nothing but my skin so nearly on Theo's own. Surely he can feel the thunder of my heart across his arm.

Neither of us speak or breathe, and I know that I should step back and move away. But I do not, I cannot, and I am silently thrilled, horrified, guilt-ridden, enthralled, that Theo does not either.

I feel a warm unfurling spiral low in my belly, and it is with shame that the tips of my breast rise, sensitive skin pressing into the chiffon that coats me where I forwent any sort of bra in my earlier haste. My breathing is shallow, chest rising and falling against Theo in quick motions.

If he feels it, he does not acknowledge, but his frozen form seems to scream to me, or maybe I am just so desperate to have someone touch me, to want to, to bring me alive and be alive with me.

Eventually the silence becomes too much and if I do not say something I think I will faint with the pressure building inside me, or worse, I will say words that I mean, that I wish I did not.

"It is," I say, drawing back to Theo's earlier words, which seem so far now that our bodies have held conversation with each other. My voice is breathy, a scratch of sound, but I am too on fire to be embarrassed because no one person could create these flames without the flint of another's desire to spark it. "One of the most famous books of all time, I'd say."

"Really?" His voice, though still deep and heavy and smooth, has taken on a matching breathlessness and to hear it is to come alive again. "I suppose I really am living history from your view, after all."

"You truly are. You're—it's amazing."

I step away because I must, because if I stay there, my body against his, we will soon come to a split in the road where we must either act or choose not to, and I cannot consider the former and cannot bear to do the latter.

The thought flashes into my mind against my will, unprovoked:

I do not want to leave.

It startles me into taking a few more steps away, until the back of my legs are pressed against the desk, and because of this thought I know I must leave. I fear that I cannot be trusted if I stay, and my trust is already so fickle, so threadbare. I turn to look out the window, at the fall of rain, and I hope that it will temper whatever it is that builds inside me. I love and hate it in equal measure and fear it all the more.

The house does as it pleases, we must bend to its will, but, for once, it seems to hear my silent screams and takes mercy upon me. For when I turn back to look toward Theo, the room around me is deep gray, the fire has gone out, and the cold draft and howling winds are my only companions.

Chapter 17

It is amazing how quickly the color can seep from me here. How easily I can slip inside, fall deep down, and become merely the idea of a person.

If Jack is bothered by it, he does not say. I wonder if he even notices at all.

As soon as I had slipped back into my own time, I regretted allowing myself to be so close to Theo, that I had not resisted the inexplicable draw to him. The want and the fear of wanting had fled, and a stone had taken their place in the pit of my stomach. The world had gone quiet once more as I trekked through the Langdon of my own time, the unwavering gloom my sole companion as I sought out my fiancé.

My fiancé. My fiancé.

I could choke on it.

I hate myself for that thought, wish I could unthink it, could unfeel it. I know that I probably cannot.

I hear faint voices behind the door of the dining room, words tight and formal from chilled mouths, and I walk through to find the three Pages seated around the table. I do not find the smiling or laughter that I had, briefly, almost come to associate with Langdon. But this is not that Langdon. This one is cold and distant and its inhabitants do not smile a tilted smirk when they see me, but rather drop their voices.

I wish that I wanted to scream, but I have already melted myself to fill the mold they have created for me. I sit beside Jack in a silence that is much louder than theirs. *How can they not hear me? Maybe they can and they simply do not care. They would not believe me, even if I did speak my truth.*

I'd managed a few days outside the bounds of Alice's gaze—whether through fate or the design of father and son, I cannot be sure. But already in such a brief time the woman has withered more, the petals or her hair drooping from gold to a lackluster yellow, her face pulling down a bit more, as though the life that should fill her skin is draining away.

Even from behind the gauze of my constant displeasure with her, I cannot help the guilt that rises forth, to see what has happened to her while I have been off in another world. I do wish that the sight of Alice worsening brought forth compassion toward her and Jack. That it created some sort of understanding between us.

But Alice's eyes still carry daggers when they land on me and all I feel is the desire to flee this room. I want to flee this Langdon, to be in the other, the one I had just abandoned out of a very different kind of fear.

It is impossible to tell how long I've been gone, how time has swayed and frayed in my absence. The only way to know is by the sky beyond the window, no longer the gray of morning but the onyx of night. The Pages poke at the food sitting on the polished plates before them. After a moment they bring a dish out for me, filling my empty placemat that had sat in my absence, as though I wasn't expected, wasn't here at all.

Blessedly, dinner passes quickly. I can hardly find it in me to engage, even with Jack. I have no energy to fruitlessly try to make them appreciate or even acknowledge my presence. The stagnation I bring to the table holds true, few words exchanged between the family and even fewer lobbed toward me.

"How are you staying busy while you've been here, Saoirse?"

"Reading, exploring the house. Appreciating it."

"Not much work to be done for that degree of yours, I suppose?"

"It's plenty of work, but I make do. I planned to take some time off while I'm here."

"Hmph. A slippery slope, more time off. Of course."

"Of course."

"Well, it's good you're keeping busy regardless, Jack needs some time with his mother. That's very important."

"I completely agree, Alice."

"Not sure what those 'doctors' of yours think, but plenty of alone time is for the best, I'd say."

"I completely agree, Alice."

Jack escorts me back to our room after and the delicate little bubbling of longing for his company, his kindness, does not come forth. Instead, there is the slight bite of irritation. I have done nothing wrong, I have hardly done anything at all, and yet his eyes and brows and mouth are heavy with disappointment as he barely looks at me. We make our way through the darkened hallways, the wind screaming on the shore.

He could not have known the truth of how I spent my day. Even if he had, there is nothing there to spark disagreeableness. I have done nothing, as far as Jack is concerned, I have done nothing. I am nothing when I am not beneath his eye.

I have done nothing wrong.

The first thing I notice when we enter the bedroom is the journal resting innocently on the chair before the fireplace and the room is not silent anymore, the one little book screaming its siren song to me.

"Yeah, you left that up in the library earlier," Jack says as he spots my gaze locked upon it.

I did not actually. It was not my hand that moved it. I left it right here, in this room.

But that is not what sets me alight with concern, the spark flaring into a low-burning flame of guilt.

"You were in the library earlier?"

"Yes?" His brows pinch together in confusion as he looks at the surprise, the maybe panic, that I try to keep from rising on my face. "I was trying to get some work done today so I popped up there. But . . . I spent most of the day in the sitting room instead." Jack turns his back to me now as he rids himself of his shirt, so he cannot see the way shame spreads across my face in a red splotch.

Why? I have done nothing wrong.

I have done nothing wrong.

If I had done anything wrong, it was because I was driven to it. Fated for it.

But I have done nothing wrong.

But that does not matter because the quiet, deep part of me that still holds a little color, the part of me that I've grown to fear and hate because Jack does, wishes that I had done something.

And that is enough—more than enough—to splash red guilt across my face.

Jack's movements are heavy with an exhaustion that I can tell has come from deep within him, a sadness, a constant stress that has bled into his muscles. The guilt intensifies, rises in my throat until I can taste it, bitter, on my tongue.

"How are you doing? With your mum and everything, baby?"

That word has tasted empty in my mouth for a long time, but now it is sharp.

"Yes, well, you know, it is what it is." He gives me nothing more than a casual, brief look over his shoulder, not even enough for our eyes to meet, for me to see in his face whatever it is that he will not put forth through words.

Jack has always held the world at a distance, known that there was power in the way others perceived him. He'd tempered and trained that image of himself. I realized later it was something his parents had taught him, the importance of appearances. But I used to be the one who he would let through the cracks, the one who was trusted with those fleshy, tender parts of himself. We were a team. But now I am not to be trusted, not even with myself. I had shown him the worst, scariest pieces of me, and it had been too much for us both.

And the fear is still there, beneath the howling of my mind and the guilt in my stomach. There is the voice that tells me I was lucky to have drawn Jack's eye, and I may not be so lucky again. That the clinging, clawing gloom in me that repels him is not the result of my mother's own distance, but the reasons for it too. That I am the problem, I am the thing to run from, irreparable.

I am trying. I'm knocking on the door that has been too long closed between us. What am I meant to do if Jack will not let me in, will not even open it a crack?

"Yeah. You know I'm always here to talk if you need it, right?"

Jack huffs out a sharp, short breath and I hear all the worst things in that release of air.

I know Jack views me as as much of a burden to his life as his mother's health. Perhaps even more. Why would I think that I could be his respite from the cold? To him, I am the cold itself, I am the chill draft that runs through our life. I wish I could be his comfort, but I'm not sure there's anything of me anymore to give.

"I know, thanks, Sersh."

He lifts the covers, crawls into bed, putting a period on our conversation. I do not know if it is love or nostalgia or guilt or all three at once, but I am still longing to knock down that barrier between us, even if I may no longer recognize the man on the other side. God knows he would not recognize me now, not really. I am merely the outline of a woman that he has fitted in his mind.

I move toward the bed but stop to linger at its foot, looking down over Jack in his stiff comfort of our shared space.

Maybe honesty is the only thing that is left to rebuild the bridge between us, to fashion into a lifeboat.

"Have you ever experienced odd things in this house? I mean, when you came as a boy?"

My voice tries for casual and misses, every syllable pulled tight like a string, desperate for the appearance of disinterest that I do not quite master.

"Saoirse." Jack's sigh is heavy, doubling the cold of the room. "Is this about whatever you think you saw the other day? The curtain business? I thought you'd gotten over these mad ideas."

"Mad" bristles me, but I am surprised to find that the word wakes me up instead of shutting me down, like his dismissal usually does. I want—I *deserve*—to be believed, for I know I'm telling the truth. If he can already write me off so easily, so carelessly, there is no reason to share my secret with him.

Is it a secret, Saoirse?

But he does not need to know the little thing I've found in this place, what this house has given me that it has never given him. He won't learn that his holy place favors me.

"No, no, I just mean it's a big old house with all this history, as your dad told me." The lie comes out easily, startling me with its smoothness. I never used to be much of a liar, even as a child, my words faltering, my pale cheeks going hot in my pathetic attempts. "I was just curious if you'd ever, I don't know, found a secret passage or something."

Jack is mollified for a moment, shrugging, the gesture pushing his shoulders up into the pillow beneath his neck.

"Nah, nothing of that sort really. It's a pretty straightforward old beast, Langdon."

I could laugh, if the sting of his dismissal wasn't so sharp as he rolls onto his side, turning his face away from me. He does not look back or fidget, as I settle into bed beside him. The tunnel of air between us is our constant bed companion, the perpetual third of our relationship, or what remains of it.

It is cold beneath these covers and cold without and I cannot deny that I am so, so lonely. It is an ache that throbs in my bones, hardening to a callous that taints me. Not just in this house, but in my life. I am so very lonely, suffocated by the constant blanket upon my mind and spirit. Most of the time it does not even feel like there is enough of *me* to keep me company. It is no wonder that I'm slipping back into the dark, familiar respite of my mind. The place of madness.

But am I truly?

I know that Jack would say yes, that he believes that he is losing more of me to myself each day. But I am not so sure. Maybe this is me finally beginning to crawl out of the hole. Perhaps I'm even discovering that the depths of my mind are not as awful, scary, detached, and disillusioned as I have been made to believe. That my mind may work differently than others', than Jack's, but that it isn't *wrong* for it. Is it not distance from myself, from the world, that makes Langdon move me through time?

This house has shown me as much. For when I am in the here that is not now, the Langdon that is not the one of my time, with the man that is not my own, I am reminded of the woman I was. The woman I still might be if I can push through the haze of my mind and make friends with my ghosts.

It is not because of Theo. Of course not. It is the difference of a new life for a little while, the ingenuity of a new time, of putting on a new identity that is closer to my old one. It is being looked at by someone who sees me in colors, as a real, solid being.

The descendant of such a man lies before me, the expansive pale skin of his back already rising and falling in slumber, shoulders caved in, tucking the tender parts of himself away from the talons that he believes spring out from my mind.

I desire that closeness, the openness that we once had before we feared what the other would do with those delicate bits of ourselves. I desire to even wish to be close with Jack again, but I do not, for he is not the same as he was, and perhaps neither am I.

But still, *I desire, I desire, I desire.*

For reasons I do not know, my breath shallows with the weight of guilt as my gaze falls from my fiancé to the journal that now sits on the bedside table. I know that it is waiting for me.

I wish that I could roll over, go to sleep, and be at peace. But I cannot, for all I want is to be within those pages again.

Not just any page, but the page on which I know—I hope— that I will see myself become a character in Theo's story.

I flip the papers gently, afraid that I will not see my name listed among his springtime thoughts. But I'm all the more afraid that I will. Want, fear, desire, and everything else that colors me in spills forth as my fingers settle on what I seek.

April 1, 1818
Something has changed within Langdon. I do not know the prompt, nor would I ever dare to claim knowledge of how this estate operates, what keeps its heart beating and mind exploring. But, at last, it has once more shown me just how living a being it truly is.

If my own eyes and my own ears are to be believed, today the house did as it has not in many years and made a fool of time and man. I stumbled upon a woman in the garden, like a sprite made of the autumn leaves, a woman of auburn and deepest green, sprung forth as though from the earth itself.

But it was Langdon that brought Miss Read from its garden in the year 1994 to this 1818. If her tale is to be believed, and I believe that it is. Langdon has done its trick once more, and despite what Iris may think, what my parents worried— to happen thrice is no madness. Only Nell believed my claims to be true when I was young, and were it not for that, I am uncertain I could trust what I see this time. What I saw and am seeing are truth, that Langdon is no mere estate.

I know that I have been removed from society of my own volition, but it was not until I was with new company that I realized just how heavy the emptiness within Langdon Hall has become. My isolation has not only faded the liveliness of my life, but that of the estate and surely the staff, who should not have to suffer my bleakness.

Miss Read's departure was sudden and haunting, an emptiness left where a woman once stood. I am most intrigued to see if our paths shall cross again, if the house shall deem it so. Even if it shall not, it has given me the gift of knowing my memories to be truth.

I turn the page and a smear of ink paints my finger black, still fresh as though the time barrier has blurred, as though the past of Theo is somehow still existing in the present, scribbling on these pages as they rest in my hands.

April 2, 1818
Miss Read has returned to the Langdon as I know it. ~~There is little to~~

It has become unseasonably temperate, a most pleasant spring. I was thankful to spend time promenading among the fresh April air, unlikely to persist for the season.

Miss Read is betrothed.

To a Page man, most likely some distant relative, birthed from some babe of Iris's own, or perhaps the child that Nell may one day bear.

It is assuring that a woman like Miss Read, of such character, will carry on the Page name in the distant future.

It's odd to see that sentiment from the hand of a Page, words that the Pages I know would never say, would never think nor feel. Yet the reassurance from this line is still as shallow as the words pressed into the page before me, for it is the next line that wraps itself around my mind, tattooing itself into my memory and pattering away in my chest.

I find myself hoping that she will return once more.

April 4, 1818
Last night I dreamt of Miss Read, and there she appeared in my study, stepped from my mind into my halls.

I cannot know the customs of the time from whence she comes; however, the way that we are with each other would be a proper scandal were she a woman of my own era. My thoughts are unseemly enough as they stand on their own, but to feel her body against mine, even the faintest of touches—

I fear that there is little innocence in it. And from a woman betrothed. Betrothed to my own blood.

It is mere foolishness on my behalf, I am certain. Of course there is no scandal in our actions nor our discourse from Miss Read herself, a woman of modernity far beyond what I can imagine. It is all of no stock, I am most certain.

I do wonder why it is that the house continues to cross our paths. I do not know the reasons for Langdon's whims, but there is such comfort in having a partner with whom to view the truth of its fantastical nature. Sometimes I see a hidden sadness in Miss Read's eyes and I think, if nothing else, the house has brought me someone who knows what it is to feel alone from the world.

If there is a further message meant to be keened from our continued, fated meetings, I am most assuredly missing it. But, nevertheless, I am grateful for this gift the house has given me.

*I wish I could do better by it. To cease the ache that comes
forth when she stands before me.*
But it is no bother.
It is nothing at all, I am certain. ~~Nothing more~~ *Nothing of
consequence. It must be nothing.*

The dark hint of words peeks through from the next page,
a peek into a future that I have not yet lived, if I am ever to
live in that time again. I think of Theo's spoken words of
the other day, his lack of desire to know what awaits him,
to know of things that he shall never see. Perhaps it is that,
wanting ignorance to things I may never experience, like the
rest of Theo's life.

It's a story I wish I could be a part of, despite the knot of
guilt living in my chest. My finger is poised, ready to turn the
page, but a nibble of guilt in the pit of my stomach makes me
hesitate. I hardly know Theo. I owe him nothing, so there is
no crime in peaking beyond, to see what is to come. Of him.
Of us. But no, that is a lie.

He is kind in a way no one in this house is in my own time,
and his words made him a friend to me before I ever saw his
face. To look ahead and see his future for him, to know more
than what he has told me, and to peek into my own story beyond what I have lived—it feels like a betrayal. It seems there
is so little in my control, but this I can decide. I let my finger
fall from the page.

I close the journal, letting it slumber back on the table as
I attempt to do the same, but closed eyes cannot hide it from
me. It is as though Theo lies in the bed with us, suddenly so
alive, so present.

It is a long time before I can drift into dreams. The desire
to turn back to the journal, to know if I am within its pages,
dims from a raging flame to a smolder that betrays me to
myself. Distant or not, I know Jack is experiencing the most
difficult moment of his life, every day watching his mother

suffer. And yet, it's not him my mind is on, much as I know it should be. It is Theo's words echoing across my mind's eye again and again, setting my heart pattering with guilt and that other burn I will not name.

As I fall asleep I think of the many paths my future could hold and could not, the words I am too afraid to use to describe my present, to describe what I hope my future holds.

As I fall asleep, I think of Theo, though I do not want to. The beast has awoken in me, the one I forgot even lived behind my ribs. I have muffled it, begging it to remain silent for days. It is a being brought back to life by Theo's words, but I cannot allow it, for it could never be.

This gift the house has given me.
This gift the house has given me.
This gift . . .

Chapter 18

I open my eyes to brightness, the shock of sunlight streaming into the room. But beside me is the familiar chill of an empty bed, the same chill still lingering within my bones. Jack is already gone, as I expected him to be, and it is okay. It's been a long time since I have looked forward to waking to the ruffle of his gold hair, to the flush of his pale cheeks.

But I did not expect to sit up and find myself not in the room I know, but in its predecessor. The canopy above me is no longer the red and gold I have come to resent, and the chairs are solid backed and new. The wardrobe is no longer shedding its skin with age.

I spring forth from the bed in a rush, my luggage nowhere to be found, nothing to my name or my time but my body and the silken nightdress that hangs off it. I do not know whether I wish to stay in my own time or if I want to keep slipping back into Langdon's past, but I cannot deny what a betrayal it is to be sprung forth now, so ill prepared.

The handle of the bedroom door begins to wobble, the creak of the hinges echoing as it swings open, and I am left standing before the bed frozen, helpless. Martha and I meet each other with matching faces of astonishment, the older woman's surprise so inflated it would be comical were the space between us not permeated so heavily by mortification emanating from us both.

"Miss Read!" she squeaks a moment before she skillfully sweeps the shock from her face, replacing it with a barely held, and even less believable, neutrality. "Oh, well, Mr. Page did not inform me that you were in his chambers."

"No! He didn't . . . I'm not . . . he doesn't—" My voice, the manner that I speak, is so staunchly different from hers, a contrast less glaring when speaking to Theo, so aware as he is of my time of origin, information that I have to assume still escapes Martha. "I have no clothing," I settle on instead, the words falling between us like bricks.

"Oh my. So you don't." Martha shakes her head, suddenly burdened with a task she did not prepare for today.

Please, please, you can send me back now, Langdon.

But maybe the house calls my bluff because everything remains the same and I remain here, even as Martha turns into a flurry of movement around me, touching everything in the room as though she's going to fashion me an outfit from the velvet drapes or the fabric back of the chairs.

"Oh, what trouble," she mutters to herself. I continue to stand before the bed, cheeks aflame, all too aware of the presumptions that must be running through her mind as quickly as her feet carry her around the space.

She comes to a stop, facing me once more, rounded features pulled together with focus.

"If you wouldn't mind waiting here just a moment, Miss Read, I'll go to Miss Iris's room and fetch you a dress. I am not certain what Mr. Page's . . . plans for the day were, but Miss Nell has arrived quite unexpectedly, and we cannot have you about the estate in your night frock."

She flees the room as suddenly as she appeared, hand clutched to her chest as she goes. It is only once I am left on my own in the room, door slam echoing, that I think to call out after her. I feel the urge to tell her that what she must be assuming from the situation is not at all the truth of it.

But what could even be said? The truth is perhaps the most unbelievable story of all, and what is the harm of letting people think I'm some bedmate of the man of the estate?

It is no difference to me, beyond the way it strengthens the teeth of guilt biting at my belly.

I look around the room, now with the knowledge of the differences I will see. The bed, blankets ruffled, is still indented on the side opposing where I woke, with the outline of Theo's form, I realize. The thought sends a shiver through me that thrills and shames in one fell swoop.

The journal still sits on the edge of the bed, in a patch of golden sunlight that filters across it like a spotlight. Its spine is unblemished, cover still crisp with youth, as though Theo himself left it here, as though he too drifted to sleep last night with it in his grasp. I almost reach toward it, almost giving in to the evil little desire to look for freshly written words I haven't read in my own time, but then the door opens and Martha returns, arms overflowing with fabric. She looks back the way she came before closing the door once more behind her.

"Off, off," Martha's voice is brisk, and she is immediately back to her frenzied business as she grabs at the edge of my nightgown, tugging it upward.

"No, no, it's all right, I can take care of it myself," I splutter. "Thank you but, really, I couldn't ask you to—"

We do a dance of confusion, me stepping away in shock and discomfort at being waited on while the older woman huffs and grabs at what little garments I have clutched to my body.

"Miss Read," she huffs at last. "Unless you plan to waltz out there in your . . . peculiar undergarments, you must allow me to dress you. These are not the kind of clothes you can put on by yourself. Come now." Her voice softens as she leads me toward the large, mirrored vanity and I allow her to rid me of my nightgown, the golden air beneath the window thankfully warming my skin, as I am still dressed in a layer of chill carried from my own time.

She makes quick work of me with the efficiency of familiarity, even as I stand complacent in my unwavering discomfort, forcing her to lift and move my limbs at will. A large fabric sack is slung over my body and she weaves me into some sort of stays, spinning me here and there by the hips as she tuts to herself. If I had wanted to open my mouth and voice a complaint, a protestation, Martha has ensured I am beyond the ability to do so.

Her mouth is pursed, sharp, brimming with little confusions and judgments that she pushes down. Instinct calls on me to defend myself, to appeal to the motherly figure, but even as I stand here knowing the truth, it sounds too absurd to be called such. So I allow her to continue dressing me like a doll.

Martha lowers my arms from above my head, smoothing the fabric at my hips before stepping back to gaze at me, walking about to take in my every angle. She seems unbothered by the small huffs of breath I've been relegated to within my fashionable confinement.

"Hmm, yes, very fine, indeed. It'll do nicely." She turns me back toward the mirror and the words are stolen from me once again as I take in my reflection in the vanity.

I could nearly blend into this time. I wear a white dress with intricate lace detailing that pillows at my chest before falling down into an empire waist. The little cap sleeves are of the same opaque whiteness, but from there, thin white lace makes its way down to my wrists, revealing the whisper of my skin beneath. It is similar to the dresses I wear daily—the same fine, pale linen, though the dress I wear now is undeniably from another time, another world. But still, it fits my body as though made for it, for me.

"I thought it best to be a bit nicely dressed today, what with Miss Nell visiting." Martha smirks at me and I want to tell her that there is no need for me to win over Theo's sister, as the type of relationship she believes the man and me to be engaged in is wildly untrue. But I cannot deny the bubbling of my curiosity to meet the sister that Theo writes so highly of, in tones so filled with regret and with the tentativeness of a damaged relationship.

But no words can come forth before I am being pushed down into the seat before me, the little woman now towering above as she looks pleadingly at the tumble of auburn curls around my head.

"How do you usually style it, miss?"

I brush my fingers over my head self-consciously, the movement doing little to quell the hair, a feeble means I already know.

"I usually just leave it down, I guess." The answering horror on Martha's face as I shrug tells me that such an answer is insufficient, and God knows what I've just branded myself as in her eyes. "It's all right, I can do it myself—"

"I'm afraid I don't have the skill for anything too fanciful. Both the Misses Page have rather fine hair, as did their mum," Martha mumbles to herself pleadingly as she lifts the hair that falls down my back, as if observing it at a close distance will change the restless nature of the strands.

After a few grueling minutes of my scalp being pulled and prodded, accompanied by the soundtrack of Martha's little huffs and muttered insistences that she can and will help, the woman steps back to reveal the top section of my hair. It has been pulled away from my face and into a long braid that sits among the rest of the hair falling over my shoulders.

"Is that all right? Best I can do, I fear."

"Of course, of course." I stroke my fingers through the strands, and somehow the red looks brighter now. As if it too is coming alive in vivid color. "Thank you."

I follow Martha's lead out the door, desperately wondering why the house has not taken mercy on me and swept me back to my own time. My time, where I can breathe, where there are no stitches binding my middle, no ridiculous, unwarranted guilt clogging my stomach and throat and chest. But here I am, headed briskly down the stairs to settle outside the familiar blue door of the sitting room, muffled voices on the other side. The scene is familiar, my chest twisting with anxiety.

Before I can stop her, Martha has knocked lightly on the ornately decorated door and nudged it open, stepping aside to allow me to enter.

Theo is seated in one of the hard-backed chairs across from a small blond woman, her large eyes brought to life by the rich blue of her dress. Even though I know full well what age women were expected to wed in this time, I'm still surprised that the woman before me, whose courtships I've read so much about, is little more than a teenager. She's eighteen or nineteen at the oldest, but the unbridled joy on her face as she looks at me makes her the picture of youth. Theo rushes to his feet in surprise before I can take in much more of the scene, his jaw slack before he remembers himself and takes a step forward.

"Good morning, Miss Read." He bends forward slightly at the waist, as he did the first time we met, a formality that feels so distant now in our times between without an audience.

"Morning." I do not know which one of us breaks into a little smile first and who is the one to follow suit.

"Miss Read, my sister, Miss Eleanor Page." Theo sweeps a hand through the air, gesturing to the space between his sister and me, and I remember that we are not alone. "Miss Saoirse Read, a recent visitor here at Langdon."

Eleanor's—Nell's—face lights up as she sees me, and she immediately rises to her feet to take my hand in both of hers, squeezing it familiarly.

"Nell, please," Theo breathes as his sister opens her mouth. The young girl's speech is thwarted by his interruption, but it does nothing to temper the unwavering smile on her face as she returns to her seat.

"Please, do join us, Miss Read." Theo gestures toward a chair already waiting as a third to their position, as though the house was expecting me.

Maybe it was, the bastard.

"I'm so sorry to interrupt, I—"

"Please." Theo's voice is gentle, just for me. "You never have to apologize for the gift of your presence, Miss Read."

Gift.

His hazel eyes catch mine, startling me with the intense sincerity I find in them. I look away because I have to, because I hate and love the fire that his gaze spreads across the cold interior of my body. His warmth is so familiar that I know I will miss it when it is gone. This man, his eyes, the upward lift of his rose-colored lips, cannot feel like home. Should not.

So I step away, taking the seat offered to me, my movements rigid and my back as straight as Nell's, forced into societal co-operation by the stiffness of the garments swaddling me.

The room is so at odds with its counterpart in my own time that had I not known it to be the same, I never would have recognized it. The curtains are thrown back to welcome the light of the blue sky, splattering the faintest gold of sun rays onto the two Pages, so different in appearance but both like a little piece of spring themselves.

"It is lovely to meet you, Miss Read." Nell smiles, the brightness of her features, her very person, endearing me to the young woman, had her brother's kind words not already done so.

"You, as well, Miss Page." I do my best to imitate the formal binds of her manner of speech, and if she notices the strained peculiarity, much like her brother she is kind enough to leave it unmentioned.

"Have you been coming to visit my brother often?" she inquires.

The question is innocent enough, but the small smile on her face and the way that her eyes cut to Theo's, as his eyes cut to the ceiling, betray the true nature of her curiosity.

I cannot help it, and I know that her unspoken assumptions are incorrect and there is no need for it, but I feel my cheeks go pink.

"Miss Read has been kind enough to become something of a regular visitor at Langdon, yes," Theo answers before I can, and if I were not so embarrassed, I could laugh at how true his statement is.

What one could call a visitor in some times and a prisoner in another.

"Well, it's no wonder you've had no desire to come to Town then, brother. Simply no need, is there?" Nell teases, and even as an outsider to the customs of this time, I can tell the bold cheek that her words carry.

Why couldn't you have swept me back another two hundred years, Langdon? Thrown me into the period that I am, literally, an expert in? At least then I would not feel so adrift, so ill informed of the customs and tingling with nerves.

But then Theo would not be there.

"Nell," Theo warns, but there is no anger in it. It is all too clear how much affection he has for his youngest sister, how he would let the girl get away with anything. I hate that it immediately endears him to me

And her words are harmless enough, or they should be, but even I know what she is implying, and I have to stop the pleasant feeling that spreads through my stomach, the small smile that steals its way onto my face at the thought of my be-

ing enough to keep Theo from the pull of being matchmade
in London.

And then here comes the quick, cold douse of shame,
shame, shame.

Feelings I cannot feel, should not feel.

Do not feel, I do not.

"Miss Read, are you all right?" Theo's voice is heavy with
concern and I look up to find both matching Page faces gazing at me, mouths twisted into frowns. I have been sitting
unmoving for far too long, mouth closed and mind clearly
far off elsewhere. In places my mind has no business being.

"Yes, yes, I apologize." On instinct, my eyes fall down
to the carpet beneath my satin-slippered feet, prepared for
the all too familiar Page family silence that will fall over the
room at my carelessness. I await the punishment of words
unsaid that will be mine to bare.

But there is no punishment, simply the tinkling of Nell's
voice, extending a hand of kindness to me.

"I had inquired if you have been enjoying your visits to
Langdon?"

"Oh, yes, very much so." The words are out quickly and I
am just as surprised to find that they are true as I am to see
the way that Theo's face brightens into a smile in response.

Chapter 19

Nell's kindness should not surprise me so, but it does. Patient smiles and playful words from the mouth of a Page are still so unexpected. They are distinct to the welcoming nature of Theo and Nell, yet so at odds with the Pages of my time. The woman made no cutting remarks in response to my odd manner of speech, raised no brows at my vaguely passed over recollections of origin. She merely inquired and beamed back, no matter the response, sending little knowing looks to her brother each time the man smiled at me. Something he did too often, painting my cheeks in a constant state of pink.

In only an hour over tea, Nell has established herself as the compatriot I wish still walked the halls in the Langdon of my reality. Though perhaps this Langdon, this time, is just as deserving of the title. It is the same home in two timelines, with me equally bound to both for reasons yet undiscovered. I want to discover them and yet am afraid to, in equal measure.

"Do you care to play, Miss Read?" Nell asks, eyes upon the piano that no longer hides broken in the corner, but sits in the center of the room, awaiting its turn to be a vocal participant.

"Oh, I haven't in a long time, not since I was a girl. And not well, at that."

"No bother." Nell stands, smile and outstretched elbow welcoming me to follow. "We shall play a tune together. My brother has never had much ear for music, truth be told. So I'm certain he will not mind however well we choose to play."

Theo laughs, the sound light. The weight that I've come to know as part of him is now lifted by the smoothing of the waves between his beloved sister and himself. Perhaps this is the kind of closeness that can be born, the confidence that can form, having just one person to believe you. I wish I had had someone like Nell in my life. I wonder how things, how I, would be different if my own family had been willing to be that for me. But I had only Jack to turn to with the shadows of my mind and the oddities of this estate, and he had dismissed them both.

"I have been blessed with sisters that play exceptionally well, as they do all things. I have been spoiled by it to develop an exceeding taste for music, ear for the art or no."

Nell throws her head back in a laugh, the formality of the room already dwindled, despite my presence.

"No man with ears would dare call Iris's playing anything above passable."

"Do not thwart your sister of her other, many talents," Theo admonishes, but he cannot help laughing along.

"Of course," Nell concedes, lacing her arm through mine and guiding us toward the wide bench of the piano.

"Miss Read has certainly shown herself to be an impressive woman in all matters to which I have borne witness. I have no doubt that she will dazzle in this regard, as well." Theo's joking manner has bled out and has been replaced by a sincerity that startles me.

Nell merely smiles at the air as Theo and I find our eyes locked on each other, the girl knowing that these words, though spoken to her, were not truly for her ears.

Nell and I take our seats beside each other on the bench, and I am grateful for the barrier the instrument has put between Theo and me, thankful that it provides somewhere else for me to rest my eyes. The air between us feels all too alive, my body suddenly wanting to drift to his as though magnetized.

Nell places my fingers upon the keys, instructing me where to press and when in the nonjudgmental, lighthearted manner that I have already come to think of as her trademark. Then her own fingers dance across the keys with ease and the room is filled with all the colors of spring upon the air. We play sprightly melodies familiar to me by sound but not by name. They ring out with an unapologetic joy that matches their creator.

It is such a stark contrast to the heavily enforced silence of Langdon as I know it, and I am amazed that so much sound is allowed in this version of the estate. Amazed that I am allowed to be a part of its creation, that beautiful colors can fill the air, air that here looks as if it could never be full of gray and tension and sharp words left unsaid.

The door cracks open and a man clearly in the Pages' employ steps into the room.

"Mr. Page," he says quietly to Theo, words barely audible as Nell's fingers continue to fill the air with the swell of music. "You have received a correspondence from the physician in response to—"

"Ah, wonderful, yes." Theo rises to his feet, headed toward the door. "Please do excuse me, I will be just a moment." His voice is apologetic as he turns to us on his way out of the room. There is a tightness around his eyes, a regret at having to step out, a fear of leaving the secret of the house seated beside his so newly reunited sister. Theo's journal has told me that Nell would believe me were I to tell her when I came from. But her relationship with her brother is still in repair, and it is clear in every movement of Theo's face how important that is to him—I would never risk it, even if it feels like no risk at all.

"It is not a bother, attend your business, brother. We are more than happy to be left in one another's company." Nell smiles at me and I find that I cannot agree with her words more, my mind no longer racing to attempt to carve a space for myself in the interactions around me, no longer regretting every word that comes from my mouth.

We play together for a moment longer, the music we create filling the room. Nell's eyes float to me a few times, her mouth opening and closing, mind clearly contemplating.

"I'm glad you are here, Miss Read. Glad that you have been here." She pauses for a moment, still weighing out her words, a self-control that seems at odds with what I've seen of her thus far. "My brother is a man who takes himself quite seriously. I understand it, of course, but I hate to think of him shut away from the world out here. But today, with you, is the most I have seen Theo smile in far too long."

I am lost, faltering to find a way to make her words untrue before they sink into me and take dangerous hold there.

"If that's true, I'm sure it's just that he's missed you, Miss Page." My words are faltering, and they do not sway Nell. The small smile on her face remains unchanged.

"I am certain that my presence has never made my brother smile like that. I hope I do not presume too much, Miss Read, but I simply wanted to tell you I'm thankful for what you have brought to Theo's life, whatever that may be."

I am flushed and my shaking fingers have slipped from the keys clumsily, missing notes that Nell does not acknowledge, dutifully continuing the piece with ease, eyes once more on the instrument before her. I can summon no response before the door opens once more and Theo returns, a grin already painting his face as he looks at us. His eyes catch mine and he does not look away, does not hide that I am the object of his gaze. My chest rises in waves, causing my skin to strain against the tight hold of my bodice, but I cannot find my breath.

The music fades to a close as Nell lifts her fingers from the keys, hand coming to her mouth to cover a yawn that does not exist.

"I must apologize, but I find I am quite worn after my journey here. I think I shall take a rest." She stands, smoothing the nonexistent wrinkles in her dress, and I follow suit, a puppet, mind still blank, filled with nothing but images of Theo's spreading smile as he walks into a room and finds me there. "I trust that you can entertain Miss Read on your own."

Her teasing smile has returned, now pointed at her pink-cheeked brother. Nell squeezes my hand once more in her own.

"It was so lovely to meet you, Miss Read. I cannot wait to continue our blossoming little friendship."

"Yeah, yes, me too."

One eyebrow lifts, her mouth puffing out a small breath of entertained confusion at the rigid oddness of my words, before she floats her way through the door. I am suddenly all too aware that it is only Theo and me now, the air still crackling with energy that I cannot identify and do not care to, and I wonder if he can feel it too. I have to speak.

"I'm so sorry." The words rush out of my mouth, for I am afraid of what else would come forth if I had even a moment of silence. I fear that I would have said the truth. "I just woke up in Langdon, this Langdon, and I tried to go back but I—"

Theo holds up a hand, his mouth tilting upward.

"I meant it, Miss Read. You never have need to apologize for your presence here. I am always happy to see you." There is a beat of silence, the room heavy with it. "Too happy, perhaps." These last words are almost too quiet to hear, spoken to himself, not me. But I hear them nevertheless, and the wildfire within me shamefully sparks to light in response.

"Would you like to go for a walk in the garden?" I grasp, desperately, for safer ground. Thankfully, the sun still peaks out between the clouds. Perhaps the fresh April air will cool the heat inside me.

"You know the customs of this time already," Theo says teasingly, quick to accept my shift to lighter fares. "I would love to."

I follow him through the house, the shock of the bright colors and pools of golden candlelight in this Langdon having worn off, replaced by comfort at the sight of them.

"Where's Blackjack?" I ask as we make our way through the tunnel that leads us out into the expansive garden. Theo closes the hall's door solidly as we step out into the chill of the spring breeze, the greens and blues opening before us.

"He's simply enamored with Nell, always has been. He'll be fresh on her heels about now, I would venture."

"I can't blame him. She's easy to be enamored with." I smile, Theo returning it as we make our way through the lush green maze of the hedges. He does not offer his arm to me as he normally does, and I do not acknowledge the little bite of longing that elicits.

"Yes, she's a lovely young woman. You two seem to have taken to each other well."

My cheeks pinken with the memory of her words, her assumptions, though there is no way that they could have reached Theo's ears. But perhaps they did not need to. Theo knows his sister and her lack of subtleties.

"I think so, yeah."

I no longer fret over each word I choose, fearful my oddities will expose how displaced I am in this time. Instead I simply feel calm in Theo's presence. Beyond, the house has been shifting with all the fickleness of spring, clouds quickly stitching themselves together into a ceiling of gray, casting a darkened hue across our descent to the garden's far edge. Raindrops patter lightly off the glass roof of the greenhouse, the sound echoing the suddenly turbulent swell of waves over the cliff's edge.

"She's difficult not to like, Nell. I take it you two are close?" I ask the question that I already know the answer to, but my words fall away to silence.

Theo's attention is elsewhere, somewhere internal, a frown unconsciously falling into place on his face. As if in response to his mood, the rain picks up, heavily pounding down upon the garden, soaking into the grass and both of us.

"We should head back inside!" I yell over the sound of the rain beating down, my footing slipping slightly beneath me as I turn back toward the house, confident that Theo is following in my tracks.

I only make it a few steps before I realize I'm mistaken.

"I know that we must sway to the house's whim, but I do not think you should return here anymore, Miss Read." I hear Theo's voice behind me, ringing out through the rain thundering down around us.

I turn to face him, his form still, unreacting, as the rain soaks his dark hair to his forehead, his lashes dripping. Despite the noise around us, his words, the practiced stoicism on his face, have created a turbulent quiet in me.

"What?" My voice is as breathy and as shocked as I feel. I almost hate him for saying what should be said, for acknowledging the truth of this little thing that I was feeding in the shadows, this tiny, hopeful thing that I was, wrongly, allowing to fill my life with the bit of light that it has so long lacked. "Why? I thought we were friends. Nothing's changed."

And as I say it, I think of how very untrue that is, of how heavy the weight of that ring on my fourth finger has become.

Theo looks at me for a moment, the rain falling in rivulets across the rises and valleys of his face, the mountains of his cheekbones, drops lingering on his lips. His chest rises and falls briskly, and then he sighs, head tilting.

"You must know that everything has changed, Saoirse."

Perhaps it is the way my name sounds on his lips, soft and sweet, or the way that I know that he is right.

But I do not think, do not stop as I stride forward, rain be damned, and press my lips to his, the taste of my name still upon them.

Maybe things would be different if we had paused, if he had stepped back, had resisted even in the slightest, most minuscule way.

But his lips come alive against mine, his fingers finding my hair, the small of my waist, and he pulls me against his body and I know that our threads have been woven together in a way that nothing, not even time, will ever be able to unbraid.

Chapter 20

There is only a moment where we pause, only one heart-beat where we separate, where our eyes are open, locked on each other, still lost to the world around us. Theo sees the words in my gaze, the hunger, the fact that I will not say no, not now and not ever. He sees that however far he wishes to push, this will never be far enough for me. Then his lips are on mine once more and I am *alive, alive, alive.*

That little part of me that still believed that this could not all be real—that Theo could not be real—is dashed by the scorching feel of his mouth moving against mine, too vivid to be anything but a most glorious reality.

I feel as though I'm finally breaking the surface, my head above water at last, and the first breath of fresh air I take is Theo's lips upon mine. I am desperate for it, for every bit of him, yet I know that I will never drink my fill.

The little spark he ignited in me is a raging flame. There is heat in every pore of my body and I am glowing as I greedily grab for every inch of him that I can. My hands fill with the silken strands of his wet hair, his exposed neck, reach desper-ately, feebly, for the wool coat that stands between us.

The rain pours down around us and on top of us and I do not care, it does nothing to temper the flame. Nothing could.

Theo's mouth meets mine with equal desperation. With desire. Lips strong and wanting, tongue gliding across my own, and with every kiss there is a new spark inside me and I can see the same reflected in him, as though we have both set off a reaction, have brought to life the energy that crackles in the air between us at last.

Look at your monster, Frankenstein. Isn't it an angel?

Theo's hand fists the loose fabric at the small of my back, and I arch into him, my chest pressed against his and it is nowhere near close enough and I want more, so, so much more.

"Please." The word is whispered, is moaned, between us and it is mine.

Theo pauses for a moment, lips pulled off mine and forehead pressed against my own, and I worry that he will not heed the call of that word, will not give me whatever it is that I am too afraid to ask for.

But then he grabs my hand in his, our grip, us, the warmest thing in this freezing world, and he is pulling me toward the greenhouse and my feet cannot follow him fast enough, my body cannot bear to allow a single inch of air to be between us. The door parts for him easily and I am ready to do the same, my body folding down onto the expanse of green chaise that he leads me to, tucked away among the writhing vines and petals. Then Theo is on top of me, body blessedly lengthening across mine, every inch of him pressing into every inch of me, and it is every brush of my hand on his, every press of my chest to his shoulder, every grab of hazel eyes upon green, magnified a thousand-fold.

Do not stop. Do not ever stop.

I beg him without words, plead with my hands that pull desperately at the buttons of his coat, that pull his hips against mine, and I feel more of him than I ever have. He hears the words my body screams, ridding himself of the thick barrier of his woolen coat with determined abandon, the layers of his dated dress falling to the cold greenhouse floor, brushing the buds of roses as they descend.

My hands cannot find every new expanse of exposed skin quick enough, my fingers greedy to feel the hard ridges of his stomach, the smooth curve of his lower spine, body dotted with coarse patches of scars, reminding me that he is here and alive and real, though he should not be so. He has so perfectly stepped forth from the darkest depths of my desires.

The rain beats down heavily upon the glass roof above us, but the anger of the weather is of no consequence in here. The pattering has trapped us in another world where there is nothing but Theo and our skin and the bloom of flowers— and we shall bloom too.

"Are you certain?" His voice is gentle against the noise, lips brushing my own as he speaks, the hot air of him kissing my tongue.

I have never been more certain of anything in my life.

I do not know if I say the words or if I merely think them, but Theo hears them all the same. His lips find my neck, leaving a trail of fire in their wake, as his teeth catch and his tongue soothes. I arch up into him, chest and hips pressed close against his own in turn, my hands knotting in his dark hair, needing to get every piece of him as close to me as I possibly can.

Our heavy breathing becomes the soundtrack of this thing between us, coming to life for the first time, the symphony of us. Theo is pushing the thick layers of my dress that rest between us up, bundling them at my hips for there is no time to rid them entirely. It would be impossible to pull away from him for even a moment. So my body lies in the pool of white silk as his mouth lowers to my breasts, wetting the fabric as his tongue flicks across the peaks that form for him.

My spine bows, head thrown back, and Theo fits himself perfectly into the arc my body has become. His hand trails down from my hip to find that place between my legs that waits, ready for him.

His fingers press into me and I did not think that my body could arch itself farther, heart lifting up to the heavens, but somehow it does for him. I am unable to contain the growing heat inside me, unable to express it in mere pants and sighs and words that say nothing and everything. My hands skate across the smooth expanse of his back, skin slick with sweat and rain and want. My fingers wrap around the thick rise of his upper arm, but I cannot find purchase—there is nothing to keep me from rising up, up, up for him.

Theo's fingers take a steady gate, rocking into me again and again, thumb lifting to sweep back and forth across the most sensitive part of me. And all the while his eyes never leave mine, his free hand roaming to drink in the exposed mounds of my body, while his gaze stays, exploring the depths of me through my own.

The tension builds, a pressure low in my hips, so much pleasure that it is almost pain. The stone of guilt and fear and shame that lives in the low of my belly is replaced by this wire within, coiled tight, ready to snap.

"Don't stop," I pant, and I could not keep the words in even if I wanted to. But Theo reacts to them tenfold, his own breath shallowing, a whispered *yes* on his lips as they press into mine.

Don't stop, don't ever stop.

"Come to me, Saoirse." His voice is rough with desire, the hardness of his body a heavy presence along my thigh, and his fingers continue to press and move and the pressure comes undone. The air in my body leaves me at once, my fingers scrambling for hold on the smooth skin of his shoulder, the delicate lace of the dress all around me crumpled in my haze of pleasure.

But it is not enough, not close enough.

"Please, Theo. I need you, need to—"

He steals my words, lips and tongue flashing hot against mine. He lifts himself above me, body against mine once more, garments and lace and skin pressing into the sparking sensitivity of my breasts.

Then Theo is pressing into me, giving me every bit of himself, and it is not a strain, not a push, not familiar. It is something I have never felt before. It is being full, being complete, being so, so alive. And for once I want more, want to stay in my body, want to be awake for every single thing.

The movement of his hips is steady and smooth and relentless, pressing into me until I can take no more—until it is all too much. His hands hike the pool of my dress up farther, fingers pressing into the softness of my hips, and I cannot remember the last time that I was so in my body, so happy to be there.

"Saoirse." My name is a blessing on his lips, and in that one word I hear everything, as though I am hearing myself spoken for the very first time. In a way, I am.

His lips are on mine, my name is between us, the damp, dark waves of his hair are drifting across my forehead, tangling into the red strands of my own.

"Saoirse, Saoirse."

His breathing builds, quickens, as hard and fast and steady as his hips and the pounding of the rain on the rooftop above us. His chest presses into mine in rapid waves, the bones that build him pressing against my own.

Then the symphony swells, reaches its crescendo, and Theo's pleasure is all around me and within me.

With one last trembling breath he slides out of my body, the absence of him already felt, but his form hovers over me on the chaise, a protective shroud from the chill of the world beyond. Theo rests his forehead against my clothed shoulder, damp from the remnants of the rain and sweat and the efforts of our jointness.

The rain lands in sharp droplets upon the glass roof, slipping and spreading, becoming larger than itself, weightless, and I feel the same way as we lie together now. Theo, almost comically hesitant now after all we have just experienced together, runs his fingertips lightly across the lace covering my arm, hand drifting down until his fingers twine and untwine and twine again with my own. I can feel the weight of his eyes on my face, and it is a moment before I find the courage to meet them with my own.

I'm afraid that I will find the distance, the disappointment that I have so come to know in these moments of intimacy.

But there is nothing but tenderness there in his gaze and a spark of excitement, of the residual heat between us. The fire within me has not dampened, not in the slightest. It only grows as I look at Theo now.

"Are you well? I should not have—" Theo begins, but I do not let him finish.

"You should have done everything." *Everything and more. I would let you do anything you want to me.* "And I'm perfect."

I could almost laugh at the absurd notion that I could be anything but blissfully, perfectly happy in this moment, as I get to experience Theo's touch both rough and lustful and gentle and tender.

"Yes, you are perfect indeed," he says, gently pressing his lips onto my shoulder. There is a delicate nature to his voice that burns much more than his desire did, that paints my cheeks pink and makes my eyes fall to our hands, still twined between our bodies.

A shiver runs down my body at that gaze. Theo sees the reaction and takes my hand more firmly in his own, guiding us up to sit.

"Come, let us go inside before you catch a chill, Miss Read."

"Miss Read? After all that?" I laugh because I cannot help it, and I am rewarded by that shy, small smile of his.

"Saoirse," Theo breathes, and I will never grow used to how beautiful and new my name sounds on his lips. Like it is a new name altogether, for a new woman, a new life.

We stand, the last of the rain's drops still on us falling to the ground, coloring the stone to black.

A foolish bashfulness overtakes me as I watch Theo bend and stretch his naked body as he redresses himself and I blush all over again, everywhere, but I turn away to give him privacy. I hear the sounds of him shuffling behind me, his still, shallow breathing echoing off the fogged walls of the greenhouse.

Then everything drops away, the pattering of rain, the muffled swish of Theo's clothes and body. There is only the sound of my small, suddenly frantic breathing.

I know what I will see, or not see, when I turn, but the air is still knocked from my lungs as I spin to find I am in another greenhouse, in another time, the blooming roses and luscious fruit replaced by cracked pots and spilled soil in dark corners. Theo is gone, and of course he is, for I have returned to my own time, and with the stillness has come the crushing, enormous realization of what I have just done.

The greenhouse door sits ajar, opening with slow reluctancy. I scramble my way through it and out into the dry January air, still covered with the warm wetness of Theo on my body and my mind. I am a survivor of a rainstorm that never existed here. That should never have existed at all.

Chapter 21

I am thankful for the shadows that dominate this Langdon, allowing me to join their ranks and make my way, undetected and unalive, to the bedroom. I do not encounter the phantom voices of Jack and his parents, and I am thankful for the respite. It gives me time to kick and hate myself for what I have done as I strip off the soaked evidence of my deceit, stuffing it hastily into the bottom of my suitcase.

I can still feel the ghost of Theo's touch on my skin, still long to feel the real thing. Beneath my shame, I still thrill at the thought that he could be here now, a phantom in this darkened bathroom I hide away in. That he is still all around me, still inside me. It is because of this that I fill the copper bath with water hot enough to scorch away every fingerprint that has ever been left on my body and force myself to sink down into it.

The sound of the water beating down into the tub as it fills is the roaring of rain across the glass of the greenhouse, and the sharp opposition of silence as I turn the tap off is loud as it makes way for my roiling guilt. My skin turns red as I step into the water, flushed with a new kind of burn, and I do not fidget, do not budge, because I deserve it.

Who have I become? Or is this who I always was? A self-fulfilling prophecy of undeservingness, cast by the Pages I have long known. The smallest bit of attention, the tiniest affirmation that perhaps I am not unlovable, unwantable, mad, and I waver away from Jack, from my commitments. But, no, I know it is more than that. And that is worse.

There are 412 stones that make the ceiling, and I count them from right to left and left to right and slip beneath the water and burn, burn, burn.

I hear the bedroom door creak open and then the familiar sound of Jack's footsteps across the carpet, the click and jingle as he removes his belt. I know he is loosening the buttons of the crisp white shirt that has become his constant attire over the years, that has replaced the tees and rugby shirts of the man I first fell in love with.

"Sersh? Are you in there?"

I cannot open my mouth to respond, too afraid of the shame that will fall forth if I do. I cannot even confess to what I have done, the circumstances of my betrayal as unbelievable as my actions.

I can still feel Theo's hands holding tight to my hair, even as the auburn strands sit in a damp knot atop my head. I sink beneath the surface, but no water can wash away the memory of his touch on me. There is no cool blast of air as my face breaks back above the barrier, the heat of the water and my shame still scalding my skin, blazing and burning everything.

When I open my eyes Jack is standing above me, looming down over the edge of the basin. I startle, water splashing onto the tiled floor.

"You didn't answer when I called." He lowers himself onto the stool at the tub's edge, and his voice is as deflated as his body.

"Sorry."

It is the first word my mouth can bring forth and I mean it. I mean it so much.

Jack leans forward, elbows propped on knees, hands running through the thick blond of his hair. His breathing is labored, not from activity of the body but from strain of the mind, of the heart.

I reach a hand out toward him, water dripping from my skin, sliding down into the crook of my elbow, pooling into little valleys between the tiles on the floor. It is a gesture I know I should make, reaching out, but I'm not sure it's me who chooses to make it.

Jack pulls back instinctually, hands rising up to block my own, as though I am a dangerous thing, my touch like poison.

Maybe it is, to him. After what I've just done, he's probably right.

Hands running across my skin, slick and grabbing, never able to hold enough of me, another man reaching out to all of me, wanting all of me.

No, no, no.

"C'mon, Sersh, you're getting everything all wet," Jack sighs, leaning away until I extract the olive branch from between us.

The apology dies on my tongue as my limbs slink back into the water, warm and safe as a womb. A protection that is shallow and fleeting. That I do not deserve.

"I'm sorry I haven't been around. I should be spending more time with you and your mum, I know—" A new way to say sorry, sorry for everything I cannot admit to, spills forth from me, the hand that reaches out to Jack invisible now, hoping to soothe what lies between us.

"No, Saoirse," Jack huffs, and I do not know what I've done to annoy him, but that constant state of his toward me persists. "Trust me, that's the last thing Mum wants."

You are not wanted here, he might as well say.

His words are cruel, leaving little lashes across my skin, but they are the truth, so he does not even see them as the weapon that they are.

"She's not doing well. Properly not, I mean. The hospice

worker stops by and I don't need her to tell me that Mum's getting worse, it's bloody obvious she is. I can see what's happening right before my eyes."

So much of Jack's life is crumbling, the foundations he trusts of family and unwavering love betraying him, and now I am too. I almost wish that the house were truly that haunted, evil thing that I once believed it to be. That the dark bath water surrounding me would house some deadly horror, that the arms of the house would grab me and pull me under. The murky depths would be a blessed escape from this reality without and the guilt deep within.

I reach a dripping hand out again to lay it on his forearm and he does not twitch, does not seem to feel me at all. Jack has tucked himself away, like I used to. But I am no longer allowed to without causing suspicion and frustration and concern. He blinks and shifts, sitting upright, arm pulling from my grasp, that mask of rigidity falling back in place. He used to let me see beneath that mask, but I can't be trusted anymore. For once, I know for certain that he's right about that.

"Mum and I have been talking, trying to plan what things will be like . . . after." His voice is as tight as his posture. I tense, sensing his next words are ones he's rehearsed. "And we think you should quit your PhD."

Whatever I had been expecting Jack to say, those words were never among them. His last moments with his parents were not spent planning funerals or missed birthdays, but trying to sort me out, to sort out what I imagine Alice and Edgar call "the Saoirse problem" behind closed doors. Despite the heat of the water around me my skin feels ice cold, chilled down to my bones.

"Mum suggested it and I agree," he continues, either missing the panic on my face or willfully ignoring it. Alice, even on her deathbed, sure to sink her claws into me even from beyond the grave. I shouldn't be surprised. "Even if you do finish and find work in your field it won't bring in much money anyway. And clearly you can't handle it mentally, Sersh. There's no point in still calling this a 'break.' Best to just step away for good now and maybe losing the stress of that will help you get better, yeah?"

His voice is casual, as if we were discussing what to eat for dinner, not that he is trying to strip me of one of the few joys I have left. He's not wrong, he is our sole support, the only money that keeps our life afloat. But surely there is more worth to what I do than that, I thought he recognized that.

"But, Jack, that's the only thing I have that makes me feel like *myself*. I do it because I love it, I thought you—"

"Anyway, once we're married it'll be better for you to be at home," he plods ahead, eyes not even on me. "The PhD will just be a distraction. You've been having fun with it, I understand that, but you'll need to learn to be a homemaker, like Mum was."

Suddenly I'm not so certain I'm the one who's going mad. All this time, my passions, my studies, who I *am*—it was all only ever a hobby to Jack, a fun distraction until I could take the role I was meant to, that he has decided for me. And the thought of calling Alice a homemaker is so laughable I almost wait for Jack to chuckle, to tell me this is all some twisted joke. Alice was no such thing, their homes managed by cleaners and nannies, a staff for every hallway. I don't want all that, I just want Jack. I want Jack to want me, but suddenly, for once, I am not sure I want to twist and change into the woman he can love, can marry.

"I just—" I pull my knees to my chest, suddenly wishing I was not so naked and vulnerable in the tub, Jack looking down from beside it. "You didn't think to discuss this with me first?"

"I'm discussing it with you now, aren't I? It's what Mum and I think is for the best. You'll want some time to get . . . in your right mind before we start having kids."

I know him well enough to read his face, to see that he

really does think he is being fair to me. That he's not doing wrong by me by deciding my fate with his mother first, as though I am unfit even for that.

Even though we both sit still it suddenly feels as though everything is moving too quickly. Theo's hands still feel fresh on my skin as Jack's words lash me, as I see how little he thinks of me. My guilt cannot stamp away my panic, my own life suddenly slipping out of my control.

But what can I say? Without Jack I have no one, no money, no *life*. I want to be enough for him, but I cannot give up the last piece of myself I still have.

"I can't do that, Jack." Water sloshes over the tub as I lean forward, soaking onto Jack's feet. My knuckles are white where they grip the edge. "You have to understand that. You're not even letting me have a say, you and your mother, it feels like—"

"I'm trying to do what's best for you. For *us*, Saoirse. Do you have any idea how difficult things are for me right now? Mum is . . . she's dying and you're sitting here, picking me apart, not even trying to make our lives easier."

My guilt returns, heavy as a blanket.

"I know it's difficult. I can't imagine the burden it must be that your mother—"

"My mother is not a burden." His head lifts with a snap, brows drawn down in anger over hazel eyes. "Not that it's really your business, but Christ, if there's a burden in my life it's certainly not her." I pull my arm back as though he has burned me, branded me with his words.

The words, spewed in a huff, leave no mystery as to who the true burden of Jack's life is. I had suspected as much—he had made me feel as much already—but to hear the words from his lips hurts. They are bitter, vile words, aimed to strike. He has learned so much cruelty from that mother of his.

He's not choosing Alice over me anymore, he is simply not choosing me. Jack never used to be like this. I would not be here if he had. Did Alice make him this way? Did I, with my shifting, slippery mind? With the struggles that bled out of me and into us? Or did he always ever see me as a malleable girl, desperate to be loved, to become whoever I needed to to earn affection? And now I'm not playing my part either, nodding and agreeing to be stripped of my parts and remade.

Perhaps this is just the inevitable truth of Jack. Perhaps this is just what love is.

The air and the guilt within me are knocked out by his anger, by the shame that he fills me with instead. I am so used to being empty, having no defense as the Pages give me their little bruises. So I am surprised to feel something hot and red and almost like anger come to the surface, though I know it is not fair, know that Jack does not mean the words that he says. I know that he is suffering. I know that I am, in truth, part of the reason for that.

"You asked me to come here, Jack. I try not to be in your way or interfere with your family time, but I am here because *you* asked."

There are so many things that you asked me that I should have had the courage to say no to.

You asked me to be swallowed up in this house, to be your bride.

"Yes, well, I had hoped that you could see beyond yourself for once." My anger is reflected back at me tenfold in Jack's eyes. "That maybe you could at least try to be better and be here for me."

He should be saying these words to me, I deserve them, but not for the reason that he believes. For that, I do not think I deserve wrath and punishment. For that, I am trying—have been trying.

But how can I ever argue with Jack over this, when what I have just done is so, so much worse than anything he ever has? He may have morphed into the image of his parents, he may have grown cold and made me freeze and shrink in the face of him, but he has not made me betray him. That I've done all on my own. And I deserve his ire all the more because there is still that little fire burning for Theo deep in my chest, a little part of me that does not regret it.

And that simply strengthens the guilt all the more.

"I'm trying, Jack." It comes out almost a cry and I only realize once the words sit between us that maybe they are a lie. Maybe they were a lie even before I let another man run his hands across me, happily let him consume me.

What has happened to the lovers Jack and I once were? When did we become this two-headed monster, always locked in a battle with itself?

Perhaps this is who we always were, even when things were beautiful. Was this beast lurking beneath the surface of our happiness inevitable?

The fight fades from Jack's body, deflating him. For just a moment I see the flash of the man he used to be, the one who held my hand, whose face bloomed for me. Then the steely exhaustion falls back into place. He pushes himself to his feet, footsteps echoing as he makes his way toward the bathroom door.

"Let's not do this right now," he says over his shoulder. "We can discuss all of this later, okay? I don't have the energy for it, and we'll say things we don't mean."

The door closes behind him, and I am left to sink back beneath the water until my lungs burn.

I have already said things I did not mean, months ago, when I allowed him to put this ring on my finger, and perhaps that is where our troubles began.

Chapter 22

My days have become a blur of gray. Countless hours have been lost to my aimless wanderings about the estate, as I slip into the gloom in my mind, afraid to see the guilt that has burrowed and taken home there. I have fallen over the edge of the reality that I knew, straight into Theo's waiting arms. But I cannot, not again. I will not.

The house has nearly returned to the captor I once believed it to be. My body is always in motion, too afraid that if I stop, I'll find I am sometime else or find the journal suddenly sitting beside me, waiting, calling to me. If it gives me any taste of Theo now, I will be forced to see how deep my hunger for him goes, how insatiable it is. So I keep moving and I hope that Langdon cannot catch me and make me look at myself. My mind is a perpetual whir of Jack's panic-inducing words, demands, and memories of what I've done, sending me down into a spiral of shame.

I spend wine-soaked days in silence, so quickly becoming once more the reckless, faded woman that Jack has too long believed me to be. As much as I try not to think, I do, I must, and it is not Jack whom I think of. The flame that Theo created in me has become an ache of longing.

I had touched Jack once since our last encounter, my unfamiliar hand tentative on his chest, the bedroom too quiet around us, the night outside too dark. I hoped that I would feel a spark, a surge, that the fire in me would have somewhere safe to go. And he'd brushed me off, the unease of our spat in the bathroom still poisoning the air between us. Or maybe Jack simply could not be bothered with me, was waiting impatiently for me to return to quietness, to malleability.

"I can't. I'm just stressed about Mum." And I was not a safe haven to him anymore. I could not ease his burden. My proposition was fueled not by desire, but by guilt, as though Jack touching me would erase the traces of another man's hands on me. And as my fiancé had stepped away from me, shame settled in his place, my new, constant companion.

I have become the mad woman in Langdon's attic, mumbling and wandering, a phantom that the Pages know is here but never see. I am thankful for every moment I remain grounded in my present hell. The only words I utter are whispers to the walls: *Please, please, don't send me back. I don't know what I'll do if I return to then, to* him.

But that is a lie. I know exactly what I would do, and it is what I should not, and that is why I beg.

All I can do is hope that if I ignore the ache, it will go away and I can lick the wounds created inside me by the guilt, can soothe and quiet the raging voices in my head.

But it is no use. Days have passed and the longing only grows stronger and I know that it will never fade and that I am not strong enough to truly wish that it would.

So the cold chill on the stone steps thrills and terrifies me as I finally make my way up the winding staircase to what I have come to think of as Theo's office. It is a place where the barrier between present and past, between Theo and me, feels thinnest. I have avoided the spot for days, have drifted past the winding staircase with my heart thumping just at the sight of it. But now, I have chosen to be here.

If the house, this wild, magic, breathing being, should bring me back there, then so be it.

I know I am not just tempting fate by coming here—I am begging it.

As I push open the heavy wooden door and feel the heat of the fireplace upon my skin, I know that fate—that Langdon—has answered my call.

Theo's back is to me, his fingers gently trailing along book spines against the wall as he searches for one. Desire races through my body just to see those fingers again, to remember them inside me. I can feel my heart pressing against the cage of bones trapping it, pounding from fear or desire, I do not know. I step into the office, closing the door behind me with a shaking hand.

I do not know what I'm doing or what I will do, but I cannot stop now that the dark-haired man is before my eyes once more.

Theo turns in surprise as the door seals itself back in its frame, a ring of finality. Of privacy.

Damn the propriety. We've already sailed past the line of what is right.

But I won't do it again. I won't, I won't.

"Saoirse," he says, immediately abandoning his search to step forward and take my hand at the exact moment that I open my mouth to speak.

"I didn't mean to come back. I'm sorry." The words are a lie, and they taste sour in my mouth.

"You're sorry? For—" The open emotion in those hazel eyes disappears as Theo guards himself, stepping away from me and letting my hand drop from his. His eyes move across my face, my body, and a trail of heat courses in their wake. "It seems it is I who must apologize then, Miss Read. You have done nothing wrong."

That is not what I meant, not what I am apologizing for. And I have done wrong, far more than he has.

Do not make me say it, Theo. Because for that, for what we have done, I am not as sorry as I should be. I'm not certain that I am sorry at all.

"I have, though. I really have." And what's worse is that I fear I may do it again, may want to, more than anything I have ever longed for. My lips tremble with the effort of taking hushed, measured breaths, my skin suddenly feeling too small. The woman who could never quite stay in her body is now brimming from it.

"Did you not wish to return here then?" Theo's gaze is on the door behind my head, as though if he were to look at me, he would crack and anything could spill forth. I know the feeling well.

I contemplate lying again, know that I still could. I could turn and leave and ask the house to take me back to the twentieth century and perhaps it would comply. But that crackling energy between Theo and me has not wavered now that we've dared to touch it. Instead, it is a live wire and I am inexplicably called to the danger of it.

"I shouldn't want to come back, but I do. I do."

For whatever reason, fate or rather, Langdon, knew time and time again that Theo and I were meant to cross paths. That we need each other, are perhaps the only ones who can understand the other. Maybe I am looking for a reason to excuse myself for what I have done, but it is hard to feel guilty for something that is fated.

We are having so many conversations at once, too many, but I know now that I am not sorry at all—not for what we did together, not for coming back. I should be, I know that. But I am not. I would do it all again.

Theo takes a deep, unsteady breath. "I'm not certain we could stay away from each other if we tried."

He does not know how right he is. As much as the house, for whatever reason, believes we are meant to cross paths, I think somewhere, deep down, I want it more.

Fated.

Theo's eyes dart across my face, and I cannot give him the assurance that he seeks because I too cannot find stable footing in this domain. But I know that I want him to run from me, but even more I want him to step closer, to touch me, *to touch me*, and he does.

When he takes my hand, now it is much more tentative, as though he is waiting for me to pull away, to tell him to stop. I do not. Theo's fingers do not shake as mine do in his grasp. He holds fast to me.

"If I have disgraced your honor, Miss Read—"

"No, no, you haven't. If anything, I did that to myself."

Theo sighs, but the sound is not one of condescension but of sympathy.

"I do not want to see you at war with yourself or with . . . I do not want to put you through turmoil. I will never touch you again, Saoirse, if that is what you wish."

Theo moves his hand from mine for one moment that has all the words in the world in it. He is stepping back, but he is not breaking our bridge. His fingertips still skimming mine, his hazel eyes still locked on me—he is telling me that it is my decision to make, that if I say yes, if I say do not stop, he will not. That he trusts me to lead us, whether it be into darkness or light. We will discover together.

I rush forward, taking Theo's face in my hands, my lips finding him with a frenzy of passion that I have never felt before. Not with Jack, not now and not ever. Not with any person who has ever touched me before but this one. It has only ever been this man who has ignited a flame of scorching light inside me.

"That is the very last thing I want," I say against his lips, the words fading as we taste each other, the sweetness of all the things that we do not need to say.

The frenzy of the first time's novelty is gone now, but the fire is not, fueling us to continue exploring the curves and dips of each other's bodies, familiarity that could never be familiar enough.

I will never stop wanting you.

Theo's hands shed the dress from my body with eagerness, nimble fingers making hastened and hesitant work through the strangeness of modern bindings. The flat of his palm is against my back as he fidgets with the clasps and zippers, keeping my skin from his strokes. The heat within me is building with the want of waiting that has been growing for days, since the last time his body was pressed against mine. Then finally he has freed me, the fabric falling to pool around my feet, the fire in the grate painting my naked body in hues of pink as Theo steps back to gaze at me, his eyes darkened.

The brush of his half-worn shirt, pulled from one shoulder in the aggression of my desire, inflames me all the more as he pulls my bare body against his, still hidden beneath cloth. His hands stroke down my back and beyond, kneading forth the shivers that course through me. Soft mountains of goose bumps rise along my skin, from head to toe, the ends of my hair tickling along my spine as I tilt my head back, letting Theo and his mouth make its way across the bare expanse of my neck.

"Oh, my dear," he whispers the words from his tongue onto mine, so loving that I am not sure it isn't simply conjured from my deepest desires, from the moisture that pools across my skin, in want of him.

My fingers shake, not with fear now but with coursing desire that I do not try to hide as I push his shirt from his shoulders. My mouth follows the trail of falling fabric, kissing and licking in its wake across every smooth surface that is Theo.

And then we both stand, naked, skin flushed and hot from the fire and from the closeness with which we press against each other. Lips alive on mine, Theo guides us both to the ground, laying us out across the carpet before the dancing flames.

There is no thought in my mind except to be closer, closer, as close as I possibly can be. That darkness within, the oil spill that spreads its sadness and loneliness so far across my mind that it seems to have become my very person—it is lessened by this flame Theo has lit inside me.

There is only a moment where we are a tangle of limbs, the hard points of my body pressing into the soft points of his, but even these little pains turn into a building pressure, a reminder that I have a body. And it is one that I want to be in so that I will never have to stop feeling the way Theo's hands grip my hips. I pull my mouth from his, his tongue darting out briefly as though still seeking the refuge of my own. I drape one leg over Theo, lifting until I am straddling him, the hard hotness of him pressing so achingly across the part of me most welcome and ready to receive him.

"Oh," Theo breathes in surprise and pleasure as I take him into my hand, feeling the silkiness of his skin against my palm. Every inch of my body that presses into him is on fire and all I want is to feed the flames.

He reaches toward me, hand ready to bring me to my own pleasure, but it is not that touch that I crave more than anything else.

"No, I need to just . . ."

With a breathlessness and a feeling that is beyond words, beyond what my mind can even make sense of now, I kneel up, aligning his body with mine.

I gaze deep into Theo's hazel eyes, his pupils blown out at the sight of me. My own gaze is wild with the thrill of this man beneath me, the way he looks at me, and I slowly sink down, my body enveloping him as I press him inside me. My hands find their way to his chest, guiding me as I lift and fall upon him, the motion of my body drawing forth a small moan of pleasure from Theo each time the skin of my thighs meets his once more.

The strong hold of his hands upon my thighs, fingers sinking into the flesh there, drives the motion of my hips faster, harder. For once, I have no thought of how my body looks, no small hand of insecurity that pulls me from the moment as I see the soft parts of me moving with our union, the skin that spills out of Theo's grip. There is nowhere for that little hand to grab, the man beneath me so obviously enthralled and enraptured by my body in all of itself, his hands drifting across it to squeeze in a constant pace, as though there is not enough time in the world for him to feel all of me that he wants to.

His hand makes its way between my legs, brushing against the most sensitive part of me, and it is mere moments before I feel the pressure in me build. My motions quicken, the air filling with the reckless sounds of our moans in tandem and then the string within me snaps and I am falling, out of and within myself, and I am free.

Chapter 23

I had been waiting for the deep sense of guilt to take hold and drag me down the moment that Theo and I pulled apart. I had been waiting for the heavy press of guilt to replace the feeling of his body on mine.

I almost wish that it had, but the shame did not come to drown me and it still has not, even as I lie in the embrace of Theo's arms, my head resting across his chest in a halo of red made from my hair and his blushing skin.

The crackling of the flames is the perfect backtrack to our frantic breathing, the air between us still too sensitive to be filled with words. Goose bumps crawl down my spine in the wake of Theo's fingertips barely kissing my skin as he glides them up and down my body. It is such mindless, natural intimacy and it does not make me shrink or roil or simply float away.

It would not have mattered if I was strong enough not to come today—if I had never come back again, never laid eyes or hands on Theodore Page once more. The damage is already done and it is irreversible—not just laying together, but my having been changed by him in ways I cannot and would not undo. I will always rise to meet him, in body and mind. I want to be changed by him, and I have been.

Theo's other hand trails down my arm, coming to rest as his fingers weave their way between mine, a tender gesture that feels far more intimate than the carnal lust that we've just shared. His knuckles bump against the ring on my finger, somehow so much heavier now, adding a weight to our tangle of digits.

My eyes fall to the ring, and I can feel that, above me, Theo's do too. The large diamond catches the flame of the fireplace within its edges, reflecting orange and red and yellow, a beacon of hell, or perhaps that is just what I cannot stop my mind from projecting onto it.

"Are you safe, Saoirse?"

Theo's words crack the silence, startling me into lifting my head from his chest so I can gaze up at his face. His eyes meet mine, waiting.

"What? Yes, of course. What do you mean?"

He takes a deep breath, my body rising and falling with his.

"Your betrothed. Does he harm you? Is that why you flee to here? To me?"

"No, no, not at all. It's just . . ."

The dark spiral of my mind suddenly looks so appealing now as I am forced to look at the truth within. It looks as though I may fall into it even against my will. My eyes close in the rising panic, but I do not need to see Theo's eyes to know what I will find in them, the look of panic and distance that has become all too familiar from the eyes of my husband-to-be as he sees me slip inside the depths of my own mind. *I should be stronger than this. I'm supposed to be getting better.*

"I do not judge you," Theo says, as though he were peering directly into my mind. "I am well aware that loveless marriages, that is to say, unions of convenience or status, are quite common of this time. Is that merely the case?"

It's not convenient, nor is it matched in status, but . . . a

*loveless marriage—is that what we have, Jack? Is that our
fate, bound by something other than affection? History?
Duty that we are too afraid to break?*

I dare to look back up at Theo, and maybe it is the shock
of seeing only kindness there, only concern not about me but
for me, that allows the words to fall from my lips.

"It's not common in my time. It's not that, I don't think,
not exactly. It's just—we did love each other, once. Maybe we
do still, in a sense." *Who is it you're trying to convince here,
Saoirse?* "But it is not . . ." *It is not like this. It is not like
my body is a flower coming into bloom instead of the dark
shadows of the night spreading between us like a depthless
sea.* "It's not really like that anymore."

Theo's free hand spins itself delicately through the strands
of my hair trailing across both of our skin as he searches my
face.

"Are you not able to leave?"

The words surprise me and I push farther up onto my
wrist, staring down at Theo, my mind unable to grab hold of
the words he says. But they should not be a shock. It should
perhaps be more shocking that the thought has never occurred to me before. That I never even considered that I was
able to do such a thing, that I do not need to wait for Jack to
release me.

But as soon as I see the door to leave my relationship, I realize it is locked. I am already hurting Jack now, in his darkest time, though he doesn't know it. To leave him would add
more pain to his life than I could bear, though he makes it
clear I already weigh heavy upon him. Besides, emotions and
guilt aside, it wouldn't be possible for me to be on my own.
All the accounts live in Jack's name. The cash is in his wallet.
The flats, the flights. I cannot drive in this country, cannot
even afford a train. I cannot leave this place, cannot even be
on my own for one day without him. PhD stipends are nothing, and even less on an extended leave. Not that I will need

to worry about that for much longer, if Jack and Alice have their way.

Money is nothing to the Pages, a given, and I had forgotten that I am not one of them, I am merely with one. Cared for by one. I have nothing without Jack. When did that happen? *Where did I go?*

Here I am, automatically thinking of Jack and our relationship in connection to the money that comes from his family, the way my life too is sustained on it—I am no better than the Pages, thinking the very same way I resent them for.

There is money and isolation and routine, and all the things beyond love that keep me intertwined with Jack. Without Jack I am a woman with empty pockets and a dark mind, an ocean away from a family who could not be bothered to help me even if I deigned to ask, left to rebuild a life with no net beneath me. I cannot even imagine what my mother would do if I called her up, told her I made a mistake, that I need money, need *help*. I'm not certain she would care any more than she ever has. Any help from my family would come with confirmation that they were right to hold me at a distance, that Jack has seen it now too. There was no amount of silence or cooperation that had made them love me as a family should and now here is Jack, the family I went halfway around the world to find, just as indifferent to me.

If I do not have Jack, what do I have anymore? Some days, too many, I do not even have myself. I have nowhere safe to fall.

I am a coward trapped in my own nightmares, and I keep Jack there beside me with a white-knuckled grip. I am trying to get better for Jack, for us, because maybe I alone am not worth getting better for.

"No."

My answer is the simplest and most complicated thing possible.

"I do not pretend to know the boundaries of your society,

nor of your heart, Saoirse." Theo's words are not measured and distant, but merely true, spoken simply. "I am asking nothing of you, of course. But it is clear that you are in pain, otherwise I do not imagine I would have the joy of holding you in my arms."

His words are kind, but they land with a sting. Not because he wants them to, as I have become so accustomed to living among the other Pages, but because they land upon a truth that I am not ready to look at.

"I do understand feeling bound by duty or society. I know it well." Theo pushes himself onto his elbows, but he merges the distance between us by gently tangling his fingers once more within the swaying ends of my hair falling down my back.

"I sense that maybe has something to do with why I'm here as well? Why there's no missus manning the estate at your side?"

I do not say the words to detract or in defense or from a place of jealousy. Instead, I see that Theo has put a small, vulnerable part of himself into his hand and held it out toward me. I want to show him that I can keep this thing safe, that I want to see it, see him, all the way down to the truth. No matter what that truth is. For there is something inside me, maybe the same something that is now inextricably woven into Theo, that tells me our truths may be the same, regardless of the centuries that sit between us.

"My name, it . . . it means something to many people. It is considered rather important."

Page important.

If only Theo could know how true his words still were two hundred years later. The sadness that drips from his voice and the frown worn upon his face tell me he would not be pleased to hear as much.

"Trying to find a wife, even to find romance, with a name such as this is a rather frivolous pursuit. Far too often women only see what I can offer, not the truth of who I am as a man. Which, to look at all I get by having this name—" He waves his hand at the estate around us, "is a shallow complaint, I know. I should be grateful that this name gives me far more than others could dream of."

His hands weave through my hair a little tighter, the tic a clear indication of his nerves surrounding his vocalization, but he does not cease speaking. He pushes himself to continue. Both for me and, I suspect, for himself.

"I have, of course, enjoyed the company of women, but even then I know that it is often the thought of what I can give them beyond the bedroom that strokes their desire." With this, a small blush spreads across his cheeks, as though talking about lust is a private thing, even after all that has flourished between us. "Romance, for me, is not only shallow, but far too much pressure. If you could not gather from my near-constant presence in Langdon, I am not the most social of men. The pressure of balls, of performing, of being the focus of every mother in the *ton* . . . it is all far too much effort for an outcome of marriage that I do not even desire."

Theo's eyes are no longer on my face, but instead lost within the colors of the fire, his mind wandering somewhere deep in his past.

"I have grown up in society, I have seen how matches are made. And I learned rather quickly in my youth that honesty in matrimony is rare for one of my standing. And as a wealthy man I have the privilege to remain an eternal bachelor, if I so please. Of course, I could not take a wife now for there are the complications of—" He stops himself, eyes on me again, full of the sudden realization that he is not monologuing for his own ears. "I simply do not want anything shallow. I crave only what is true."

There are mysteries in his words, question marks painted on doorways that I want to peer between the cracks of, want to bang down. But all these desires are swept away by the way that Theo looks at me now, a fondness in his eyes that is not desire but affection.

I have been so afraid of honesty but now that it has forced me to look upon it, I find that I, too, only want the truth. I simply wish I knew what the truth was.

But something about this, whatever this is between Theo and me, feels more truthful than anything else I have come to know. As though this honesty is my life, and the world of shadows and howling winds in my own time has been relegated to a mere memory, a dark dream.

"So it seems our situations aren't so different after all." My voice is quiet, afraid that my words will push one or both of us back into ourselves and break this tender, fragile thing we are creating. But we have not created sharp edges between us. There is nothing here that could do harm.

The thing that Theo fears being saddled with is the thing that I have—and we both feel bound to our paths by an inability to choose. Yet our paths have crossed nevertheless, despite everything between them, and here we are, choosing to wind them even further into one another.

"Yes, I believe so. And I am sorry you do not have the luxuries I do, that you are bound to the decisions you have made, ones that I have so avoided."

But am I truly bound? Is my ending already written for me in ink and blood? Have memories become unbreakable vows? The diamond ring pulls my finger into my lap, my hands twisting around each other.

"Though if there is anyone who could change things, I believe it to be you, Saoirse. I can tell you most assuredly that you have irrevocably changed things for me."

Theo's words now are as delicate as the hand that brushes across the nape of my neck, his motions a whisper on my skin, as if I too am a delicate thing—not because I am unsteady and volatile, but because I am treasured. It has been so long since anyone has been delicate with me, has seen me as being worthy of such treatment. I cannot help but lean forward, pressing my lips against his and tasting the sweetness of his tongue against my own.

"I do hope I have not spoken out of bounds," he says as we part.

"You haven't." I trail my fingers across the stubble on his cheeks, over the sharp lines of his jaw. "You couldn't."

"No, it seems as though all bounds between us have already disappeared."

"I guess so." This time I smile as I press my lips against his, and I feel him do the same.

I tuck my head back beneath the dip of Theo's throat, the April rain pounding onto the window outside as we lose hours to the sound of each other's voices, meeting each other in mind as we have already done in body. And when I drift to sleep, it is to the rhythmic sound of Theo's breathing beneath me. When I wake, I find my cheek pressed into the carpet, the angry howl of a twentieth-century January outside. But the bleakness of this time cannot reach me, not with the echo of Theo's touch still sizzling within me.

Chapter 24

The footsteps that echo around the bend of the hall this morning could belong to Jack in their heavy, familiar trod. But I choose to believe that it is Theo's steps I hear.

Bring me to him, Langdon.

I pause a moment outside the bedroom door, just in case it is my fiancé who awaits me at the hallway's end, blond hair and dark eyes that I do not want to see. But it is not because I worry that it will reignite the guilt inside of me. The guilt is missing now. Or perhaps it is not gone but it is buried between the warmth, the light, that Theo gives me, far enough that I can pretend I do not see it for now.

I want to stay in the light.

After a beat, I continue down the hall. *Theo, Theo.* As I turn the bend, the harsh yellow electrical glare on the dark walls fades to the golden glow of candlelight. It is under this halo that I find Theo Page, hands clasped before his body, eyes open and peering through the hall, somehow expecting and awaiting me.

A smile softens the sharp edges of his face as I step into the light.

"Hello, my dear." He rushes forward to meet me, hand

familiarly finding the small of my waist, pulling me into his orbit. "I thought I heard your phantom footsteps coming."

Before I can reply, he is pushing me to the wall, where candlelight cannot reach. My body presses into the stones at my back, and Theo's body presses into mine, mouth and hands hungrily finding me.

I have hardly parted from you and yet I missed you, I do not say.

The dark silk of his hair is smooth between my fingers as I fold into him, holding his lips to mine, and rising to meet him with the same intensity and unbounded desire to *live*.

This is what it is, what it should be.

I do not think it will ever matter how many times I have felt the hard press of Theo's body on mine, within mine—I will always ignite for him. And it seems, he for me too.

Theo's hand grips the curve between buttocks and back, bunching the fabric with a tight fist, the other hand moving across the swell of my chest, rising and falling with my hurried breath.

Mine. More.

How quickly I can come alive for you, Theo.

His mouth works against mine, opening me up. The fire burns, pushing us onward, together, but there is no rush. There is no ticking clock, both of us placing trust in Langdon to let us enjoy the union it has brought us to—we may drink our fill of each other.

Theo pulls back, breath still tickling across my face. A hand moves from my body to grip my fingers, pulling me through a doorway that lies waiting beside us.

"Come," he says as he guides us through to the other side of the door.

And I follow him happily, as I am beginning to think I always will.

*   *   *

Thankfully the room is pleasantly mild, for I have lost sight of my dress since Theo stripped me of it, tossing the garment from us. My skin is still flushed from the lingering heat of our satiated lust, but nevertheless I feel the chill of absence as Theo untangles himself from me, pushing to stand from the chaise lounge beneath us.

I cannot see Theo as he moves through the room, clearly familiar with the space, even in the dimness, but I can hear the padding of his footsteps. I can feel him even without sight, as though our bodies are already inextricably interwound with each other, entities attached even when they are not. How oddly quickly, how naturally, we've become twisted in one another when it feels as though fate and history have conspired to bring us together, again and again. There is the dull clank of metal upon wood and then a flare of orange light casts across Theo's face from the candle held aloft in his hand.

"There she is." He smiles as he raises the candelabra out before him, letting the golden rays fall across my body where I still lie, where my bones and veins and nerves have not yet settled enough for me to move. I can see that Theo has adorned himself with his trousers once more, though his torso remains bare. The sight does nothing to ease my still-pounding heart.

Between the light of the flame and the silver rays spilling in from outside as Theo draws back the curtain, I can make out the varied inanimate occupants of the room around us. A large easel rests opposite me, wooden legs bowed out beneath it, a small stool holding paints at the ready beside the canvas.

"Is that yours?" I nod toward the setup, pushing up onto my elbows.

Theo looks from the easel to me, stepping forward and holding up a hand to still me.

"Wait, wait, do not move." He steps up behind the easel,

the dark wave of his hair just visible over the top as he bends to gaze at the empty canvas. "May I paint you?"

Rain begins to patter lightly on the windowsill, filling the room. My heart, just barely slowed, kicks up again at the question, at the thought of being portrayed, perceived within this body that I know, but often forget, to be my own. I feel a pinch behind my rib cage at the memory of seeing myself in photographs—or rather seeing a photograph that I know is of me, yet seeing only a stranger. It was like observing an unknown body, a form that I do not always feel like I occupy, a reminder that I am tethered to something that I often feel anything but connected to.

Theo mistakes the heaviness of my quiet for self-consciousness.

"I would like to show you how I see you, through my own eyes. Not that I am much of an artist—it is a hobby at best and often one with rather unattractive fruits for my labor." He chuckles and the mood lightens just a bit, as I know he intended. "But nevertheless, I would like to preserve on the canvas the beauty I see within you."

Beauty within is not something I'm sure can be found where I am concerned, especially as of late. But if there was ever one who could find it, if there was ever one who I trusted to poke around inside the most vulnerable part of me and try to find something worth memorializing—well, I have already let Theo in. It is him.

"Okay," I nod, though the pattering of my heart has not slowed. "I trust you." I wish I could make a joke in return, but I have not yet found my footing in my mind. I am still scrambling with unease.

It will be all right. It is Theo. How easily trust comes when it is fated to be.

I am rewarded by Theo's growing smile as he immediately takes a paintbrush into his hand.

"Lay back down as you were, my dear. I want to capture that pink glow still on your skin." He smirks at me, the memory of what caused such color flooding back to us both, and suddenly I know that more pink has arisen on my skin to guide his brush.

Theo's motions begin slowly, eyes trailing from the canvas to my lounging form. His brush moves from easel to paint with the intentional slowness of precision. But as time passes and the light beyond the windowsill shifts, his pace quickens, his gaze falling invisible to me from behind the edges of the easel before him, hand moving briskly.

He emerges from behind his post to gaze down at me, eyes sweeping across my body like a trail of hot kisses. Theo steps forward, kneeling before me so his face is aligned with mine as I lie on my side. His eyes bore into mine, unwavering, as he gently lifts a strand of hair from my shoulder, dropping it to trail across the bend of the chaise behind my back. Theo's hand drifts down my body and he must feel the way that my skin rises in little bumps of desire, must hear how my breath quickens and shallows, for he smiles and his eyes never once stray from mine.

His hand trails down into the curve of my waist, up across the rising swell of my hips, his touch the barest whisper across my body. He curls his fingers around the thick of the back of my thigh, guiding my leg forward, knee to the front, pressing his hand flat to my skin to tell me to hold this position. I can feel the swoop in the depth of my belly, the heat and moisture that gathers there immediately at his touch.

"Perfect," he breathes, rising to return to his easel once more.

And then I lose him again to his art and perhaps he loses himself too, time passing quickly as I watch the ease of his movements, gaze at the peaks of him as he floats in and out of the world around him in the artist's fog of creation. Never before have I sat so still and silent with myself without a book, or the hum of a television, or just anything to keep me from that fearful thing that I worry may emerge from the quiet.

Even as a child I have always been in motion, body needing to race as quickly as my mind. It has only ever been getting lost in my work that could make me quiet. But I suppose Theo makes the stillness calm, makes the quiet of being with myself something akin to peace.

Just when I think that I can wait no longer, when my muscles have begun to ache dully with the strenuous labor of stillness, Theo steps back, head tilting to admire the easel before him. He sets the brush down on the stool, a movement of finality, before stepping forward and taking my hand to guide my body up off of the chaise. The green of his eyes is a bit darker, the pupils shrunken, the man behind them not fully come back yet from the haze of his craft.

I stand before him naked, hair falling across my shoulders and back, but I cannot find it in me to be self-conscious— not of the appearance of my body nor of the fact that I have one—as Theo gazes at me as though I were Aphrodite herself, emerged from the sea.

He guides me to the other side of the easel, his hands resting on my hips as he stands behind me, allowing me to observe the Saoirse Read who has been created by his hand. For a long moment, I do not speak.

"I—" Theo breathes, stepping forward, reaching out as though he is going to take the painting down, hide it away. "I realize it is not quite true to life. It is simply . . . well, this is how you appear to me." His cheeks have colored amidst his stammering, so uncharacteristic of the Theo I am coming to know. But I understand why. I can see the vulnerability in each stroke of paint, can see the truth of Theo's gaze on the canvas. The truth of his feelings.

I place my hand on his arm, stopping his obstruction of the portrait.

For he is correct, this is no realistic portrayal. I lie on the canvas composed entirely of swatches of petal-pink skin, flaming hair, eyes the color of ivy, casting a shadow of sapphire blue across the gray of the couch beneath me. I am a splash of every color found in nature and in love, while everything on the canvas beyond me is in shades of gray and empty white. As though I am the only thing alive, beyond the dull hues of reality.

I can look into my own eyes, there on paper, and for once, I can see myself.

"This is how you see me?" My voice comes out in a whisper, as though if I speak too loudly, say too much, I could blow the colors away.

Theo is not looking at the portrait, but at me.

"Yes."

I step forward, taking his face in my hands. I feel the rigid press of cheekbones and jawline against my palm, the warmth of blood flow and vulnerability beneath his skin. I lean my forehead against Theo's, feeling our breath intermingle with each other, before pressing my lips to his, hoping that my mouth can tell him everything I am still too afraid to say.

I want this always. I want to see myself the way that you see me, always.

Chapter 25

I have been consumed by Theo Page in the most beautiful, intoxicating way. I've spent days and nights in his embrace, as we bloom into each other within the crystal walls of the greenhouse, fingers interwoven as we stroll through the garden, sunlight pouring down on us and from us. I had forgotten what it was like to feel that flutter of newness settling into golden comfort. To live in contented anticipation of the next moment of reunion.

My minutes are occupied by Theo, his presence more constant in my life now than Jack's, his era nearly washing away my own, and his journal still my secret, constant companion when the man himself cannot be, when our dearest friend Langdon keeps us apart in brief snatches. I see so little of Jack, and even less of his parents, that I do not have to think of what I am doing. I can lose myself in Theo and the past and pretend I do not feel the recurring nibble of guilt. Jack and Alice and Edgar have become the dim memories of my life, days passing without the sight of their faces. My moments in that time are so fleeting that the most I see of them is Jack's back as he crawls into bed at night, awakening to a cold side of the mattress, if I even wake in the twentieth century at all. I think I understand now why Langdon brought me here, to the beauty and the joy that awaited me.

Even as I drift through the halls of my own time in a yellow daze, my ears are always tuned for the creak of an empty floorboard or the whoosh of a curtain to know that Theo is nearby, even if it is in another time. I am calmed knowing that the house keeps us connected, that there is a strand of me, and a strand of him, woven into each other. Even when we part, I can still feel the estate's walls breathing around me, but being lost inside this living creature is no longer fearful but a comfort, a friend. It is the reminder of Theo's rising and falling chest, a memory and a promise of what is to come.

We spend so many days tangled into each other that it is nearly a surprise that we can even sit as we do now, our only contact my head resting upon Theo's lap as we lie among the flowers in the garden. Thick clouds drift across the blue of the sky like boats through the sea as I stare up into it, my toes pressing deep into the cool grass beneath us, and I cannot believe there was ever a time that I did not feel alive.

Theo's voice is the steady soundtrack to our afternoon, words of romance and longing falling from his mouth, lifted from the leather-spined book of poetry in his hands. The pages contain names and titles considered to be the academic classics of the nineteenth century, but who are merely Theo's contemporaries. They are men and women who have passed through Langdon's halls at his own invitation, who have too found themselves the talk of London society. But the book in his grasp now is one plucked by my hands from the Langdon library of my own time, slipped into the past with me, bringing words from a near future.

"'Art thou pale for weariness, Of climbing heaven and gazing on the earth, Wandering companionless . . .'" Theo's voice washes across my skin with a warmth to match the April sun above us. "'Among the stars that have a different birth, And ever changing, like a joyless eye That finds no object worth its constancy?'"

The fresh sea air carries the caw of a passing bird over to us, the sound and feel drifting across the exposed skin of my feet, my ankles, my hands twined around Theo's. How is it that things could be so perfect?

You deserve it, Saoirse, you do. You deserve to feel . . . wanted and blissfully, perfectly happy in the arms of another who wants you to be no one but exactly who you are.

"'Thou chosen sister of the Spirit, That gazes on thee till in thee it pities . . .'" Theo trails off, his voice always smooth and gentle, but still with the practiced tone of a storyteller.

"You've got a good voice for that, you know," I say, eyes closed, basking in the warmth both from the sun and from the man above me, as my head rests upon his lap, chin tilted up to the light, one hand trailing aimlessly across his arm as he holds the book I've brought him.

"In her girlhood, Nell loved being read to. I had opportunity aplenty to perfect my power of storytelling."

"And perfect you have." I lift his free hand to my mouth, planting the lips of my smile against the smoothness of his palm.

When I look to Theo, he does not smile back, eyes still wandering across the page, dark brows pondering.

"Who wrote this?" he asks, eyes still searching the page. "It reminds me of a piece by Sir Philip Sidney. Is it not his own?"

"I think it was inspired by him, yeah." I used to remember nothing, could hardly even remember who I was. But now that Theo has guided me up into wakefulness, into living, I find the depths of my mind undarkened. I can easily reach the words of some undergraduate seminar back in Boston and pull them forth. Remembering things I did not even realize I ever knew, remembering things I did not even know I had forgotten. "The moon and its longing sadness and whatnot. That one's Shelley, though. Percy."

I am surprised I have so many words now, so many opinions. I have become so used to slipping into my mind that I forgot just how vast I am, how much brightness and color can be contained in me too.

"Ah, of course. I do enjoy his work as well. In fact, he's just published a fascinating new piece that printed in the *Examiner* this winter." Theo smirks down at me, mouth tilting but eyes still full of the same tenderness that I have not yet accepted can be for me. "Quite the rebel too, he was. No wonder you so enjoy his work."

How alive I am in your mind, Theo.

"I have not heard talk of this piece, though," he continues, stroking a hand through the red of my hair, fanned out across his lap.

"No, I guess you wouldn't have. It was only published after he died. In 1822, I believe."

Something in Theo's face slips, the happiness and teasing falling from it with a thud, replaced by something that wipes the color from his cheeks.

Missteps seem to be all that I am capable of. What a fool I am, to not learn to swallow my words, to keep them tampered down.

"I'm so sorry. God, I am sorry. I know you hate knowing about things that haven't happened yet for you, here. I spoke without thinking."

A heaviness has tumbled into Theo's features, his face pulled down in worry and fear. For once he looks so like Jack and it makes my stomach flip, guilt and regret flooding in. I feel his breathing shallow beneath my head, eyes roaming across nothingness, moving as quickly as the thoughts he does not vocalize to me. I scramble up, leaning on my bent wrists instead, body tenting over his as I watch his face astutely, wishing I could push my words back down my throat and choke on them.

Am I really any different here?

"I'm s—"

"Do not apologize, Saoirse, truly. You have nothing to be sorry for." Theo leans forward, planting a kiss on my lips, taking some of the shame and hatred away with the gentleness of his touch. When he pulls away his face is one of calm beauty once more. Whatever pain I have relegated him to has passed. "I am certain my knowledge of the death of a poet whom I have never met will not greatly affect the state of the world. It is merely a sadness for a life lost so young." His voice scratches forth as he speaks.

At first I think that grief has wedged itself in his throat, his words rough and strained. Then, as if the concern that has overtaken him needs to be free and come forth, Theo slips into a round of ragged coughs. The sound echoes across the hues of the garden, not the first time I have heard Theo caught in such a fit.

I rub my hand across his back as Theo's shoulders curl into themselves with the force of expelled air, the motion overtaking him. It makes him appear almost frail, delicate, so at odds with the man of strong body and mind that I have come to care for. Like a storm cloud, the fit passes, Theo once more uncoiling himself up, the garden returned to little more than the sounds of springtime.

"The April air has a bit of a chill, that is all," Theo says, though he has not yet given me a chance to ask. "The flowers in bloom can quite overwhelm, as well."

"I'm sorry—"

I have learned well enough that the blame for all things will fall upon me.

Theo's brows raise in admonishment.

"I meant it, Saoirse. There is never a need for you to apologize to me, you have done nothing wrong."

Forgiveness, so unexpected that I did not realize how much I longed for it until it was brought to me in gentle hands.

I bring my hand to rest against his face, fingers along the peak and valley of his cheek, my palm fitting to the sharp edge of his jaw. He leans into my hold, silky dark strands falling across my fingers.

"Are you all right?"

I watch the green at the edge of Theo's eyes spread and brighten as he gazes at me, backlit by the brightness of the sun breaking through the clouds. He has a small smile on his face that I cannot help but mirror.

"I am with you, my dear. I am more than okay."

This gift the house has given me.

The fire that Theo lit in my belly has simmered into a honey that flows through my veins, keeping me warm, and I cannot believe that I once thought that the cold was all I could ever know, that the winter would never pass for me. Now here I am, living in the springtime green of those eyes.

Theo leans down to kiss me, my lips rising to meet his mouth, his tongue.

"Thank you for allowing me to read the beauty of this poem." There is a heavy sincerity to the words he speaks against my lips and I do not know why, do not know how to soothe the little weight of sadness within him. So instead I push my body up into him, mouth alive on his.

It is never close enough. I want to be one with you, Theo.

"You said you read to Nell when she was a girl?" I ask. I want to know every piece of Theo, every small corner of him, every crease and fold of his heart. And I know his sister, despite the frayed relationship he had detailed in his journal, is close to his heart.

Theo nods. "All sorts of tales. I was never much of a reader as a boy, but I would take any reason to be in the company of my sister." A private smile lights his face, eyes made gentle in thought of the younger Page.

Theo settles back down into the grass, pulling me onto his chest, my chin propped on his sternum so I can look up at him, his dark hair offset by the cerulean sky.

"Have you always been so close?" I ask. Much as I love to see the lightness on Theo as he speaks of his sister, I cannot deny the knot in my stomach as we lie together. At something like jealousy—no, longing—that my own brothers do not hold such fondness for me. That they did not try, that they did not mourn a loss of our closeness as I know Theo did with Nell, for my own brothers were never really close to me at all.

"When she was a girl, absolutely." Theo's chin tilts up farther, but I do not miss the tension in his jaw. "But our parents passed when she was young, both lost to illness within a year of each other. I have more than ten years than Nell, it was only natural I would step into the position of the parent that was left behind. She wanted a joyful brother, but I struggled to be that anymore. It was more important I care for her, that I keep us alive and safe."

I think of his journal, those early entries I read. It was important he keep her protected, see her happily wed to the right man—a role that he had to take, done from love, though it would never seem as much to a teen girl. When it seems Theo will say no more I dare to fill the silence, to show him I understand him, that I have, in my own way, been where he has.

"My father died when I was little too. I was barely seven, but my brothers were already in their teens, like you were." I pause for a moment, swallowing heavily around the lump in my throat. To continue is to risk Theo seeing the worst of me, seeing the lack of love that made my mind into darkness, made my body a stranger. But, as Langdon knows, Theo and I seem to be one in the same.

"I wish one of them would have taken on the role of a parent. Or taken on any role at all. They had each other, though, they didn't really need me," I continue. "My mother . . . she had a tough time coping. She couldn't really be bothered to take care of a young kid. I tried to be useful—be good at school, help around the house—to, I don't know, earn her attention or affection or something. But it never really worked. It still hasn't worked, if I'm honest. I don't know what I need to do to make her love me like family is supposed to."

It wasn't until I was older, until I saw the way others' families treated them, with attention and love without conditions, that I realized I have never known the same. By then I'd pulled so deeply inside to find somewhere that felt safe, so far that I'd lost that sense of self in the process. I could not look at myself and see all the flaws that made me invisible, unlovable, if I could not even recognize myself. I could know all this now, could see the path to where I had landed, lost to my body and to reality too often, my diagnosis making it official. But it was too far gone, that the coping, the escape sometimes felt like it was me all the way down, whatever me meant.

I had fled to a new country, but the distance from my family meant nothing when I still had to sit with my swirling dark thoughts. Struggling with the awareness that it was because of my own faults, and none of theirs, that my family only loved me as far as I bent myself to fit their shapes. I really do think they try their best to love me, in the ways that they're able. I feel guilty that it's not enough for me. I feel guilty that I cannot become easier to love, even though I've spent a lifetime trying. *I swear, I do try.*

My family probably thinks they love me, would say they did if asked. I've just never seen it, never felt it. It is still an ache like an open wound to think of my mother sometimes, such a deep-boned desire for her affection that my stomach hollows at the thought of her. At the thought that I was not enough, am not enough, for her love.

Jack's love and attention may be like the shifting beam of a lighthouse, but that still means it falls on me every so often, even if not as much as it had in our early days. Still, it was more than I'd gotten elsewhere so I had worked desperately to keep it. *I will do better, will claw my way out of the depths of my mind any way I must, to keep it.*

It wasn't until I met Jack that I really felt like I got attention, love. Sometimes I think Jack can see that desperation in me to be loved, in truth, for once. That he can see that the people who were supposed to love me most, unconditionally, could not be bothered. That he pulls away because he can detect the cracks in who I am, not just a woman whose mind is her own personal terror, but the dismissals that brought me to that place.

And I know Jack can't relate to that, could never even imagine not being the unquestionably adored star of his parent's life—their only child, their proudest achievement simply for existing. I'd been drawn to the way Jack and his parents truly just loved each other, and I am so desperate for them to take me into the embrace of that affection. But I am the only thing about Jack that his parents don't love—the stain of me is ruining him too.

I had thought maybe Theo would understand, that he had ached for the love of his family the way I had, had lived with the absence of it, the loss, even if briefly. But as soon as my words are out I regret them, my stomach knotting into a fist. All I have done is show him the truth of me, the truth that Jack already knew, and my brothers, the truth that my mother must have spotted even when I was a girl. Now he will see the cracks in me too and will float away. There is no amount of fate or magic or whatever Langdon is, that can make him want to stay close to me.

I cannot look at Theo, so I stare instead up at the clouds drifting past, blinking away the water that's trembling in my eyes. Perhaps if I don't move, don't say another word, my confession will float away on the wind. Theo won't put the pieces together and realize I am too flawed for my family, for Jack, that I have not made myself into a person to be cared for.

Theo's fingers brush the tears from my eyelashes so gently it tickles. He tips my chin up to face him and there is no horror or disgust there. There is not even pity. His eyes and jaw are set almost in anger.

"You do not need to do anything to be loved, Saoirse." His tone is as fierce as his expression, a hardness I have never heard there. It startles me, though his loving touch as he cups my face tell me his ire is not with me. "That is a flaw in *them*, not in you."

"It's no big deal, really—"

"It is. Love should not come with conditions. Their failings are not a reflection of you. I'm sorry you were treated that way, my dear."

I tamper down a rising sob that catches me by surprise in its heft, in the hollow ache that seems to have cracked open in my chest.

Theo holds me tight to his chest until my own seems to still, until his words can seep into my skin and my breathing can steady. Until I can knit myself back together again in his arms and do my best to believe what he says. Every day it feels like there is a new condition I must meet to get Jack's love, so familiar from my family that I hardly noticed until now.

I realize Theo has never given me one prerequisite for his attention or affection.

Theo's fingers run across my head in a consistent rhythm for so long that I come to expect the gentle touch. That I almost come to feel I deserve it.

As the clouds shift above us and time drags by, I hear his heartbeat slow beneath my ear. I know that the songs, the books, rave of the thrill of making someone's heart race, of being their excitement. But as I lie here with Theo, the crack in my chest slowly mending, listening to his heart mellow, I think that maybe this is worth much more. All I'm doing is being here, as I am, without a thought. And yet, somehow, I've become his peace.

There will never be enough of you for me, I will always want more.

I will always want to touch all of you and be touched by you.

I will always want you.

I will, I will.

I return to my body and it no longer seems like such a scary place to be as the colors of sunrise, of fire, reds and yellows and oranges, spread from that part of me that Theo knows best to encompass my body. Until I am nothing but the rising sun, and it is all because of him, for *him, him, him.*

Chapter 26

I am the ghost of Langdon Hall now.

It is nighttime when I return, the house honoring my reluctant wish, placing me back into the twentieth century through the arch of a door, the feel and taste of Theo and his sweet words and his skin and *him* still on my tongue and in my mind. There is a smile on my face as I allow my body to bleed into the shadows sewn along the walls, weaving my way through the endless hallways.

I do not know where it is I'm going here, for I do not even feel like I belong here anymore, but it does not matter, this place, this time, is not what's real anymore. But I know I must return, must fade in and out of this time. I cannot simply disappear, though the truth of me exists only in the distant past now, while in the arms of another man.

As I creep my way through the darkened halls I swear I can hear the whispers of Langdon in my ear, in my mind. Or maybe it is Theo's hushed voice, the echo of his gentle words. Or perhaps there is no difference at all.

My joy fills my body and spills out, blocking my senses, and I do not hear the floorboard crackle beneath my bare foot or the clearing of a throat like gravel rolling until it is too late.

Until I hear the voice call my name, heavy with disappointment at my very existence, as it always is.

"Saoirse." Alice's words are not a question but a statement, her resentment carrying the end of my name downward. And immediately I go with it, down, down.

The gasp that slips from my mouth is quiet but still echoes back at me in the heavy silence all around. I step back, peering through the open doorway I'd just passed to see Alice sitting in the blue tea room. She sits, still, in the darkness, her face lost to shadow. Even with her illness, her posture is rigid and uncomfortably formal, or perhaps that is merely her response to seeing me haunting her beloved halls.

I want to keep moving, pretend I never heard her. I wish to hold on to this dream that I've been living in where nothing is real but me and Theo and the springtime, and his hands and words on me, gentle and loving.

But the illusion has been shattered. The curtain closes on the brightness I have come to know and I am once more left in the dim gray of my own life.

Alice does not move, her predatory stillness quickening my breath, the weight of her gaze piercing me. I step through the doorway toward her because I must, because I am small once more, and I am left with no decisions here.

How I longed to be seen just weeks ago, and now I wish I could be anything but.

You are not the ones I want to see me. You do not see me, you never have. Any of you.

The wind howls, rattling the windows in their frames, nature ready to do the older woman's bidding, to carry me away from this place and her home and her son. To make me part of the haunting emptiness of night, reflecting in the deepest parts of my mind.

You do not need to go back there, Saoirse. There is brightness within you now. Remember, remember.

"Why don't you sit, Saoirse?"

It is only once I'm within the room that I hear the shallowness of Alice's breathing, the way that her voice is strained, trying to make its way through the illness that clogs her lungs. The sympathy that rises up in me is nothing compared to my fear at the very sight of her, and it dissipates quickly as she snaps her harsh words across my skin.

"Now."

I do not want to, but my body has been so trained to follow her orders that I immediately sink into the chair at her side. I cannot believe that this is the same body that so recently knew such pleasure, the same hands that wove into earth and man and joy now tangling within themselves with unease. My knuckle cracks, the sound slicing the dense, expectant air.

Alice looks at me, eyes sharper than her body, patiently torturing me to break the silence she has prompted between us. Neither of us moves to bring light to the space, hovering in the quiet of nightfall and the weapon-sharp tension between us.

"Hi, Alice." The fear is clear in my voice, but I do not know what it is that I am afraid of. This woman, too weak now to lift a weapon to me? But of course she's not. A hard facade and cutting wounds are not what she does but simply who she is.

I wish I could stop it, but there is still that tiny river of shame in me as I look at her, features grayed not only by nighttime but by the life seeping out of her. There is so much of her gone now, and I have not been here to see it leave. Have not been here to hold Jack's hand as he surely watched the same. My fiancé may not have supported me in a long time, but it is all too clear now how absent I have been from him, when he needs me most. But it was Jack who tucked me away into tiny rooms and shadows here, who made me shrink myself until Langdon found me and took me somewhere new. I am not certain if this is a reason or merely an excuse, a displacing of my own guilt.

"I didn't expect you to be awake. Are you all right? Do you need help getting back to your room?" I ask.

Alice's responding laugh is hollow and rumbling and it shrinks me.

"No, dear, I most certainly do not need your help."

Dear, dear, dear.

Her favorite weapon of all.

"I get so little sleep these days. I'm often awake and wandering in the night, best as I can. I do so love every corner of this house."

I am surprised that Alice will even acknowledge that she, the strongest matriarch of all, is weakening when the ears of her son are not there to elicit sympathy and place all of his focus upon her.

"Not that I imagine you would have noticed. It seems as though you're hardly in Langdon these days. It feels like weeks since I've seen you truly."

It is then I see that Alice has set a trap and I have walked right into it, like a scared, trembling creature. And now I am caught.

"I've done my best to be less of a bother. I don't want to get in the way of your time with your family."

The words are not entirely a lie, but they sound like one and I know that Alice hears it too. The dark line of her brow quirks, pulling on the wrinkles that have formed around her eyes, thick lines somehow doubled since I saw her last.

"It is a big house, but I know it well. Harry says he's seen you sneaking about, wandering the halls at all hours. What is it you're doing, Saoirse? Where could you possibly be hiding away?"

The wind screams outside just as I do within.

Alice has eyes everywhere, even when they are not her own. From the start, I have felt like the house was watching me, judging me—maybe Alice is the ominous being I feared Langdon to be.

"I'm not hiding. I spend time in the garden, working in the office. Sometimes I'm just in the bedroom reading."

My fingers ache, they are so tightly twisted into one another now. It is as though I think if I can hold on to them tight enough I can hold on to this conversation, on to the reality I have come to know, slipping between my grasp with every suspecting word from Alice's mouth.

"I know Jack is of little concern to you these days, but he could use your support. If you can find the time to give it to him, that is."

Lashes, lashes, do they ever end, these little wounds this woman inflicts upon me? Worse, because now I have brought them upon myself. I am no longer an innocent to their unfounded cruelty.

"I was under the impression Jack could use some space and time to spend with his parents. That's all I'm trying to give him."

"Mmm." Alice's answering noise is noncommittal, skeptical. What does she know?

Does she realize the guilt and shame she has reinflicted on me, how she has reminded me of the weight of this ring on my finger, on a hand that has been held by another?

"I do hope your illness isn't getting the best of you again, Saoirse. Even I've heard you skulking about, whispering to no one. You must see how worrying that is. A bit scary even, like you're in a whole other world. What is it you think you see here?" Her tone is mocking, she is baiting me, or is that simply what I hear? What is the truth anymore?

You know the truth, Saoirse.

You know.

I know the truth—and this is not it.

Do not let them make you into the madwoman they treat you as.

With a creaking from the chair and her frail bones in equal measure, Alice pushes herself to standing.

"We all have nothing but concern for you is all," she continues. "But I'm certain you'll feel better once you're back in London. No more worrying about your little degree anymore will be good for you."

She must be mocking me, seeing how she has the power to pull everything out from under me. Her whispering in Jack's ear, how powerful that can make her. How powerless I am, Saoirse who roams the halls like a ghoul, for they do not see what I see and think me mad.

Surely I am not. *Please.*

"I should be off to bed." Alice steps toward the door, walking slow and labored, brushing off my touch as I stand to aid her. "I can do it," she snaps, and I know that it is not from a place of anger with me, but frustration with herself, with the way that life is slowly moving further and further beyond her desperate grasp.

I can nearly see the clock ticking above her head, yet she uses the moments she has left to incur more injuries upon me. How very fitting of her. How very deserving for me.

Alice makes her way to the door and the weight on my chest becomes heavier, even as the distance between us grows. I cannot see her face through the shadows, but the night still carries Alice's words to me.

"Be careful, Saoirse. You are not as invisible as you may wish to be. The gaze of the Pages is sharp within Langdon." And with one last haunting look from the dark of the hall, as though she is already a ghost of the past come to warn me of my future, Alice is gone around the bend.

She cannot know the truth, surely. She cannot know the way the house guides me through time and reality, cannot know the shape of Theo's hand in mine, his persistent presence in my mind.

But it does not matter, she has done enough with what little she does know, whatever it is. Alice has put a fracture in the veil of happiness that I have worn to hide from this reality. And now darkness has begun to seep in through the crack, thick as oil and dark as night, and it has come to stain this thing that I have held so close to my chest. It is as though Alice's words have woken me from a dream, sprung me awake into the gloom of this Langdon, into the nightmare I have created in the wake of my decisions and my indecision. She has reminded me that my belief that I could have it all is so foolishly impossible.

I am Icarus flying toward the sun, edging too close and wanting too much. Now watch me fall, for these wings cannot last forever.

There can no longer be a separation between this time and the past I so often visit, Alice has made sure of that. I can no longer pretend that this, now, is not my reality too. Or is it *too* at all? How can I be sure of what is real anymore?

The shadows seep in and my grip loosens. I am falling back into the depths of my mind, my illness lurking and waiting within to snatch me. Alice has turned off the light and I can no longer see the colors Theo has painted me with. It is all darkness.

Chapter 27

Sleep did not come to me, much as I called with my desperate, hoarse voice. It evaded me, leaving me to stare at the ceiling, the bed hardly able to fit us all—me, Jack, and my growing guilt and unease. As the grayish white of early morning began to creep across the house, I did the same, sliding from the bed to wander the dimly lit halls, eyes stinging with a restless night.

My hands have not stopped quaking, and the tremors have little to do with the cold of this place. All I want is to be taken into Theo's arms, yet this has become the very thing that I fear most. Maybe I do not know what it is that I want, but the house does not give me time to contemplate. It instead trips me into the past as I turn the bend in the upstairs hallway. The large room at its end transforms into a ballroom with pools of golden candlelight reflecting across the floor in the blink of an eye.

A faint wind drifts over to me and even in the mildness of spring it meets my skin in a chill, goose bumps rising across my arms, my fingers pulling the edge of my sweater down over my hands. Is it true, is it real, does this bodily reaction prove it to be as much? Or am I so deep in my mind, lost in the delusion and guilt? I cannot deny that my time in the twentieth century is reality, but does that make this time any less so? How can I know the truth? Do I *deserve* for this to be reality too?

I lift my head at the sound of footsteps and see Theo striding across the ballroom toward me, lit by the green of the garden visible through the open glass doorway of the balcony. The sun is bright outside, but it is brighter in his face, as it blooms into a grin at the sight of me.

Both of my hands are taken in his, a kiss pressed to my trembling lips, and it all feels so real, it does. Theo rubs his fingers across mine briskly, and the little fire inside me that is branded with his name wants to rise, but there is so much fear, so much confusion dampening it. But even then, there is nothing that could extinguish my flame for Theo entirely.

"Your hands are ice, my dear," he says, voice full of tenderness. "Though I suppose they always are when you first arrive." He brings my fingers to his mouth, warming them with his kiss.

It is true, and it reminds me of just how thin the boundary between my time and this one is.

"It's very cold in my time. It's always so cold." I can hear how empty my voice sounds and I am terrified to hear that it is not my voice, but that of the woman I was a year ago. The woman who was hardly a woman at all, hardly alive, so lost in her brain, wandering the cramped halls of her London flat, unable to see her fiancé, the world, anything in color anymore. Reality was a dream that felt like it was slipping from her mind.

Please, please, I do not want to be that woman again. I cannot be that woman again, I will not survive it this time. Please, please.

Theo's hands fall from mine, coming instead to cradle my face, tilting my gaze from the floor up to meet his. There is so much concern in those hazel eyes, so much kindness that I do not deserve. But I cannot deny that I want it anyway, that those eyes on mine guide me just a bit out of the darkness, pull me back up into myself, help me find my way back to the surface for now.

"What has happened?"

"Nothing, it's just . . . I'm not sure."

I want to tell him the truth, but I do not know what the truth is. I simply know that I do not know where the line sits between reality and dreaming, do not know where I am anymore within that. I do not know how I was ever so certain, even with that brief, fleeting assuredness that Theo gave me.

"That'll be a symptom of your condition, Saoirse." The doctor's voice was so steady, his eyes looking at me with pity that I was at the surface enough then to hate seeing. "Things can feel without consequences because they don't seem real to you. It can play tricks with your memory."

What is reality when everything appears as a dream?

Try to remember your senses, Saoirse, try to ground yourself.

I can feel Theo's skin against mine, can hear the sound of birds swooping joyfully above the garden, can taste fear on my tongue. But I am numb all over, can feel the nothingness spreading like a poison through my veins, hollowing me out, slipping, slipping.

Theo sighs, face pulled down with the weight of his sympathy, with concern. He kisses me on the forehead, warmth seeping out from the point of contact, and maybe I can feel a bit of my body again. His fingers lace into mine once more and he guides me toward the open balcony door, my feet following through the fog that clouds my mind.

"Come, my dear. The freshness of the air will help you."

And it does, the air more like summer than spring. The sky is so blue that it casts the garden before us into vivid streaks of green and pink and red, and I cannot believe that such beauty can be real. Theo guides me to sit on the marble steps leading down toward the grass, his hands gentle as ever on my body. Not as though I am breakable but as though I am precious.

Perhaps I could be both, for I do not feel enduring now, in this body I hold onto by mere threads and this mind that feeds the dread it nests. But who could tolerate such flaws, such fractures—Jack cannot. I can't expect Theo to look at me so gently still, if he knew how deep my cracks went, the darkness that flooded my mind through them. But I had shown him some of those gloomy, tender parts of me just yesterday, and he had met me with only protectiveness, kindness, not one hint of disgust or regret.

Dark coils of ivy weave their way around the thick stone railing, their leaves wobbling in the breeze as it passes by.

I find my body naturally leaning into Theo as we sit, my shoulder pressing into his, trusting him to keep me upright when I cannot do it myself.

He does not speak, does not ask more, does not push me. He gives me space, but he does not ever make himself distant from me. Slowly, carefully, I wade up to the surface a bit more.

I look at his face, at the way that the affection in his eyes softens those features sitting among the sharp angles of his face, and I am home. I do not know if this place, this time, is the truth, but Theo is. He must be.

And so he deserves to know my truth too.

"I should tell you. There's something about me you don't—" My voice trembles and I cannot stop it. "I . . . I'm often not well. Sick, I guess, in a way." His eyes widen, concern and something else I cannot quite recognize, something urgent, overtaking them. Fear, perhaps. Nevertheless, I push on, fingers trembling to think that Theo will meet me with the same wide eyes Jack did by my side in the doctor's office. "Not physically, but in my head. Mentally a bit struggling, I mean. Sometimes I can't quite tell what's real and what's . . . not. I just . . . I have a hard time sometimes. A lot of the time."

The mystery falls from Theo's eyes and the concern shifts into something more open as he takes my hands once more, presses my knuckles gently to his lips in a now-familiar gesture.

"When I first saw a person from another time in Langdon I was so overjoyed I ran to tell my parents. They thought me mad, truly, were certain there must be something amiss in my brain. That what I saw could not be real. It made me question myself, if in fact I was unwell. But then it happened again and again and I knew that, no matter what anyone thought of it, of me . . . I knew the truth. And now I could not be more thankful for Langdon's little slips in time." He smiles, stroking a finger over my knuckles. "What I mean to say is that experiencing the world in a way others do not does not make you mad or ill or flawed, Saoirse. I believe you, as you should believe yourself. If you struggle, I will be patiently by your side regardless. I do not care what scars you wear, my love, in your skin or in your heart."

The word floors me and tangles up with the sorrow inside me.

Mine.

Love.

Love.

"I know your mind and it is a beautiful place. I know that you have the strength within you to endure, and my hand will always be in yours to help as you do."

I want to believe him, I do, so desperately. But will his hand truly always be in mine? Can it be?

"Of all the times and all the people, Langdon brought *us* together for a reason. You are not alone."

Each of his words has weight and they hit me with full force. I cannot remember the last time that I did not feel alone.

But I remember that ghost of hurt that crossed Theo's eyes the very first time we met, and I remember that he knows what it is to have your words, your reality, mistrusted. That maybe it was this, first, that made the house weave our paths together. Before affection and desire, there was understanding in a way no one else could.

Theo's hand in mine, the way his finger strokes softly across my knuckles, feels too real to be anything but.

You decide, Saoirse.

This is the truth.

I want nothing but the truth.

"Thank you." My words are a ragged whisper, but their quietness is not lost as I press my mouth to Theo's, letting his affection fill me.

His hand falls from mine, reaching into the pocket within the white folds of his trousers. When it emerges, a tiny box of dark wood is resting in his palm. I can see the slight shake to his fingers as he opens it.

Nestled within the box is something I know well. I look to my own hand and yes, there it sits, resting on the fourth finger of my left hand, and yet there its twin is too, in the box before me.

"After seeing that ring on your finger weeks ago I sought it out, in my own time, of course. I had long hidden it away, a reminder of what I did not have. What I did not want." There is such a sincerity in his voice and the faintest touch of nerves that endears me to him all the more. I did not think it was possible. "I do not speak of matrimony, of course, it is not possible and I know far too quick. It is just . . . I do wish I could have been the one to put this ring on your finger. Someday."

His words are honey sweet and they are all I ever wanted to hear, all I ever wanted to feel, when a man held a ring out to me, a desire undiscovered yet never quenched. Yet my stomach tilts with guilt, with the realization of how true my longing is. How it will never fade or falter, no matter how much time or distance is between us.

It is not love, not yet, but whatever it is now, between Theo and me, it fits me like the piece I never knew I was missing. It smooths the sharpened edges of myself that so often cut me. It is the last rung of the ladder that allows me to climb out of my own darkness and be in the world, allows me to be in my body and not feel trapped. To feel that there is someone waiting for me, waiting with me without judgment, in the moments that I cannot help but float away from myself and the world. It is all quick, I know this, and yet these feelings that could be, this comfort, does not feel rushed or shallow or temporary.

Theo does not reach to put the ring on my finger and I am glad. I could not bear the sight of it, his hand on mine, those two rings a mirror image on my fingers, a visual reminder of the duplicity, the duality that my life and heart have become. My eyes shift from the ring on my finger to the twin held in the hand of another man and they are the same, yet there is a world of difference between them. An object split in two, just as I have been, the truth obscured in the lack of singularity.

How is this what my life has become? Who I have become? How is it that there is no part of me, not even the faintest whisper, that wishes for this to truly be my madness, that wishes that this were not the truth, despite the guilt that still whispers inside of me?

This is the truth.

I would not give up the way that Theo's eyes move across me for anything in the world, and the realization opens a pit in my stomach that tells me I will never know peace again.

Chapter 28

The air is cold against the thin skin on my feet, even as I tuck my ankles up, folding deep into the chair before the bedroom fireplace. Some modern bestseller sits open and forgotten in my lap, my gaze instead fixated upon and lost within the flames and myself. Even though it is all I want, even though my mind and heart reach out to me and beg for it, I whisper pleas to the house to keep me here, in the coldness of my own time, for now.

I cannot lose my grip on this reality again. I must sit in the cold, let it bite at my skin and not let me forget the truth. I cannot keep moving, slipping between time so much that I fall within. It is time to stop, to pause, to think.

If this—now and then—are both the truth, I am not fool enough to think it can continue forever. I must not slip away into dreams. I must find my footing, find myself, before I am swept away. I know it will not last forever, but God, I am not ready to give it up yet. Not just Theo, but this here and now too. I am a nostalgic creature of habit, I cannot forget what Jack and I once were, and I am realizing that, somewhere, I am still hoping that we can be that again.

I am a selfish woman and I cling desperately to both. I will not let go until I must.

The bedroom door creaks open and my heart kicks up speed, but it is not the phantom of a man that comes through the doorway, but the all too real form of my fiancé. I have nearly forgotten what Jack looked like, it has been so long since we've been awake in a room together it seems, though I know it could really only be a couple of days at most. But, no, he is still beside me in bed every night, isn't he?

I have grown so accustomed to a taller, broader, gentler form filling the doorways of this house. Grown used to the shape of a man who reaches his arms out toward me, who greets me with kind words and a smile on his face.

That is not what I see before me now. Jack's movements are as heavy as the look upon his face as he makes his way toward me, as though he must, as though we are still bound to each other, dragged toward each other forevermore.

But still, I can feel Theo here with me, as though he has become the house itself or it, he.

I am almost surprised Jack can see me at all, surprised that I am not simply a ghost, in truth. He opens his mouth but I cannot hear his words through my shock that they exist at all. When was the last time we had spoken? Have we ever spoken at all? I cannot remember.

"Sorry, what'd you say?"

"I just asked how you are," he sighs, and I don't think I'm imagining the taut tension in his voice.

What does he know? Has Alice spoken to him?

"I'm fine," I say.

I'm not.

"Good, yeah." Jack sits down in the seat beside me, back pressing into the clothes he's left strewn across it. His knee is bobbing up and down, a dance born of unease, his fingertips dancing atop it. I rarely see Jack nervous because Jack is never nervous. The last time I saw him like this was the day he proposed, but now the jittering is not interspersed with charmingly shy smiles thrown my way.

Today we wear matching frowns.

I am nervous too, afraid of what it is that's making its way from his mind to his mouth. The guilt in my stomach twists around nerves, the two tightening into a knot.

"Look, I know you've been keeping yourself sparse lately, and I do appreciate that." *He cuts wounds even when he thinks he is healing them.* "But I'm sure that means you haven't seen just how bad Mum is doing. She's . . . yeah, she's really not well. Might be happening, and whatnot."

He pauses and I do not know if he expects me to respond, so I don't. I should probably have the urge to reach out to him, to squeeze his hand in comfort, but I do not. Is this how Jack has felt all these months when he's left me on my own, hand swinging empty? Obligation not as strong as desire, or the lack of.

"So I've been thinking that maybe we should get married."

"We're already engaged, Jack."

And we are, but why is the reminder still a punch to my gut? The guilt there roils in response.

"I know that, Saoirse, of course I do." That short, sharp sigh of his. "I mean we should get married now. While Mum is still around. I'd like her to be there for it, and I think she'd like to be as well."

She wouldn't. I know she wouldn't. Jack probably knows it too, really. He has no concern for my own family being present, writing them off as they've written off me. He does not think that maybe I'd want someone who cared for me, someone who was mine, awaiting me at my wedding. Because he thinks that he is the only one who fits that criterion in my life and sometimes I am not even sure he does. But he's wrong, I'm realizing.

You are not the only one who is loved, Jack.

It takes a moment before Jack's words actually make their way through the fog of my mind. He is still talking, but I cannot hear him through the ringing growing in my ears.

This is the path we've been walking down for months; it should not be such a shock that Jack expects us to reach our destination.

But, God, I thought I had more time.

I need more time.

It shouldn't be surprising, it shouldn't steal my breath, but still it does. I knew that the universe, this house, whomever, would not let me continue much longer. I could already feel the tension of the truth brewing before Jack walked through that door today. Jack is realizing just how limited his time with his mother is and yet my sympathy feels distant behind the howling of my panic, of what this means I, too, will come to lose. I can no longer be indecisive, having two realities, living in the present and the past.

"It wouldn't be too difficult to get someone in to officiate, I imagine. And there's the ballroom, or really anywhere in the house that we could . . ."

Through the pounding of my own heart, through the screaming knots in my stomach, Jack's voice drones in and out. And it is a drone, words spoken with no emotion behind them, merely going through the motions.

That's all we ever fucking do. Go through the motions.

He cannot possibly want this.

Please, please, don't do this. Just let us be free.

It is all too clear to me now that we cannot get back to what we had, what we were. Even clearer that that is not what we—either of us—really wants.

Why are we simply going through these motions? Why can we not break free of this cycle we have created? What was once our horse-drawn carriage has become a car racing toward the edge of the cliff, and we are both sick from the motion, both clinging to the wheel and pressing the gas, unable to let go.

Marriage at last. A contract signed in my blood; my freedom traded for the Page name.

Wiping me away just a little bit more.

I should think of Jack. Of us. Maybe I should even think of Alice.

I do not. It is only Theo's face that comes to my mind. It is Theo's hand that I want to take in mine, Theo's voice that I want to soothe me. It is Theo. I am no saint, I have proven that tenfold, but to marry Jack feels like finality. It feels like saying yes to one man means I no longer have an excuse—that I must finally say no to the other.

If I am here a minute longer, I think I'll be sick from the guilt and shame and hatred, so much hatred, for myself and Jack and my life. It will bubble up and burn the skin right from my bones. It will leave me as exposed as I already feel.

"Saoirse, are you even listening to a word I've said?"

No, I am not. Because I'm not here. But I'm not with Theo either. I'm deep, deep down in my mind and the slope is slippery and dark, but I cannot stop falling down into it, away from my body and the reality that I cannot bear to face.

Will no one save me?

"Of course."

"Good. So as I said, I'll give you a day or so to really think on it and get ready. I know it's not the wedding in a museum you wanted, but Mum wouldn't have signed off on that anyway. Right, I'll need to get everything in order quickly." Jack leans his elbows onto his knees and for a moment I think that maybe he'll touch me.

But he does not. This tilt of his body is the closest we've been in too long anyway.

Is this really what he wants? Is this the life, the future, that he wants? Every day more of this—me, Jack, and the memories draining the air between us of color?

Good God, I would rather die.

I would rather finally, truly, go crazy, if I have not already. But the grief is awash on his features, and I've always been a coward and I cannot deny that little voice that is still in my head telling me to do what I must, be who I must, to keep Jack, to keep the only person who keeps me from being alone. To be better so his worry can settle, so he can love me. But *better* feels too far off in the mind and body that feel less like my own with each passing moment.

Once more I cannot say the truth to Jack around the dimness that floods through my system. I do not want to have to make a decision. I want to continue on in this purgatory where I can have both and do not yet need to decide, need to change. For without Jack I am without my life, my home, everything I've come to know, entirely on my own. But I fear that without Theo I am without my heart. I do not want to decide, even if the stagnation comes with the darkness within me, at least it is familiar.

Things with Jack may not be perfect, but it is better than being on my own. I am not certain I can keep Theo, and I have never been able to keep myself, whoever that is. But still, the thought of losing Jack is overwhelming. Too much would go with him—my life, the memory of those moments we were good, any ability to convince myself that I am, or ever was, a good person. I do not think I would survive myself again.

"Okay, I'll think on it," I say.

Inside I scream. I am surprised I can do that much, that the blight inside me has not already stolen every kind of voice that I have.

I cannot breathe inside this body, cannot exist inside this skin.

It is a good thing Jack doesn't touch me. I am not in here anyway.

I fall into a memory, it must be three years ago now, Jack and I in a pub in some corner of London, the sounds of our friends laughing and strangers hooting all around. The world did not yet overwhelm me then, not all the time at least, and we were smiling at each other. Jack's arm was strewn across my shoulder in mindless, casual intimacy, regardless of the eyes around us, so proud of and comfortable in the *us*. Jack was telling some story about a passer-by or pubgoer with a face worn to swirls in my memory who had laid a hand on my waist. Jack smiled as he told the table how I snapped at the man, how I stood my ground, how "my girl is a tough one, don't mess with her." How my body used to be a home I would fight to protect.

I want to go home.

Would the doors of my body even open for me anymore? What a fool I was to think that Theo had brought me back there. Here I am again, so quickly, lost on the streets, left to the cold, floating adrift with no tether back. As bad as the doctors always warned I could get.

Jack's voice, "My girl's brave."

Brave, brave.

Mine.

When did I stop being my own and start belonging to everyone else?

I do not know that woman anymore. I am not brave. I am not anything. I have fallen away, and I didn't even go kicking and screaming. I simply faded.

What a waste.

Is this life with Jack a reality that I actually want enough to bring me back to the surface, put me back in my body? I do not know.

I think of Theo and sun-drenched floors and the soft burgundy flower petals swaying in the spring air. An impossible meeting, an improbable pairing, but maybe it could be, maybe it is what I want, what I need.

Maybe, maybe.

But that is not my reality now. My reality is a man with sandy hair and dark hazel eyes and a tightly pursed mouth sitting in front of me asking me to make true on the bargain I struck a year ago. My first love, but it seems not my last, after all. And if I say yes, I will be saying no to that other man, that other life, that other maybe. It was my cracking that drove Jack and me apart and now the cracks are back, deeper, and the shadows slip through and through.

I can feel myself fraying at the edges.

How much longer can you hold on, Saoirse?

So I am lost in the haze of my mind, cannot see the path forward, but I know that I must find it regardless. I know that I must choose.

Chapter 29

At the edge of my vision, I see Theo's hand resting against the side of my face. But I do not feel it, there is no warmth across my skin beneath his touch. There is nothing, or if there is, it is very little. It is not enough to reach me down here in the cloudy depths of my mind. It is like a touch you might feel when a hand sits atop your leg, buried beneath layers and layers of woolen blankets, so far from your body that the touch is silenced.

The house did not give me a moment to breathe, not one. Jack walked out the bedroom door, his words still echoing in the room and in my mind, and then I thought I saw Theo's journal by the bedside. It is a companion I had, at some time, set aside for its counterpart made of flesh and blood. And then the gray light shifted to pinks and purples, my bare legs in a square of incoming light, painted in the sunset. I numbly watched it splash across my body.

Then the door creaked open once more and when I looked up, I was in a room that still breathed life, that still felt like it had a future, the furniture strong and sturdy instead of melting into its age. And then Theo strolled in like an image of my wildest dreams, so perfectly beautiful, eyes made greener by the golden light of the evening and the candelabra fixed to the wall, dark hair sitting in those same smooth waves.

I felt nothing. I wish I could, but I wasn't at the surface anymore.

I only return to my body, to the moment, when Theo's hand disappears, coming instead to cover his mouth. His body shakes with the power of the coughs that wrack through him, that he cannot seem to stop, a sound like sandpaper and gravel in his lungs, a scrape and ache that wakes me up, my body so viscerally connected to his that I can feel a phantom pain in my own chest.

Oh, my dear, my dear Theodore.

The air rocks through him, spine curving in a show of fragility, the sound echoing across the stone walls and being thrown back at us, a horrifying reminder of something I do not know. And then the moment passes and there is a long beat of silence. There are only the waves crashing against the cliffs beneath us and Theo's deep, labored breathing, the sound of jumbled rocks still buried there beneath the surface. Has that haunting noise always been there?

Then the man straightens back up, looks at me, and my concern pulls me forth a bit, just enough to see that there is more than green and gold in Theo's eyes. There is moisture gathered at the surface. There are thin arms of red veins hugging the edges and the faintest look of sadness, deep, deep within.

"My apologies. I can be rather sensitive to—"

"Don't tell me it's the weather or the garden, Theo. It's not." Why do my words sound like an accusation?

"It is nothing, my dear." Still so calm, he brings my hand to his mouth, kisses my knuckles, placing a seal on the envelope that he will not allow me to open.

I want to hold on to this, want to push it open, but my mind is barely strong enough to keep me near the surface. So I must let it go, but I do not think I will forget the way this mystery scrapes at the side of my brain, wondering what it is that must ail this man.

Theo smiles and I can see his mouth moving, but I hear nothing, his words—even his—unable to find my ears from whatever little dark, damp corner of my mind I have fallen into.

Help me, Theo, help get me out of here. You're the only one who can.

I want to tell him, want to show him every little fleshy pink piece of myself, inside and out, every little bit that I fear and loathe and love. I know, he has proven, that he will hold all of those pieces gently in his hands, cradle them with reverence and without judgment. I thought no one would ever, that Jack's affection was a fluke, was luck, but then here is Theo giving me so much more.

But Jack's words, Jack's question, is not something I can find the bravery to bring to my tongue now.

So instead, it sits in my mind, piled atop Alice's piercing, accusing gaze, weighing me down within my mind, holding me in the dark depths. The guilt could consume me whole.

I know that I must make some sort of decision. I cannot live two lives like this. In this state not only can I not truly belong to either man, but I have found that I cannot even belong to myself.

I want to belong to myself again. And maybe I want to belong to Theo too and want him to belong to me in return.

It is not only whether to marry Jack now that I must decide upon. Jack's question has snowballed into another decision— to say yes to Jack is to say no to Theo. Perhaps forever. What happens? A marriage, a death, a car holding the newlyweds driving back out of Langdon's gates? The moment I leave this house is the moment I leave Theo.

And that feels as inconceivable as saying my vows to Jack.

I must do something, must say something.

I bob back up near the surface of my body and hear Theo's voice fade away, filled with unspoken concern for me.

My words come forth without me asking them to.

"I won't be at Langdon much longer. I imagine it will only be a few more days until I'm expected to leave the house."

And what a gruesome, cruel way to discuss the worsening of Alice's health. Her name and her life are not even in the mouth of my concerns. But what a gruesome, cruel woman I've become. Everyone is the villain in someone else's story, and it is no surprise that I wear that role in Jack's. His family wrote that part for me long before I became a person who could fulfill it.

I want to see Theo's eyes widen, want him to grip my hands tighter, tell me we will figure this out. I want him to tell me he will not let me go.

Instead, he sighs and his lids fall down over his eyes and there is no determination in them, only sadness. Only resignation.

Fight for me. Theo, fight for me because I cannot fight for myself. Not on my own. I need you, I think I may always need you.

"Yes. I knew our time was limited. I had simply hoped that we could have more of it." His small smile is not teasing now, is not a smirk, but a mask for his sadness. Theo strokes his long finger across my knuckle and even now, even buried as I am, his touch still stokes the fire inside just a bit.

I cannot let this thing go.

I will never stop burning for him.

So let the fire eat me. I will be consumed by you and be happy to burn.

I spent so long thinking I was lucky to have Jack, that no one else would want me, even before my shadows consumed me. What we had was lucky, yes, once—it is no more. If Theo's affection has taught me anything at all, if there is a reason Langdon knew we must be woven together, it is that I do not need to rely on Jack's crumbs to feed me.

"Perhaps it's for the best," Theo sighs, and I crack—all the way down through my mind, through my heart, every inch of my body split in half. Theo has never made his words a weapon before but here they are, slicing me deeper than any phrase ever spit at me by his descendants.

"How can you say that?" The pain does not silence me, I do not shrink beneath it, but rather rise to the surface, the push of outrage at my feet. "What, am I just another woman you've gotten bored of? Are you ready to move on already?"

My words strike to hurt, to maim, but Theo does not allow them to make contact.

"You know that is not the truth, Saoirse." My face is in his hands once more, but despite my anger I do not shake him off. I melt into the touch and tears come forth, frustration and fear. "I never want to be parted from you, not for a moment. When I told you that I would love to give you that ring one day I meant it. You know the weight that that carries from me. But I do not see a way that we could have this future together, much as we may both desire it. And I do, my dear. I desire every moment of my life to be with you."

He presses his lips to mine, our mouths dancing together for a long moment before we part. For once, for the first time in a long time, I have something that I do not want to let go of.

Jack has given me a decision to make, but . . . is there another choice? Could it be possible?

Could I say no to Jack, could I disappear in the night, slip between Langdon's walls and back into its past, for good? A missing woman in my own time, but a found one in another century.

Could I spend my days and nights by Theo's side, ritualistically begging the house to let me stay here, to not take me back? Making sacrifices to Langdon to keep its favor? Doesn't this house bring us to where, to when we're meant to be? That could not be anywhere but here, with Theo, surely.

There is nothing to go back to. Was there ever?
Could it even be?
It is all I want.
I want it so badly that it feels impossible to have.
You are all I want, Theo. Only you.

Chapter 30

I fell asleep in no arms but my own, but I was still present, floating around within my body. I can see the two paths; I merely have to choose which route to take. But I have time— even if it is only one day until I have to choose to add a ring to my finger forever or remove the one I already have. But still, I have time, little as it may be.

Perhaps I should still feel guilt for what I have done, what I am doing. But I felt nothing but confusion and the faintest spark of excitement as I lay in bed staring at Jack's back last night. Excitement at finally, maybe, having a choice. No longer simply following Jack, too much darkness inside to see clearly for myself. But I can do it now, I must.

I had hoped that when I woke I would see the slashes of springtime light falling across the linen. See the sturdy backs of new, nineteenth-century furnishings. But I did not, instead I drifted into consciousness with a brain and a window full of fog.

I step from the bed, the duvet sliding across my body, springing forth the memory of Theo's hands running across this very same skin. Of his hands perhaps running over my skin forever.

I am still not in my body, not really, but I could be—I can see the surface, I could do it, I could become real.

Another day. I have another day to decide.

I do not need to walk down the aisle to Jack yet, there is no car idling in the driveway waiting to take us away.

I have time.

I pace to the window, but nature has hidden the world beyond. There is nothing but dark gray fog swirling, hovering in the air, condensing on the glass surface of the window, as though this house is the only thing that is real. As though nothing lies beyond these stone walls.

Against my will, my stomach begins to somersault, my Gran's old stories echoing down to me in the depths of my mind.

"The fog brings change."

Please, Langdon, keep the fog out there, do not let it be back inside me. It may waver now, but I know the world looked so clear for weeks, Theo bringing it all into sharp focus. I cannot lose the clarity, it is already slipping through my fingers with indecision.

I will not lose it.

It is as if the fog has spread inside as well, a stillness brought within. The weight of silence is all around. It is not the absence of sound but rather the heavy, poignant sound of nothingness. Goose bumps rise across my naked body in tandem, and I know immediately that something is not right.

I do not want to know what it is, almost wish that I could sink back down into the ignorance of my frenzied mind, but my coursing anxiety will not release me.

I gather the nearest clothes onto my body, shame joining my bloodstream as I slip into the dress I wore on my picnic with Theo back when I had first begun to wake up, stuffing a jumper of Jack's on top. It cannot conceal the guilt, cannot hold it in, but maybe it can keep out the icy chill that is running through the house.

I push my way out into the hall, out into the nothingness. I do not want to go—do not want to know what awaits me out here—but nevertheless my feet carry me down the hall, down the stairs, my mind a victim at their mercy.

I hear a collection of muffled voices behind the wall of the tea room, the room in which I first saw Alice, and the room where I saw her last.

Will I find the woman seated there, her son at her side, waiting for me to walk into the trap, caught and exposed? Will I enter to see Jack at the end of an aisle made of worn carpet, Edgar holding forth a bouquet of frozen flowers, me the bride stepped straight from my nightmares?

But I find none of these things as I pass through the doorway. Instead I see Edgar slunk deep into a chair, head down, fingers caught in his gray hair, his guard down in a way that has made him appear human for the very first time. A woman who I do not know is lurking by the window, eyes downcast upon her fingers, as they twist into one another. She must be Alice's hospice worker, a face I have never seen before, as I have not been here, not really. Not at all.

And then there is Jack, pacing against the far wall, blond hair standing on end in the way it often is after he's anxiously run his hands through it. His chest rises and falls, the movement shallow and quick, as if he's afraid to take in too much air, afraid of what will come out of him if there is ammunition to feed it.

And I do not need them to tell me what has happened. Because I already know.

How could I have thought that there was time? How very naive.

The clock has struck twelve.

I make no noise as I enter, but Jack turns to me immediately, body attuned to my every move, just like it was back when our bodies knew each other better than anything else in this world. My eyes lock on his, pupils nearly black, the whites streaked with red, the creases of his face filled with pooling tears.

The sadness comes first—my heart, even after everything, springing out of my body and reaching toward him. And then comes the heavy smack of guilt. Jack may have forgotten that I was human, but I have forgotten him to be the same.

All that he has gone through, months spent already grieving the inevitable that has occurred at last, and I have not been by his side.

Jack has not held my hand, but I have not reached out to hold his either.

How could I do what I have done? How is it that, even now, I fear that I will keep doing it if given the chance?

Neither of us is better than the other. And I know, deep down, I know that the timer has buzzed, that I may just make myself even worse. I might commit the biggest betrayal of all, if fate will allow me it.

Jack and I cross the room toward each other and he falls into my arms, the dam within him breaking, his tears coming forth freely. His body feels so unknown to me, my hands drifting atop him, unsure of where to settle. He is made of unfamiliar juts and ridges and I am not sure I have the right to touch them anymore.

"She died," Jack chokes out a brutal whisper, saying the words I already know. "In her sleep. She's just gone. She's gone, Sersh."

Jack cries like a young boy, curling himself against my chest like a child to their mother, already feeling the new chasm of his life, a place that can never be filled again. My chest aches beneath his cheek, with the weight of him, the weight of his grief, of everything that has come and everything that I may bring about. I do not grieve for Alice, and there is guilt in that, but the woman showed herself to be human so rarely to me that I am not sure what I could even grieve. I did not know her at all.

But I do feel that same deep, empty sadness for Jack. I have lived through what he does now, even if I was too young to remember it properly. I know the gap that will now forever be left in his life, even if he does have another parent left whose love will buoy him. I know that there's probably a tunnel Jack could slip down into in his mind now too, become a living ghost as I have been, even if he will never share the diagnosis that follows on my back.

I hold him for a long time, for once supporting us both on my shaking legs. Minutes, hours, days pass as I hold him. Who could know, when the world beyond the window does not shift, and the world within is no more? Time no longer exists in Langdon—it has run up. We are out of time on so many things. Who even knew the clocks were ticking until the sound has disappeared, plunging us into this haunting silence? For the first time, the estate itself seems to hold its breath.

At last Jack pulls himself upright, the flat of his palm wiping the water from his face, the movement like that of a small child. Lost, lonely, too fragile.

He is so hurt, and I know that I will only hurt him more. If I stay or if I go, I will hurt him.

Jack's gaze cuts to the empty chair that Alice so frequently haunted in this house, a woman of such fierceness that even now it is almost as if her presence still lingers there, a fresh, cutting remark ready for me on her tongue.

"I don't want to stay here any longer. I think it's time to leave Dad, yeah?" Jack's voice crackles, pain cutting into every word. If I long ago dulled the natural gleam of Jack Page, it seems the loss of his mother has turned out his light entirely. "It's—she's here still and I just . . . I can't be."

A sob racks through his body. It is so clear that no matter

how many brave faces Jack has put on, no matter how many times he said he was ready, that he had accepted it, he did not know the depths to which there was still to fall.

Edgar clears his throat, the noise echoing through the room, the grounds of Langdon for once not screaming in their haunting aerial voices.

"Yes . . . yes." He sounds lost, here but not. "We'll leave the day after tomorrow to start on the funeral preparations."

The day after tomorrow.

No, no, no.

"All right." Jack steps away from me, as though he's just now remembered the air that is meant to live between us. He makes his way toward the door, and I stand in my shock. "I just need to . . ."

I do not know if he passes the doorway without finishing his sentence, or if my panic has simply made me fall away from him.

Spencer—the name comes to my mind unburdened and it takes me a moment to remember that it was the one Alice wore before Page. Alice Spencer—was that a different woman? Could she have been if she'd stayed that way?

This is not the only path.

I can hear Edgar speaking distantly to the hospice nurse, but it is as though through a tunnel, echoed. *"Thank you for all your help, Martha."*

"Of course, Mr. Page. She was a wonderful woman."

I hardly hear it. My mind is somewhere else.

My own thoughts are screaming and echoing within my head, telling me that I have no time at all. I must decide.

And when the time to choose is staring me in the face I realize that there is no decision at all. I have already made my choice.

I am sorry to Jack for it, but I suppose it doesn't matter. He'll never see my face again to tell me as much. Maybe being rid of me will allow him to live at last.

That is what I tell myself as I make my way back through the hallways toward the bedroom, talking to the house in my mind all the while, calling to Langdon to wake up, to take me back into its familiar embrace.

Take me, take me one more time.

Take me and keep me.

Chapter 31

I wish I could say that I hadn't thought about it, that I was simply acting on instinct—that I wasn't foolish, merely ill prepared. But that's not the truth. I've been thinking about this decision for days now. Maybe even weeks. And it was never a decision at all. I was always going to do this.

I spin in the center of the empty bedroom and I have never felt as awake as I do now, a tremor coursing through my body and I can feel it all. Surely there must be some item here that's dear to me, something that I couldn't bear to part with forever.

But there is nothing. There is no one.

That's the problem.

Should I leave Jack a note? Try to ring my mum or my brothers, shock them with the sound of my voice after months of Jack being the only one who could muster the energy to pick up our phone? Would they even care?

No, no. I said goodbye to them without saying anything at all months ago. It just makes it all harder. I've made my decision and I can't look back.

I just need to go.

I strip hastily, trembling fingers shoving Jack's jumper far from me, not because the smell of his skin on it disgusts me but because it does not, despite everything. It still smells like home, but I have chosen a new one.

The house is so still, choked by the fog outside. There is not a crack of a floorboard or the creak of a wardrobe door. The house is giving me nothing, it will be my confidant no more, will no longer tell me if this decision I've made is the right one, if it will be the guide I need it to be.

It does not matter.

I fish the crumpled white form of Iris's borrowed dress out from my suitcase and pull it over my head, not caring that it halts and bunches on my form without the smooth guidance of Regency undergarments. *I do not care, I do not care, I just need to go.* This house, this time, it is suffocating me. If I don't get out now I'll fall into my head, fall into the hollow woman I am in this time, and I'll never get out, I just know it.

I need to go.

You need Theo.

I squeeze my eyes shut so tightly that the tears I did not realize had collected there sting relentlessly.

Please, please. Take me to him.

There are many things I can bare to lose, but I know that Theodore Page is not one of them.

When I open my eyes, the fog has lifted. Rain is pattering down on the window and maybe down my face as well, and I could kiss Langdon's freshly polished floors because, thank God, it's done it.

Thank you, friend.

I'm here. Exactly where I need to be.

"Theo!"

There is no time for subtleties. I cannot wait, it is all starting now.

"Theo!"

My voice is manic. Perhaps so is the smile on my face. I do not care.

I push my way out into the hallway, gold dancing across

the walls as the flames of the lit candles waver as I pass. The presence of the future, of the past, of things I cannot look at, is hot at my heels. There is fear inside me and worry and guilt, but if all of that is what brought me here, then it does not matter.

Then it is all joy, so much joy, yes.

The velvet on the stairs slips beneath my bare feet, my dress dancing in the wind behind me. I must look pulled straight from the pages of a Brontë novel. To think that a scene so similar once caused me so much fear. To think that it was mere weeks ago. To think that there was a time when I did not know Theo, that I was left alone to be trapped in my head, in this house. I would still be there now if not for Theo. He's given me the torch and I can see the path out of my own darkness.

I can see him at the end of it.

The frenzied, frantic search has taken shape in the shallow, quick breathing in my lungs. This run through the house consumes me, corners and halls and stairwells, but then I round a bend and there he is.

And of course it is there—sitting in the tea room in which I just held the sobbing, grieving form of my fiancé—that the dark-haired man who occupies my mind is sitting, as though he is waiting for me.

Theo rises to his feet as I cross through the doorway. I can only imagine what a sight I make, with my ill-fitting dress, haggard breathing, wild curls, and wild eyes full of visions of the future I have chosen.

"Are you all right? You look startled." Theo's wide steps bring him to me quickly, my hands lifted into his, the concern in those hazel eyes so at odds to the look that must be in mine. "My dear, are you well? Are you harmed?"

His gaze sweeps over my body, searching for the harm he fears, but there is nothing.

It is joy, it is all joy.

It is guilt and pain and the deep, nagging feeling of wrongness in my belly, but it does not matter. I have made my decision.

"I am wonderful."

I surge up, press my lips against his, slow to respond, hesitant in their still lingering concern for me.

"I've left. I'm staying."

Theo steps back in shock, but he does not release my hands and I do not know if it's because of my own grip or because he wants to be here, holding me, with me. His brows pull down, face heavy.

He doesn't get it. Why doesn't he get it?

"You've left your fiancé?"

No, yes, it does not matter, I am here. I'm here now. I'm here and I'm not leaving.

"I'm here. I'm staying here, with you. We can do it, Theo, I know it's not easy and we'll have to figure out how it is Langdon brings me here, I guess we'll need to ask the house every day to keep me or something. I think it brought me to you because we're the only ones that could understand each other and that's still true, so maybe it will just keep me here. I don't know yet, but why would it not? It wants me here, it clearly does. We'll figure it out. It brought us together, didn't it? It's just . . . I can't be parted from you. Not yet." Not at all. "I can't."

The concern on Theo's face breaks and he steps back into my embrace, brings his lips down to mine, tongue and mouth so alive with want, and I can nearly taste the joy there, the joy and hope for our future passing between our jointness. His hand finds its way to my hair, long fingers lacing into the auburn, tight at my scalp, holding me to him.

Do not let me go, do not ever let me go.

But then he pulls back and I can see that flicker of sadness back in his eyes and I hate it. There is no sadness here. There should be no sadness. This is supposed to be the beginning of our happiness. We deserve a happy ending, but this is not an end, this is our beginning.

The guilt is mine to bear, the shame is mine, and I will bear it happily if it means I have Theo's arms around me.

Please do not make me give this up. I'm above the surface at last. I've tasted the air, the fresh, sweet air, because of him. I cannot go back to the dark damp of my mind.

Theo's hands are on my face, thumbs stroking across my cheekbones, and why is there dampness there? Why does my body seem to know that my decision is not enough? Why has it produced tears for a cause I do not yet know?

Why must the other shoe always fall?

"Oh, my dear, there is nothing that I want more, in this world or the next."

Your words say this, but your voice does not.

"Theo, don't . . ."

Do not finish that sentence, do not say no, do not push me away.

Hold me, keep me, love me.

Say yes.

I have chosen, I have sacrificed what must be given for us.

Say yes.

"You cannot stay here, Saoirse. You know this."

"I can!"

My voice cracks, throat clogs.

The conversation has barely started yet I already feel my grip slipping, feel myself losing, falling.

No. No. Please, no.

"You cannot. I wish it were possible, you know I do. But it is not. Have we not always said Langdon is a fickle thing, a mystery? I believe we were fated to find each other, I do, my dear. But we cannot know for how long. We do not know how it brings you here, we do not even know if staying is possible unless the estate wills it. Besides, you have not lived in this time, you do not know the truth of it. When we are together it is . . . we are beyond time. But if you stay, we cannot hide away in this house forever. Even if you could somehow remain here outside of Langdon's walls, it would not fit, my dear. You are a woman of your era, you are not meant to be one of mine, much as I wish it could be."

The pad of his thumb strokes across the swell of my bottom lip, but I will not be silenced. I speak around his touch.

"I will become a woman of your time then. I will become whoever I need to be to stay here, with you."

The sadness in Theo's face blooms, eyes brightening with moisture.

The corners of my mouth pull down to mirror his unconsciously.

"I do not want you to be anyone but yourself, Saoirse. You need to be yourself, at last, and you cannot do that here. Our illicit affair has been beautiful, but I fear that that is all it can ever be. That that was all it was ever meant to be. I do not want your survival, your happiness here, to be dependent on me. It is not fair to you."

"It all depends on you already, no matter what time I'm in!" Like trading a fire for a flood, that's all it is. "You say the house might not keep me here forever, is it . . . do you think you will not *want* me here forever? Is that what it is?"

Theo shakes his head, his hand finding my face even as I flinch.

"I swear to you, that is not it, my dear. But Langdon does not always give us what we want, so much as what we need. What is meant for us."

And I am not sure this is meant for us much longer, he does not need to say.

Fated and doomed in equal measure.

The words fall out of somewhere deep within me. The truth spills forth at last, as it always will.

"But—if I go—it's just . . . I fear that if I leave you behind, I will always wonder what could have been," I finally manage. "I worry you may be the great love of my life."

Theo's eyes simply get sadder, gaze heavier on mine, so at odds with the small smile that has turned up his mouth.

"I worry you may be the great love of my life too." He is somber for a moment, eyes shining with wetness yet to fall.

I did not know I could be that for anyone, that I was even qualified for such a role. For being significant to someone. But as I look at the naked sincerity in Theo's face, I think perhaps I am worthy of that, in the right arms, the right life. If only I could keep it.

The thrill through me is a splash of color, it is the orange of every sunrise I have ever seen, the pink of every flower petal, the deep navy of every crashing sea wave, the green of every strand of grass that has kissed my bare skin.

But still, I know that it is not enough.

I can practically hear Theo's unsaid words in my head. *Do not make me say it, Saoirse. I cannot bear it. Do not make me speak.*

You said you wanted honesty, the truth. So be it. Then tell the truth to me, Theo, tell me what is hidden here, what the hearts in my eyes have kept me from seeing.

He hears what I cannot say as well, and it only makes the heartbreak crack a little deeper, to see the truth of how woven we have become. Threads braided together that can never be broken.

"And that is why I must tell you the truth. And the truth is that you cannot stay here and spend your life with me because my life is nearly at an end."

Just like that all the color drains from me, not only the hues Theo has painted me with, but every color I have ever possessed. It is darkness and it is grim and it cannot be true.

"No, you're not dying, Theo."

"I am, my dear. I am. Even if I were not, I would not allow

you to leave your family. You miss them, you should be with them, work to mend and rebuild. I know how important it is to hold family dear. You cannot let them go on my account."

For a moment all I can hear is the slightly haggard tilts of Theo's breath, but screams and pleas pass from our eyes.

I chose you, I chose here and this and now. I did not leave you. You cannot leave me. If I lose you, I may lose myself.

This was not how this all began; this is not how it's supposed to end.

"No. No, Theo. It's fine, I've decided. And you're fine, you are."

"No, I am not. I have been ill for quite some time. The lungs, I fear. It is incurable. I cannot say for certain how much time I have left, but I know I am worsening every day. I imagine it is mere months at the best."

"Stop talking about this like you're dying! You're not!"

"I *am*, Saoirse." Theo presses his forehead to mine, as though this touch, this place where we meet, can pass the love that could have been between us. The tears come to my eyes, spill forth, and I do not stop them. "I have known since the autumn. I have already stolen more time than the doctor told me I was promised. Perhaps I was kept here just so I could have what little time I've had with you."

I could not stop the tears now if I tried.

"And we can have more! I want every moment by your side, even if it is not many moments at all."

I press my lips to Theo's, feel the warmth there, feel the pulse of his tongue, everything that tells me he is still alive and so am I. We pull away and as though to banish any hope from my body, a cough rises out of Theo's mouth. And I can see that the fragility I saw before was no illusion, it was nothing temporary. It was the truth. He wore a mask of health around me—the entire time we knew each other—and I believed it because I wanted to.

I wish I could still believe it now.

"You will always be by my side, my dear. Even when you are not here in person, but simply in spirit."

"No! Come on, please, you know what I mean. Stop saying goodbye without saying goodbye. I'm not leaving."

"Then what becomes of you when I pass? You will have no life here. You do not belong here." Even from the depths that I am slipping into, drifting to cope with the pain of this moment, his words sting me deep.

"When that time comes, I'll go home then. Back to my time. But not now, not while I can still be with you."

I am begging, any shame or conscience that was left in my being has gone. I regret nothing but the moments I chose to be anywhere but here. My pride is gone, thrown out into the rain, and I beg him, I beg the house, *Please, please, do not take this thing I have just found.*

"But you cannot! Who is to say what you will return to? You have left without a trace, you have abandoned your fiancé, your life there. You will return to nothing at all. You cannot do that." Theo's voice is sad, heavy, but there is firmness there. I can push and push and the man will not budge.

"I don't care. I'll do it happily. Just let me stay here, with you, while we can."

The wind screams outside the window, taking the sounds of my heart right from my body. But it is not right. There is not meant to be howling winds or the darkness creeping into my vision here. That is not this Langdon, this is a Langdon of sunshine and springtime. But the shadows have found me, even here, even now. Maybe the darkness, the illness, the numbness, are all I am.

"If you stay until I am no longer . . . I cannot take your life from you that way, Saoirse."

"You already have my life!"

"But I should not! Your life is yours. You must live it. It is all I want."

"And all I want is you!"

"And what of yourself, Saoirse?" Theo sighs, the sound heavy against the rain beating down outside. "You cannot give your affection and devotion entirely to me, with no regard for yourself."

My breathing is shallow and I feel panic rising, clawing its way up my throat and across my entire body in an icy spread. I cannot feel my hands where they grip Theo's arms. *No, stay here, Saoirse, stay in your body.* "You can come to my time. A doctor in my time can fix you, they can undo this, I'm sure of it."

"That was never how it was meant to be, Saoirse. And it is not what I want. I have accepted my fate. I wish it were different, but it is not, and I will not take your future into the darkness with it."

"Do you really think there could be anything but darkness in my future without you?"

"Yes, my dear, I do," Theo sighs, and I know that this is the last word. He will say no more and there is no more that I can say. Theo has found the flaws in my brash logic, discovered the tears in my sails, and there is no way for the wind to blow through me anymore.

He is right, and how desperately I wish that he were not.

Our lips find each other once more because we both know that there is no more left to be said. Not now and perhaps not ever. I feel the cool moisture of my tears fall to pool between our lips, swirling into the dampness of our tongues as we find each other for the first time not with joy, but with desperation and fear and maybe a bit of the love that will never be allowed to bloom between us in truth.

But, oh, what could have been.

Theo's hands are exactly where they belong, making their way all across my body, thumbs stroking me to peaks, palms pressing into the swells of me. I wish those hands would never leave my body—what if I no longer have a body in their absence?

But I do now, and oh how I do, a body that Theo worships as he so often does. A body that he has made feel worthy of worship.

He guides me to lie upon the chaise, angling his body atop mine, hips pressed to hips, knees locked and tangled just as we are. The tears stream down the side of my face and I cannot stop them, would not, and they fall to dampen the spread of my hair on the pillow beneath me.

"Please." It is a whisper from my mouth, spoken directly into Theo's.

One hand holds my face, the other gripping the fabric by my hip, the dress I wore when we first became one and the dress I will wear as we join for the last time. Theo moves down my body, tongue and lips finding my neck, my shoulder, my collarbone, kissing the skin that pulsates with the pound of my heart beneath it. All of his motions are filled with such devotion, with such finality that it haunts me. The tears cannot stop and I am not sure that they ever will.

Our hands meet, fingers skating across one another, mine undoing the laces crossing his breeches that keep him from me, his hands deftly pushing up the hem of my dress. The fabric bunches around my hips and it is all too familiar and it is too much and never enough all at once.

His fingers find my warmth, but they are not what I need. I need more, as much as I can get.

"Please, please."

He pushes inside me and the feel of him is so familiar now but no less thrilling for it. The arch of my body presses my chest against him as it always does. I hasten the white linen of his shirt from his body and he does not stop his movements as I do. I'm in a frenzy to hold as much of him as I possibly can.

His lips pillow against mine, that dark hair tickles against my forehead, teases my eyelashes. His left hand meets my right, fingers weaving of their own instinct, for it is where they belong, sewn together. The fingers of my other hand press into Theo's back, nails reddening the smooth skin there, holding him to me and inside me as though maybe I can hold true enough to keep him here.

Theo presses his forehead into mine, and we are touching each other all the way down and still I wish that we could be closer, that we could merge into one, that I could heal him.

He continues on, our bodies flowing in and out of each other in waves, steady and sure and powerful. I wish I could open up more of myself, all of myself to him, but this is what I can offer us now.

My legs lift and wrap around his hips, lifting and holding him to me everywhere.

Stay, stay right here, beside me, inside me. This is where you belong.

His movements become shallow, but the pace reckless and quick, and I know that the end is coming though I wish it were not. And then there is one final push, the last bit of air knocked from us both, swirling between our open mouths.

Theo removes himself and the emptiness inside me is so much more than it has ever been. He rolls beside me, body pressed along the length of my own. It is then that I see that tears have fallen from his eyes too, damp trails left down his cheeks, a path of sadness over his cheekbones and down into the hollows beneath.

I wish you could have been the one.

How will I ever survive you?

With one hand on my jaw Theo guides my face to his, bringing our lips together. There is no more urgency, no more desperation. There is only gentleness and sadness and acceptance, and something on my tongue that tastes a little like love that will never be, bitter and sweet.

I cannot open my eyes when we part and my head finds its way back to the pillow.

Maybe I will stay down here, in the deep dark of my mind. Give up and free-fall.

I feel the absence first, feel the parts of my body that had touched Theo now pressed only to the air. Then it is the cold, the chill on my skin and in my bones, the ice spreading its way across me, snowflakes cracking the surface of everything that I am.

This cold will become me.

I know that I will never again feel the comfort of Theo beside me.

The tears fall faster, pooling in my eyelashes, and still I cannot lift them. I cannot yet see the truth that I know will greet me.

"Goodbye." My whisper is only for my ears now, I know that.

It was not my wish that the house obeyed, but that of its owner.

I thought that I had made my decision, but now Theo has made it for us both.

Oh, how I wish I could have kept you. Even if not forever, I wish I could have kept you just a little bit longer.

Chapter 32

I cannot be in this room any longer. Not without him.

I pull my dress down to cover my skin once more, and how foolish it feels, to have dressed for the future, within the past that I wanted so desperately. But perhaps I always knew, deep down, that I would not get to have it. I am wearing the dress of another time, the embodiment of my loss and grief, like a bride left at the altar, still haunting the halls in white.

The Langdon Hall of the twentieth century is cold, dark, and so much lonelier, so much deeper in this sadness, than it has ever been before.

As I make my way toward the stone staircase up to the library, I know I will not find Theo there.

I will never find him again. I know that too, with a certainty that stabs me deep in the gut, deeper than my guilt ever had.

But I cannot be in that little blue room where Theo and Alice have both said goodbye, cannot be entirely in this time either, not yet, so I will go to the place that seems somewhere in the middle. I know that I will not cross paths with Jack or Edgar there in the library, and I am thankful, for that is a feat that I am not yet ready to face.

I cannot look in Jack's eyes as I am now. I cannot yet choose the next path for myself, for us, as I know I must.

I cannot hold his grief in my hands as I should—they are already so full of my own.

The stone steps are chilled, my footsteps echoing back at me in the vast tunnel traveling upward. But there are no phantom footfalls, no curtains rustling from passers-by unseen. It is merely an old house filled with two men, a woman neither of them sees, and the memories of their beloveds.

The large office door creaks in its opening and booms in its closure once I have slipped inside.

And maybe it summoned me here, or maybe I called out to it, but of course the dark, decorated face of Theo's journal is sitting on the empty seat, waiting for me, exactly where it was when I first met the man through those words upon paper.

My hands shake as I lift the journal and settle into its now-vacant seat. The fire doesn't dance beneath the mantel as a reminder of Theo's presence in this space in some other timeline. But I do not expect it to, not anymore. The house has given me Theo and now the man himself has decided that we should be parted. There will be no more phantom echoes of a lover for me.

The words on the page are difficult to read through the tears still gathering in my eyes. But the words make themselves known to me, as I knew they would, for they are meant for me and perhaps they always were. Seeing the labor of Theo's hand does not smother the fire smoldering in me, does not dry the tears. It wrenches me open, flooding my mind and eyes with memories that I will cling to. It stokes that little flame in me that I know will always flicker, casting light across the shadows within the deepest depths of myself.

Oh, my Theo.

April 11, 1818
The truth of a thing can be seen in earnest by gazing upon what one hides even from oneself. For me, there is much I

have kept hidden—from those I love, from the page, from myself.

My feelings for Miss Read, for Saoirse, are of a strength and depth that is undeniable now. I fear that she is what I have long sought, what I believed could not be true, what I thought would never be meant for a man such as myself. Yet, here she is. And still I fear putting the truth down upon paper, as though taking my quill to ink and saying these words makes them so.

What a fool I am to believe that they are not—that she is not—already having a hold upon me.

It is not merely the barrier of time and society that divides us, no. For my affection for Miss Read has cast the light of truth upon my life, and I can no longer deny the grim that lurks, awaiting me.

I am on borrowed time, as I have been for too long. I believed I had accepted my fate, come to peace with what will inevitably come to pass. But Miss Read has shown the shallow falsehood of these beliefs. As long as there is a way to hold her hand in mine, I will never truly accept that I am to be no more. For once, I truly wish to live.

Time is not the greatest deterrent of love, nor society, riches, mothers of the ton. *I was a foolish boy to believe as much.*

It is death, above all, that stands in love's way.

If I am to speak the truth to this page now, then yes, I must admit, that it is love that I believe it could have one day been. Had only fate looked upon us with a different face. For fate is what it must have been to bring us together, despite it all.

The sob that racks through my body echoes back to me from the curved walls of the library, and the wind outside howls its grief to mirror mine. How will I ever live with the weight of our what-if? Theo bears the burden of his ticking clock, its click within these walls. But I must learn to live the rest of my life, always holding the hand of a ghost of a love that never got to be.

The pages are soft on my fingertips and I imagine Theo's own hands here, those fingers that I know so well, that I long for and perhaps always will, stroking across these same rigid edges, creating these little forgotten pools of ink.

But I will not forget. I will never.

April 24, 1818
I preach the value of honesty and yet today I cannot find it. There are no words today, and I am not certain I will ever have words again. I have made the decision, I have reclaimed what little bit of power fate has left to us. I have given Saoirse her life, and in doing so I have taken her from mine.

The ache in my chest now cuts much deeper than whatever that being is that grows inside me, eating my life and taking it from me. From today on, I fear my life has already gone.

May 2, 1818
I have barely accepted what shall come to pass. But I could not allow my sisters to remain in the dark, to one day receive a letter from the staff and learn that I have slipped away in the night, with them both ignorant to the fact that I have long been fading.

Nell wept and wept and I fear that she will never stop weeping. Even now, she roams the halls, the sounds of her grief for a life not yet taken are as constant as the wind in wintertime. Iris expressed her sorrow, but she is of a more pragmatic character. The distance within her that has always kept us apart is now the very thing that will survive the Page name when I pass. She and Charles shall be with child soon, and I speculate that I will not be here to welcome the babe.

We have agreed that, in my passing, they will take up residence in Langdon and the ownership and power of the house shall pass to her. Their son shall bear the name of Page, important to both me and to the family legacy. A legacy I cannot carry out, but such is not my course.

It is all too clear, even through my grief, even through the anger that I hold toward Theo for making such a decision for us, that every word he said was in truth. Much as I may wish that it was otherwise, his words are there on the paper. His decay is before me, just as he said would come to pass. He did not cut me off because he wanted to. He let me go because he knew that he must.

It is a comfort that does nothing to quell the pain throbbing within my bones.

May 14, 1818
The edges of life feel a bit thinner now. The veil between the Theodore Page that is and the Theodore Page that is no more seems to flutter every day, and I find I am trapped between. The pain is regular, the sadness constant, but there is peace too. I believe I have finally come to peace with what shall be.
It is for the best, ~~as I fear~~
No, I know that my time is soon.
My hands have caught a chill that has gotten into my bones and has yet to release me. My days are spent abed, walks in the garden with Blackjack by my side a rarity.
It feels as though everything that has made me feel alive, that has reminded me that I am, is falling from my grasp piece by piece. I am lucky to have my sisters still by my side, their love keeping me.
I hold too the memories. Memories that I could not hide from within Langdon, not even if I so desired.
It is this that keeps the fire within me burning, that keeps me present.
One memory, perhaps, the most powerful of all. My time passes, so often trapped in this bed, but in my fevered dreams

*Saoirse is beside me. It makes the pain lessen, even as I know
I will wake alone once more.*

*But I shall always remember that, once, I was not alone here.
I had my Saoirse, though I hope that she no longer finds herself
within Langdon's halls in any time. I hope she finds herself out
among the world in truth.*

The words stop in the middle of the page, the stretch of
nothingness, that expanse of yellow parchment taunting me,
for all I want is more. More of Theo's words, Theo's touch,
more of Theo. All of him would never be enough.

I do not attempt to assuage my flow of tears until the droplets of water slide from my face and splatter upon the page in
my lap, their moisture making the ink of Theo's words, his
last words, bleed out into an ocean of black. I pat the page
hastily, my fingers coming away smeared in dark ink that
must streak across my cheeks as I frantically scrub the tears
from my face to keep more from falling, to keep them from
stealing the words.

I cannot lose these words; they are all I have left of him.
They are all I have left.

And in my haste the thick of my hand pushes back the
pages and there, after several swatches of blankness, is that
handwriting I know once more. More swirls of ink across the
page, waiting for me.

Waiting for me in truth for there, atop the page, is not a
date but a name. My own.

Saoirse,
*I hope that these words bring you comfort. There are so
many things that I wish I could have said to you, that I could
still say to you. Not on the page, with centuries between us,
but that I could have said upon your lips, holding your hands
in mine.*

I have thought about that decision I made every day since.

But I do not regret it. Given the chance to do it all again, I would, exactly as it was, even our most painful parting. For I know, deep down, that though it aches, it was for the best. Perhaps not in my own interest, but in yours. And you are what matters to me, far more than the temporary beating of my own heart.

I hope that you do not fault me this, my dear. I hope that you see that in sending you back to your time I cut the cord of Langdon that bound us physically. Not because I desired it, but because I knew I had to. But nothing, not time nor death, can ever break that woven thread that ties us together, that wraps around each of our hearts like the ivy upon Langdon's stones, and keeps our hearts, our very souls, connected together for all eternity. No matter how soon eternity may come to pass. Our strings were always tied to each other, our paths were always meant to cross. We are inextricable from each other. As we are meant to be.

And for this, I will never forget you, not while I live and not in death. Nothing can make us part in truth.

Know that I will think of you until my last breath. But still, I cannot find it in me to regret sending you from me. For it is not you that should be by my side when I release the last of the little air that resides in my lungs, just beside the heart that will always be yours. Though I cannot, you, my dear, should be living.

You are so much more than the things that darken your mind and make you fear and forget yourself. If others cannot see that, it is their loss, not your folly to remedy. I know you, Saoirse, perhaps more than any other soul could, brief as our time together may have been. I have been where you are, feared myself as you do. It is not darkness within you. It is truth. It is.

And it is only you that can decide what binds you and where your life shall go. I have set you free as best I can. I made our decision, but you must make your own now.

Know that you do not need anyone else, do not need to see the world the way others do, to have a life worth living.

I hope you have decided to find your freedom, my dear.

And then there is nothing but blank pages, empty parchment until the back cover of dark leather.

Theo has said his final goodbye.

You will always be my greatest what-if, the most beautiful almost love of my life.

I am afraid to find anything at all in this world where Theo Page does not exist. But he never did in this one, not in truth. Here I have only myself. And perhaps I can finally find out who that is once more.

For he is right, I must make my own decisions now. There was a third option I never even considered, could not see through the pain. It was not just the choice of Jack or Theo, past or future. I could have also chosen myself. I still can.

Fingers still shaking, eyes wet and cheeks streaked with tears, I stand from the chair. I contemplate taking the journal with me or tucking it away into the endless array of books upon the shelf to perhaps be found generations from now, by another woman who may one day be a Page.

But in the end, I set it back down upon the empty seat.

This journal found me, time and time again. If it is meant to find me once more, then it will.

I will no longer be leaving my life, my fate, in the hands of any Page or the estate that they have long called home. But just once more, I will leave something up to Langdon to decide for me.

After all, it has never led me astray before.

Chapter 33

Maybe I should wait a day. Sleep on it. It's no small decision, I know that. I've felt it rattling around inside me for
months, years maybe, long before I knew what it was. I've
had to do this since the moment that Jack got down on one
knee before me. I should have done it then, but if I had I
wouldn't have met Theo.

And now it is time for one more parting. A decision that
will be entirely my own, though am I ever alone, when I can
still close my eyes and feel Theo's hands on me, feel that little
flicker of light burning within me?

For you, for you.

I wish that the timing could be different, but it cannot be,
so I take it for what it is. And I am sorry to Jack, though I
truly do not believe it will give him another thing to grieve.
It is not another death in his life, the loss of us. It is merely
exposing the slow demise that has been *us* for too long now.
We have already done our grieving.

I stalk the dimmed halls for him, my pace quick, feet desperate to take me to him, to make my decision, to speak it
aloud and bring it into being.

My hands tremble, but the nerves that do this are old, they
are a memory of a fear I held for so long, not the fear itself.

My footsteps echo off the empty halls, the house silent within, the world silent without, beneath the blanket of falling snow that covers us now that the fog has lifted.

The fog has lifted.

I wouldn't have spotted him if the place didn't mean so much to me now, if the balcony beyond the ballroom wasn't tethered to my heart, woven into the tapestry that is Theo and me. And on it now sits a different man who gave me the same ring as the other, hunched back to me, shoulders and golden hair dusted in the white of a late January snowfall. Positioned like that, hunched into himself, his grief sitting on his shoulders and pushing them downward, Jack doesn't look so much like the villain I've come to think of him as in my life.

He looks like a small boy, lost, alone. I hate to worsen that for him, to add another weight upon his back. But I suspect that, if anything, I will lighten the load he carries. I will be stripping him of the decay he has dragged behind him, that we have both dragged behind us and between us, for years.

We are both, in a sense, guilty of holding a dead thing in our hands for far too long. We hoped to give it life, but instead were the victims of the monstrosity it became.

I slip between the crack of the open doorway, the snow melting and scattering beneath my feet as I make my way to Jack. Those empty places where the granite flashes through the snow in the outline of my steps reminds me that I am alive, and oh, I am. I am now. I do not want to go back into the nothingness. I want to have this body, I want to see the mark that I make as I move through the world.

And it is only you that can decide what binds you and where your life shall go.

I do not know if Jack hears me as I walk, if the snow muffles my footsteps, or if the screaming of his grief does. But he does not look up at me once, not even as I sink down onto the cold stone step beside him.

It chills me, right through the thin fabric of my dress, the backs of my legs taking on the numb bite of winter. But I can feel it because this is my body and I am alive. I am in here.

"Hey." I do not try to put a smile in my voice. It would be a shallow gesture, twice over.

A sigh.

I will not let the weight of Jack's breathy agitation at my very existence push me down until I hardly exist at all. Not anymore.

"Hey." His voice is empty and even now, even after everything, I only feel sorry for him.

Jack still does not look at me and I do not look at him. Both of us gaze outward, toward the decaying, crumbling form of the garden maze, toward the darkened cliff drop, toward the ocean, restless and angry but free.

I can almost see Theo there, Blackjack at his heels, strolling carelessly between the hedges, dark hair lifted in the breeze, his feet leading him, always, toward the cliff, toward the sanctuary that is his greenhouse. This Theo would turn to me, his eyes easily and immediately finding me despite the acres of grass between us. And I would spot the way his lips, those lips I can still feel dancing against mine, tip up at the edges into that flirtatious smirk, an expression just for me.

My heart lurches and I feel a deep ache in my chest that I will never see that sight again, not really. But even this pain holds me to my body, Theo keeping his hand in mine always, never letting me fall entirely into the rabbit hole of my mind.

I wonder if Jack is seeing his own phantom among the empty grounds.

I wonder if we will ever not be haunted by all that has happened and all that we have done.

"I wanted to talk to you—" I start.

"Can it wait? I don't have the energy for a meltdown or something right now, Sersh. I really don't."

I am strong enough to deflect the weapons of his words

before they puncture me now, before they can create a hole through which all of the air within me, all of the *me* within me, can seep out.

"I'm sorry, but it can't really."

A sigh, sharp and scratching. I can still feel it, but it does not cut the same. I do not shrink to fit what he wants me to be.

"All right, fine." Jack still gazes out at the garden, all life frozen from it, withering. "Is this about leaving? I'm just as eager as you are to get back to London. Like Dad said, we'll head off as soon as we're able. A day or so, all right?"

"It's not about leaving."

Is it not, though?

"Well, what then?"

I look at Jack at last. At the way his pale skin and hair melt into the white air of winter, at the smooth slope of his nose, at the puff of lips I used to love kissing, a jawline that used to feel like it was made to be cupped in my hand.

My God, Jack, how did we get here?

But I know I cannot stay with him, even if I am staying in this time. I have been loved twice, and I have loved as many in turn—love will find me again. I will try to give it to myself. I deserve that. I am no longer the person Jack believes himself to be engaged to, promised to, and I'm not sure I ever was.

"I think we should split."

I look at Jack and he still does not look at me, and that, this moment here, that's the truth of it all, isn't it?

"What're you on about? I just said we'll leave in a few days. Please, Saoirse—"

I fight the urge to lean into the misunderstanding, to stay silent, to stay with him. I do not want to hurt Jack more, not when I know he already aches. But if I stay all I will do is hurt us both. All I have done so far is hurt Jack, through my actions and just in who I am. I must act, for both of us.

"I mean that I think we should split up, Jack. You and

I." A beat of silence. The air filled with the white clouds of frozen breath, coming quickly. "I think we should break up."

As though I've woken him from a trance, and maybe I have, Jack sits up straighter, his eyes open a bit more, and finally they turn to look at me.

"Are you serious?"

It is not a plea to stay, not a reaction born of shock and hurt. Maybe it would have been if either of us had been brave enough to do this when we should have.

But I'm doing it today, at last, and Jack's response is a flicker of hope behind his dark eyes. It hurts to see but finally, it is the truth, even if he has not yet realized it himself.

My grief meets Jack's, and there we can finally find a middle ground. Maybe we can see each other in truth for the first time in a long time.

"Yeah, I'm serious."

For a moment we do not speak, both brains whirling through memories and finding that they're all that's left. The howling wind tangles the blood red of my hair and Jack's sigh is not sharp with condescension, or rounded with acquiescence, but large and relieved and honest.

"Wow. Um, okay. Are you certain? I know there's a lot going on at the moment, what with Mum . . . and I know how overwhelmed you can get, Sersh." There's a bit of kindness returned to his voice at last. It is not a return to the boisterous, outgoing man he was years ago, but the gentle, caring being he used to be in our private moments. We are both still human. We are both just human.

"I really am sorry to do it now." I think about reaching my hand out to him and for a moment it hovers extended between us and then I draw it back to my lap. Why make false moves of empty comfort? I wish him well, but I do not want to be the one to see him there. Yes, I think I understand Jack a bit better now. "But I'm certain, yeah."

"No, that's . . . yeah, okay."

"Are you all right?"

"Yeah, yeah, right. I'm fine. I just . . . I didn't see this coming, Saoirse. You never gave any warning sign of this."

I gave so many signs, so many times, you had simply learned to tune me out.

You had seen it coming, you just thought you would be the one to do it, thought I was too asleep to be the one who woke up to us first.

"I guess I just realized it was time. And it is, don't you think?"

"Is there someone else?" Jack's words hit with me a spark, glinting off of the buried truth.

"No, it's not that."

And it is not. I should have broken my path from Jack's even without falling into the arms of another man. I cannot say for sure if I would have had the foresight, much less the bravery, to do so without Theo, without seeing the potential for love, honest love. If I would have realized I, as I am, might be worthy of that. Still, this is not about Theo. No, this, finally, is about me.

"That's good at least, I suppose."

Another breath out.

I'm sorry I hurt you, Jack. And I'm sorry that you hurt me too.

"But it's for the best. You see that, yeah?"

Jack thinks for only a beat before he responds. He already knows.

"Yeah, I do."

There are so many things still buried beneath the history of us, years' worth of words still left unsaid, yellowing bruises we've left on each other's hearts and minds. But I do not need the closure, not from this. It is closed and it should have been long ago.

This is not the relationship I'm losing right now, not really.

Maybe this is not the way it should have ended, Jack and

me, not after all these years, not with me grieving the loss of another love, not with words like weapons always pointed at each other, not with both of us living our lonely lives in parallel with each other.

But this is how it has happened nevertheless. And I am glad that I was the one to do it first, for it was always going to be done.

See how strong I can be, Jack?

The bitterness is still there, and I suspect that it always will be. But the wounds we've inflicted on each other run deep and they will take time to heal and even when they do, we will both be left with scars. But that is okay. Jack and I are in the process of healing now, regardless. This is not the worst loss either of us are suffering now, anyway.

There are no hard feelings because I almost regret to say that there are no feelings at all. We have both been, silently, in our own ways, grieving the death of us for many months. The body is long since buried, the funeral has been held, we are simply only now reading the eulogy.

But it's for the best. It's for the best.

You can be rid of me now. I will no longer be the wrinkle in the pristine press of your life.

I set you free, Jack.

I set you free, Saoirse.

Every step, every falter and slip I took on this path with Jack brought me to this house, to myself. And for that it will always be worth it.

Finally, Jack reaches his hand toward me, the tight, icy skin of my fingers meeting the same in his. He gives my hand a gentle squeeze and I am reassured at last.

Chapter 34

My hands are empty as I make my way down the stone steps that guide me toward the mouth of Langdon Hall. Jack has taken my bag this time, his footsteps a steady beat behind me, following my path for the very last time. Maybe the very first time. I have never been the one to lead before.

My goodbye to Edgar had been easy, brief, so many years in the making already. So many years and yet there was little to say to each other. Nothing was new in that regard. I could see the relief in his face as I'd said goodbye. And as I began my trudge to leave his beloved estate, I realized I would grieve the loss of the place more than the family who now resided within it.

The woman had never given me anything but vitriol, but I almost regret that I could not have said goodbye to Alice, that she had not been here to see this. To see her son and her family be rid of the woman who did not deserve them. It could have been the last great joy of her life.

What a bitter, bitter woman I have become. But I have become.

I can see the big stone doorway now, can already hear the rumbling engine of the cab Edgar has called for me, patiently waiting in the driveway beyond. I am so close.

But then, from high up on the wall, I feel a pair of eyes looking upon me. Not the cold, dreaded kiss of all of those hazel Page gazes, judging me from behind the paint, finding me unworthy. It is *those* eyes, the ones tinged with a swirl of green, even if the artist failed to capture it, those eyes that have roved across my body and soul, those eyes that see deep into me, even now.

One last time I look into the beautiful face of Theo Page, still and peaceful and captured in paint strokes to sit on the wall here, where he will always remain. He looks different there in stillness, more like a distorted memory of the man I knew, but the same one nevertheless. I wonder if the portrait he created of me is tucked away within Langdon somewhere or if, like the woman off the canvas, it will fade from the memory of this place, blissfully forgotten.

I will meet you again. You will always be in my heart and in my mind.

Looking into those eyes one last time, I swear I can hear Theo's voice, feel his lips tickle against my ear as he speaks words meant only for me. Perhaps this is the last gift that this place will give me, one last shock of energy through that connection that binds us.

I am so ready to step out of this house now that I nearly miss it. In the highest corner, tucked away far from the chandelier's reach is a portrait made of rich colors, swirling hues so much brighter than every other face on this wall. Because that portrait was painted with love. I stand on the stairs, looking up at the painting of me made by Theo's hand and I recognize myself in those spring shades now.

The portrait is slightly dulled with age but looks at home where it sits, like I have been sat upon that wall for two centuries. It's as if Theo could not leave Langdon, leave life, without ensuring I had a permanent place in the estate. For just a moment I linger and look at that Saoirse, made of rose and ivy and cerulean, a woman who was just beginning to wake.

Theo ensured I would remain in Langdon, and the house it-self has made certain that I will see this beautiful memory one last time before I leave.

Oh, Langdon, and its little quirks, its long reach through time.

Goodbye, my dear.

Goodbye.

I continue down the steps and I do not turn back, I do not waver. I open the door, an echoing creak splitting through the stone hall. The gravel drive sits before me, the green stretch of cliff past the gates of Langdon. The world beyond looks so bright now, such a contrast to the gloom within the estate. For a moment I stand there, on the precipice of two binaries, two lives. Then I step through the doorway and out into the world.

I stand beside the car as Jack jimmies open the boot of the cab, dropping my bag inside with a thump. Then he turns to me, the weight shed from his hands. We can finally look each other in the eye now, no longer afraid to see the truth. It is what it is. Perhaps we finally see each other as human again, not just the villain of the two separate stories we have each been writing within our minds.

Jack's face is different now, and it is not only because I feel as though I can see him in earnest for the first time. He is darker, etched with the loss and grief that will always be written into his skin, that will sink in and become who he is. He has always judged the twilight in me, but maybe now he can understand the life I have to live a little bit more. Maybe he will understand that sorrow racing through the bloodstream and weaving into the brain isn't a flaw or a chal-lenge or a mark that can be wiped away—sometimes it just is. Maybe I can understand that now too. Some are born with our shadows and others grow over time.

It does not matter, not anymore. But it is now, as we will part, that I think we can both finally remember what it was like to truly love each other, all those years ago. It is a shame it took all of this to bring those memories back.

Jack steps toward me, hands opening to his sides, shoulders rising and falling. *That's it, folks,* his gestures say. *The show is over. The curtain is closing. Please take all your belongings on your way out the door.*

As always, I cannot help but be his opposite, my arms sitting close to my body, my fingers still twisting against one another. Unease is all I have come to know around this man, even in our final moments. But they are that, our final moments at last.

My nail strikes off of something hard and oh yes, there it is, the ring still sitting on my finger. That growth, the barnacle that took hold in my skin, the metal circlet that acted as my handcuff to this family. That round of diamonds perpetually branding themselves into my skin, making me another property under the Page ownership, another thing that they would wish to cast aside into the depths of the attic, to rid themselves of.

But now the ring does not feel so heavy. It feels as light as I do, and maybe I don't hate it so much anymore, now that I do not look at it and remember the sinking stomach of saying yes to a man I do not wish to wed. Instead, I can imagine bright green eyes and a smooth-skinned palm, that ring sitting in the outstretched hand of a man whom I wish I could have held on to with the devotion that this silly little piece of jewelry is meant to symbolize.

But still, I slide it off of my fourth finger, flexing my hand, testing the new weightlessness, the freedom. I feel the cold air of the clifftop lick at the bit of skin that has been covered up for a year. I hold the ring out toward Jack. He looks at it, then to me, and for a moment I see him contemplate, see him consider his words. In those dark hazel eyes, I see the memory that we share, that spring afternoon in Hyde Park, the way the sun lit up the gold of his hair as he got down on bent knee before me. I see the way he huffed afterward, worried that the grass would stain his trousers.

I see Jack and remember it all. I wonder if he knew then, as I did, exactly how this would end. If in our future he saw a stark period, a stop on the page, in a story that we had once hoped would never end. If he knew that maybe this ring was meant to be mine after all, but never like this, never from him.

Jack takes the ring from my hand and the diamond winks at me one last time before he tucks it into the tiny pocket of his button-down, where it can rest over his heart, recharging before it finds the finger of the next girl, who maybe will be worthy enough to wear it.

The free fall before me makes my heart pound, liberation taking the vacant seat by my side that fear has left.

"Can you . . . will you be able to find your feet on your own, Saoirse?"

"Yeah, I think I'll be all right."

And I am shocked to find that I actually believe the words that I say.

How lightly the truth can come forth now, now that these weights have been lifted from me.

"Bye, Jack."

I turn, hand on the cold metal of the door handle, when Jack reaches out and stops me.

No, no. Let me be free.

But when I look back at him there is no plea or remorse in his eyes. But there is the journal in his hand. Theo's journal. It has made its way back to me one last time.

"I figured you'd want to take this, yeah?"

"Yeah." I take those beloved words, my first friend here, hold it to my chest.

"I didn't realize you were, but I'm glad to see you're writing like your counselor recommended for . . . you know, your health."

"What?"

Jack points to my chest.

"The journal."

The wind around us picks up.

"What are you talking about, Jack? I'm not writing. This journal isn't mine, I was just reading it. We found it in the attic, remember?"

Those dark brows before me pull down.

"Well, no, I know, there's a few entries in there from, like, centuries ago, but I flipped through briefly and all the rest looks like your handwriting, Sersh."

"What? No, I've never written in here."

No. No. No.

My heart is in my throat and I cannot breathe around it.

I feel a heat rise in me and the journal feels like it could burn me, could melt the tender skin of my hand to it, merging us forever.

"I'm fairly certain that's yours . . ." Jack continues pressing the point, though I try and fail to blot his words out. "I didn't read any of it, if that's what you're worried about. But it's good for you, Sersh. It's really good, I think."

Jack's words latch on to something in my brain, but I do not want them there, I do not want whatever lies sleeping there to wake.

"Christ," Jack had said to the doctor, "what the hell is depersonalization-derealization disorder? That sounds . . . serious."

"It is," the doctor had said, and his stoic face mirrored his words. "But there are ways to cope. Environment will be important. As well as support."

Jack had dropped my hand then.

The memory is an echo in my mind.

No, no. He wants you to stop believing yourself.

Do not stop believing yourself, Saoirse.

A crack begins to split through the center of my chest, halv-

ing me, pain such a physical, visceral beast now that I live in
my body once more. My breathing quickens, shallows, the
air stinging through the angry red path in my chest. Theo's
face rises in my mind, his eyes, his hands, *him* fading to mist.
Fading to shadow, to nothingness, perhaps as he always was.
Emptiness is already starting to set in, held at bay so briefly
since Theo told me of his illness. That deep, weeping chasm
that takes up home inside you when someone you love is no
more. Or never was.

Maybe I should have grieved Alice, grieved the parting
from Jack, but, oh, has the grief come for me at last, Jack's
words waking it like a snake to twist around my chest. Rob-
bing me, breaking me.

It cannot be. It cannot. Or perhaps it could. Who I am
to know what is truth? Perhaps there is no being a waking
woman for me, perhaps I am too far gone, too lost. But once
I was not, once I was not alone.

If it was all in my head, tell me now, someone, please, before this ache in my chest rips me in half, pulls me back down
into myself, my body lost again, my mind and heart a mocking villain. I have worked so hard to come back to myself,
we have worked so hard, Theo. I cannot lose it again. And I
cannot, will not, lose you either.

That's your hand . . .

If I can just go back inside I can spot my portrait on the
wall again, proof that Theo was real and what we shared was
real. Undeniable proof in aged paint right before my eyes. I
step forward, muscles poised to dash in, trembling with the
need to be reaffirmed.

But I stop before the gravel can crunch beneath my feet,
before I frantically prove to both Jack and myself that I do
not trust my own idea of reality.

Jack may have lived in this house, may have a birthright
claim to it—but I *know* Langdon Hall. While Jack and Alice
and Edgar moved through the estate like they owned it, I am

the one who truly lived in it, the one who made a friend of this place. Langdon showed me its secrets in a way the Pages' hubris, their vanity, would have never allowed.

I know Langdon and I know it plays tricks, wrinkles time and reality and expectation. I know this house's wily spirit. Maybe it is Jack who the house deceives and confuses in its humorous way, makes his eyes see writing that is not there, gifts him a duplicate of a journal I know well because it knows he could never, ever believe such a thing is possible. But I know it is.

Or maybe it's only my own mind that plays tricks. But for once, for the first time, given the choice of whether to believe Jack's reality or my own, I am choosing myself. I don't need to prove myself to Jack anymore. I don't need evidence to make him believe me. I don't even think *I* need evidence to believe. I know Langdon Hall, I know Theo Page, and I may even know myself too. This is what I choose to believe. What I *know*. It was all real.

Jack will not take another thing from me. *It is not true. You do not have to believe him. You know the truth, you know.*

So no, I will not open the journal now, will not pore over each letter and perhaps I never will again. But to look at its cover, the coil of that Celtic Tree of Life, its branches woven into one another—I know the truth.

"Right, well, anyway, I should go."

I will keep moving, nothing can be in my path, not anymore. I breathe in deep, push the grief from my chest along with Jack's words from my mind.

Jack shrugs, wipes his hands clean of me, lets the weight of me and my problems fall from his shoulders.

"Yeah, good luck, Sersh."

With one last smile that neither of us truly means, I retreat into the cozy interior of the taxi. The driver does not turn to me, but we begin our journey at once and I find myself once again born out into the fog and the greenery beyond the protection of glass and metal around me. The winter howls, but it cannot reach me in here.

We approach the looming, wrought iron gates that will lead me out of Langdon Hall for the very last time and I hold my breath as we approach. What will happen when we pass through them, already sitting ajar, as though the house is steering me on my path once more? Will I turn to a puff of smoke, a memory forever bound to the walls of this estate, the place I truly came alive?

But miraculously, nothing happens. Nothing at all. We drive through the gates as we would anything else, leaving the estate sitting where it always will, in the rearview mirror. I cannot help myself, twisting in my seat to look through the back window at it once more.

As Langdon Hall shrinks behind me on the other side of the glass, it does not look like the daunting, living, breathing monster that I feared would devour me those first few days. Nor does it appear the best friend I have ever had, reaching its arms out to guide me to my destiny.

It is still. It is just a building. And maybe it was never anything more than crumbling stone held together by the strong northern winds and the sheer stubbornness of the Page legacy.

But it does not matter. It was all real, nevertheless.

It was all real, of course it was.

With the journal still held tightly in my hands, hands that no longer tremble, I say goodbye to Langdon Hall one last time. I bid the house and everything and everyone and every time that it holds within its sinking walls farewell and I know that it is for good.

Then I turn in my seat, facing forward at last, and I do not feel the icy burn of Langdon's gaze on my neck anymore.

There is no diamond ring on my finger, the hand of no Page man is woven with my own, and I am free. To fall or fail or fly on my own. It will be all right.

For I am free, I am untethered from my fear, yet still held close to myself.

Look at what we have done, Theo. No—Saoirse. This is my beginning.

I am free.

Author's Note

The first seed of this story—and the heart of it—has always been to show what life with depersonalization-derealization disorder (DPDR) can be like. Before the plot or the romance or the shadows of Langdon Hall came to me, I knew I wanted to write a story about the realities of living with DPDR. I was diagnosed with DPDR in the Autumn of 2020 and, as is my instinct, tried to find fiction that featured this disorder— I found little that named the disorder directly or resonated with my experience. Which, of course, is unsurprising as DPDR, like most experiences with mental health, can be quite unique to each person.

So I decided to write a character who was living with DPDR in some of the same ways I was and am, whose dissociations were not used as a villainous plot twist. Instead, she learns to trust herself not despite her disorder, but by coming to accept it and herself. Saoirse is flawed and often makes self-serving, harmful decisions not because of her mental health struggles but because she is an imperfect person in a difficult situation. I wanted to create a character whose DPDR is not a villain or the sole motivation or scapegoat for all of her decisions, good and often bad, but rather, whose DPDR is simply one factor of who she is and her life, even though at times it feels all-consuming.

So much of this disorder can be isolating, as Saoirse's experience shows, and writing this book was equal parts a means to hopefully connect with others with this diagnosis and to allow a part of myself to be seen on the page. DPDR is a dissociative disorder, a particular area of mental health that is often stigmatized and misunderstood. I believe the first step to destigmatize it is to be overt and educational. Though my own diagnosis felt like a validation, for Saoirse it is terrifying—it is only toward the end of the book, as she is learning to accept and stop fearing her DPDR, that she is able to name it directly. This, above all, was of the utmost importance to me. I wanted others with DPDR to potentially see themselves in Saoirse's unconventional worldview and not have to wonder if she was like them—for her disorder would be named right there on the page.

Many adults will experience an, often brief, episode of depersonalization or derealization at some point in their lives. However, the persistence and severity of these episodes, enough to be diagnosed as DPDR, affects only about one to two percent of the general population. Despite this, I would guess that many people have not heard of DPDR. This lack of information in itself can be quite challenging, as DPDR is a disorder that often only presents itself in young adulthood and the onset of it—as seen in my own experiences and Saoirse's—can be terrifying and maddening if someone doesn't understand what it is that's happening to them.

The onset of DPDR is most commonly caused by turmoil and trauma in childhood, particularly emotional neglect, physical abuse in the home, and the sudden loss of a loved one. In adulthood the disorder often presents itself in "episodes" triggered by change of environment, lack of support, or stress, no matter how minor. Though depersonalization and derealization can be categorized and can occur separately, it is not uncommon for both disorders to happen in concurrence.

It's a disorder that seems to align instinctively with the hallmarks of gothic literature, and *Where Ivy Dares to Grow* bloomed quite naturally around that basis. Depersonalization can cause feelings of detachment from one's physical body, as though the person's mind and *self* exist merely on a tether to their body that grows or shrinks depending on episodes. Much like the classic gothic heroine who sees phantoms in the mirror or feels her own mind become a terrifying, unfamiliar thing, those with depersonalization can experience hands that can look completely unfamiliar, like that of a stranger; they lose interest in former passions and things that made them feel "like themselves" and feel as though they no longer have a sense of self; they can fail to recognize their face as containing themselves when looking in mirrors or pictures; and their mind and emotions can feel detached, and therefore untrustworthy and inconsistent, giving them a hollow or robotic feeling.

Where depersonalization regards a detachment from the self, derealization runs a parallel track, separating those with the disorder from their reality. Many who regularly experience episodes of derealization—including myself—describe it as feeling like you are, constantly, within a dream; movements of themselves and others seem slow, unnatural, or fleeting; vision often makes everything look hazy or two-dimensional; light can look too dark, too bright, or vignetted, creating the illusion of moving shadows; it can feel as though there are constantly eyes on them; they may have memory issues; they have a distorted perception of time as, during an episode of derealization, they feel as though they are moving through the world in a different reality.

DPDR, clearly, has so many natural alliances with gothic literature—but some days it feels as though the ghosts are born from your mind and your own body is the haunted house. Much like Langdon does not turn out to be this evil, sentient being Saoirse must escape and overcome, her DPDR is not so terrifying as she initially believes, nor is it something that she can or should "escape" from.

There was never, and could not be, Saoirse's story without having DPDR at its center. I wrote the first draft of this book in February 2021, just months after my own diagnosis, and in many ways, for a period of time Langdon Hall became like a real place to me too. As you see Saoirse come to terms with her diagnosis and learn that it does not make her abnormal or unlovable or villainous, I was discovering those things alongside her.

Marielle Thompson
August 2022

Acknowledgments

Writing a manuscript can feel like a solitary experience, but writing a *book* truly takes a village. I've been lucky to have such a great one.

First, a thanks to my agent, Jill Marr. Whenever I wavered or panicked (which, let's be honest, was often) your enthusiasm for this story brought me back on track. Your patience and knowledge are unending, and it's been wonderful to always feel like I have someone in my corner.

A thank-you to my editor, Shannon Plackis. From the first time we spoke I knew I wanted to work with you—and not just because you immediately recognized this book's countless Taylor Swift references. You've seen the heart of this story from the beginning and your vision and feedback have pushed this book to become better and better.

Thanks to the rest of the wonderful team at Kensington: Alex Nicolajsen and Lauren Jernigan on the Digital Team; Vida Engstrand, Michelle Addo, and Kristen Vega in Publicity; Kristine Noble in Art; as well as Lynn Cully, Jackie Dinas, Adam Zacharius, and Steve Zacharius.

This book was once just a chaotic manuscript submitted for my master's thesis, and I cannot thank the entire cohort and faculty at my Creative Writing MSc enough. I had a wonderful writing group in this program who deserve so many thanks, alongside the other friends who lent early eyes to this book and ears to support its journey—Lindsay, Becky, AV, Daniela, Paulina, Morgan, Rosa, Alex, Kathia, Karolina, Michelle, Mary, and Paulette.

There have been so many friends—across many countries—

who have had unending support and enthusiasm for my writing. I'm so lucky that there are too many of you to even name but know I appreciate every one of you so much nevertheless. I would hug you all, if that were the sort of thing I did. A specific thank-you to Claire for your characteristically unwavering enthusiasm and love during my entire journey to publication, as well as for letting me drag you on countless graveyard strolls in the name of "historical research." Also a notable thanks to Danielle, who took my dreams of being a writer seriously before I ever did, and pushed me to take the leap.

A huge, huge thank-you to my family, specifically my mom, for nurturing my lifetime of dramatics and constantly having my nose in a book, two traits that are finally paying off. There have been few people in my life as excited for my wins as you—thank you for always reminding me to be excited too. To my dad, who may not be here to see it, but always encouraged the little girl who had some fantastical story to tell. To my siblings, who I'm also lucky enough to call my best friends, who have both taken my dreams seriously and, somehow, never wavered in their belief in me. Also, of course, thanks to my niece, who's too young to understand what I do, but still declared me the aunt who tells the best stories—sometimes the confidence boost is needed.

Despite working in words, there doesn't seem to be enough to thank Beau. From the first day we met (the second time) you've been passionate and interested in my stories like no one else. I know you wouldn't describe yourself as patient or sensitive, but the way you have been beside me, holding my hand through every high and every low of the journey here, shows that you are. Thank you for believing in me every minute of every day, and for creating a life for us where I can be myself and do what I love. I'm so grateful I get to go through life with you. This story may be dedicated to you, but all the rest of them are too—every beautiful word I write about love I learned from loving you.

And finally, thank you, readers, for picking up this story and being here from the beginning.

Where Ivy Dares to Grow

Marielle Thompson

ABOUT THIS GUIDE

The suggested questions are included to enhance your
group's reading of Marielle Thompson's
Where Ivy Dares to Grow.

Discussion Questions

1. Author Marielle Thompson references several nineteenth-century novels throughout *Where Ivy Dares to Grow*, including *Frankenstein*, *Wuthering Heights*, and *Jane Eyre*. Do you notice any similar elements or ideas between these stories and Saoirse's?

2. What do you think is the symbolism of the title *Where Ivy Dares to Grow*? Ivy imagery is recurring throughout the book—why do you think that is?

3. *Where Ivy Dares to Grow* uses a time-slip plot device to for a story that is ultimately about loneliness, longing, and legacy. Why do you think the author chose to use a time slip vs. another device, such as flashbacks?

4. How does Saoirse's experience with depersonalization-derealization disorder align with the use of time slips as a plot device?

5. The novel uses a journal as the mechanism for Saoirse's time-slip travel. Why do you think the author chose this item? What is another item or device that the author could have used?

6. What did you know about DPDR or dissociative disorders generally before reading the story? How have your assumptions and thoughts changed since?

7. A character in its own right, Langdon Hall brings Saoirse and Theo together because they both need the same thing: a friend to believe them. If Langdon Hall brought you to another time, when would it be and what would you be seeking?

8. An important theme in the book is isolation and the extremes of emotion that it drives people to. Saoirse feels

very physically isolated in Langdon Hall and emotionally isolated in her relationship with Jack and her family. How do you think other characters in the story experience different forms of isolation?

9. Family history and legacy is a key part of the story, particularly the value that the Pages place on their history versus Saoirse's own lacking familial connections. How do you think Saoirse's interactions with the modern-day Pages would be different were she closer to her own family?

10. Saoirse travels from her own time in the 1990s to 1818. How do you think her experience in Langdon, with her mental health and her time slips, would have been different if she were from the 2020s instead?

11. Discuss the prevalence of different kinds of love in this book—romantic love, familial love, and self-love.

12. Because the story is told from the first-person perspective of Saoirse, the way we see other characters is heavily influenced by her perception of them, herself, and the world. Take a moment to discuss Jack and his mother, Alice—did you find these characters to be at all sympathetic or redeemable? How do you think the story would be different were it told from either of their perspectives?

13. The book opens with a quote from *Frankenstein*: "The whole series of my life appeared to me as a dream; I sometimes doubted if indeed it were all true, for it never presented itself to my mind with the force of reality." What connections do you see between this quote and the book, particularly Saoirse's experience with depersonalization-derealization disorder?

Visit our website at
KensingtonBooks.com
to sign up for our newsletters, read
more from your favorite authors, see
books by series, view reading group
guides, and more!

BOOK ||||/||| CLUB
BETWEEN THE CHAPTERS

Become a Part of Our
Between the Chapters Book Club
Community and Join the Conversation

Betweenthechapters.net

Submit your book review for a chance to win exclusive
Between the Chapters swag you can't get anywhere else!
https://www.kensingtonbooks.com/pages/review/